Spence was so near to her that she could feel his heat

Thea tried another tactic. "Let's just agree on two things. We won't squabble. And there will be no unnecessary touching. No kissing. Nothing."

"Well, that's hardly fair, Thea, after you spent the gondola ride groping me."

"I was not groping! I—"

The corner of his mouth lifted in a half smile. "Okay." He relented. "Call it holding on. I just think I ought to have the chance to return that favor."

"Don't..." His blue eyes warmed as he gazed confidently into her face, and she felt herself responding, wanting to smile back at him. "Don't even think about it, Spence."

"I've got a few conditions of my own," he said. "Number one—we stay in the present and not dwell on the past. Number two—we both keep our minds open. Number three..." He obliterated the distance between them in a single step. She should have pushed him away, but her arms went around him and she wanted the taste of against hers.

Dear Harlequin Intrigue Reader,

Cupid's bow is loaded at Harlequin Intrigue with four fabulous stories of breathtaking romantic suspense—starting with the continuation of Cassie Miles's COLORADO SEARCH AND RESCUE miniseries. In *Wedding Captives*, lovers reunite on a mountaintop... unfortunately they're also snowbound with a madman!

And there's no better month to launch our new modern gothic continuity series MORIAH'S LANDING. Amanda Stevens emerges from the New England fog with *Secret Sanctuary*, the first of four titles coming out over the next several months. You can expect all of the classic themes you love in these stories, plus more of the contemporary edge you've come to expect from our brand of romantic suspense.

You know what can happen *In the Blink of an Eye...*? Julie Miller does! And you can find out, too, in the next installment of her TAYLOR CLAN series.

Finally, Jean Barrett takes you to New Orleans for some *Private Investigations* with battling P.I.'s. It's a regular showdown in the French Quarter—where absolutely anything goes.

So celebrate Valentine's Day with the most confounding mystery of all...that of the heart.

Deep, rich chocolate wishes,

Denise O'Sullivan
Associate Senior Editor
Harlequin Intrigue

WEDDING CAPTIVES
CASSIE MILES

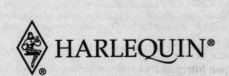

HARLEQUIN®

TORONTO • NEW YORK • LONDON
AMSTERDAM • PARIS • SYDNEY • HAMBURG
STOCKHOLM • ATHENS • TOKYO • MILAN • MADRID
PRAGUE • WARSAW • BUDAPEST • AUCKLAND

ISBN 0-373-22649-7

WEDDING CAPTIVES

Copyright © 2002 by Kay Bergstrom

Visit us at www.eHarlequin.com

Printed in U.S.A.

ABOUT THE AUTHOR

Cassie Miles lives in Denver, one of the fastest growing cities in the country, with the traffic jams to prove it. She belongs to the film society and enjoys artsy subtitled cinema almost as much as movies where stuff blows up. Her favorite entertainment is urban, ranging from sports to museum exhibits to coffeehouse espresso. Yet she never loses sight of the Rocky Mountains through the kitchen window.

Books by Cassie Miles

HARLEQUIN INTRIGUE

HARLEQUIN AMERICAN ROMANCE

†Colorado Search and Rescue

Don't miss any of our special offers. Write to us at the following address for information on our newest releases.

Harlequin Reader Service
U.S.: 3010 Walden Ave., P.O. Box 1325, Buffalo, NY 14269
Canadian: P.O. Box 609, Fort Erie, Ont. L2A 5X3

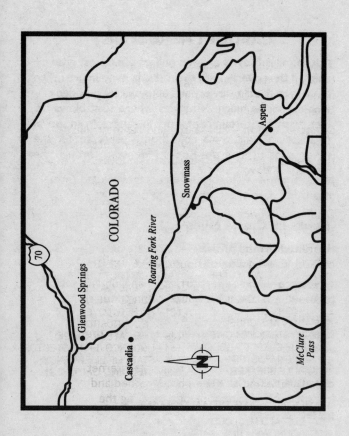

CAST OF CHARACTERS

Thea Sarazin—She comes to the castle as a bridesmaid, never expecting to face her former fiancé, never dreaming she'll be threatened by the revenge scheme of a madman.

Spence Cannon—His search-and-rescue training might be the difference between life and death for the wedding party and the woman he loves.

Jenny Trevain—The bride's wedding weekend turns into three days of terror.

Dr. Mona Nance—The psychiatrist knows too many secrets and reveals none of them.

Reverend Joshua Handy—Before he became a man of God, he lived a mysterious life.

Lawrence—The butler carries a handgun and seems to know little about his housekeeping duties.

Travis Trevain—The bride's younger brother, an Olympic-class freestyle skier, believes he's the best at everything.

Gregory Rosemont—The reclusive Internet billionaire has never been photographed and has spent his life and fortune preparing the perfect revenge.

For Cheryl McGonigle.
Couldn't have done it without you.

Prologue

Beyond the carved stone entryway to Castle in the Clouds, the shadows of a winter night bled and puddled along the edges of the snow-packed pathway. Rolling clouds churned across the face of the full moon and obscured the glimmer of starlight. The cloaking darkness suited the purposes of Gregory Rosemont, the owner of this stately manor situated on a high crest surrounded by glacial Colorado peaks. He was not ready to reveal himself. His flashlight beam hardly penetrated the tapestry of icy haze, yet he strode with confidence. He knew every inch of this rugged mountaintop, every stone, every tree. He had memorized the cliffs and precipices that isolated the castle, making it accessible only by a ten-person ski gondola hung from a tensile steel cable.

His light shone against the walls of the gondola house, constructed from locally quarried granite to match the crenellated ramparts. Tomorrow, the gondola car would make its last ascent. Tomorrow, he would mount his final revenge.

For years, he had arranged this event with compulsive attention to detail. He had amassed a fortune to finance his goal. And now, his plan was perfect, an exacting test

for the remorseless specimens of humanity who were to
be his guests.

Inside the gondola house, he slipped the backpack from
his shoulders, took out his tools and went to work. Ignoring the huge metal cogs and wheels necessary to haul the
weight of the car, he concentrated on a precision piece of
machinery that would slice through the cable at exactly
the right moment to send the gaily painted gondola car
plummeting hundreds of feet into the chasm below.

In his vivid imagination, he heard the shattering of the
fiberglass car, torn by jagged teeth of stone. Tomorrow,
the screams of terror would echo endlessly against the
cold, unforgiving mountains. It would be a spectacular
crash.

As he adjusted the coils, the spring-loaded severing
mechanism squealed, metal against metal. The gloves he
wore to ward off the sub-zero chill impeded his efforts,
but he was glad for the cold, the promise of snowfall. A
January blizzard would hamper any rescue attempt.

His task completed, he allowed himself a smug grin.
He'd thought of everything, left nothing to chance.

As he hiked back along the path, moonlight spilled
through a break in the clouds, illuminating the turrets and
sculpted ramparts of the fanciful medieval-style castle. The
only light shone from the high window of the bridal suite
above.

Chapter One

In the fading mid-afternoon sunlight, Thea Sarazin trudged uphill toward the small stone house where a ski gondola would transport her across an impossibly wide chasm to the Castle in the Clouds.

In addition to her small suitcase, she carried a garment bag containing a floor-length gown. After this weekend, she'd add this brocaded creation in sunrise orange—a color particularly unsuited to Thea's olive complexion, hazel eyes and dark brown hair—to the other three godawful bridesmaid dresses that hung, swathed in dry cleaner's plastic, in the back of her closet.

Though she'd sworn never again to be part of a wedding party, she couldn't refuse when asked by Jenny Trevain, her co-worker at Lloyd Middle School in Denver. Not only was Jenny a good friend but the wedding meant spending a weekend at this fabled mansion where she would finally meet Jenny's reclusive fiancé, Gregory Rosemont.

The whole event was simply too fanciful and romantic for Thea to resist, especially since Jenny was also thirty-four, and had likewise resigned herself to the odds against ever finding true love. And then, seemingly out of nowhere, Jenny had been swept into every woman's fantasy romance, a whirlwind courtship by a rich and mysterious captain of industry.

Rosemont was...okay, an *eccentric* multi-millionaire who had earned his fortune with one of the first online shopping Web sites. Just for this weekend of fancy, Thea preferred to think of it all as exciting and exotic. Jenny's love affair rekindled the hopes and dreams of every almost-a-spinster like Thea. She sighed.

A dream come true. Thea knew better. She was sure she knew better. But an engagement ring from Tiffany's! Marriage to the modern-day equivalent of a prince. The guy owned a castle, for goodness' sake!

On the other hand, Gregory Rosemont also had the reputation of a genuine twenty-four-carat recluse. There were no existing photographs of him. Not even Jenny had one. He never gave interviews. He ruled his business from afar, keeping in touch through the highest of high-tech computer innovations. Privacy was a big deal to this man who chose to live on a mountaintop which could only be reached by a mile-long ride on a ski gondola. No doubt his communications with the outer world required satellites...or something. Computer technology wasn't her forte.

The extreme cold bit at Thea's nose. Around her, in the below-freezing chill of the clean, crisp mountain air, rose mountains as old as time. If she hadn't just driven the wickedly iced-over access road several miles from an interstate highway, she could believe she'd crossed over into some frozen other-world, never to be seen or heard from again.

Where was Jenny's car? Where was anyone?

Thea's feet were freezing, her fingers already numb. She told herself to get a grip and keep going. Maybe the stone house for the gondola was heated. Thea was beginning to worry about the cold, the isolation and—most especially—about dear, sweet, naive Jenny who planned to change her fiancé into a marginally sociable human being after the wedding. Thea couldn't believe it. Jekyll and Hyde belonged in fiction. Hoping for a metamorphosis on that scale was like hoping to transform Colorado's rugged fourteen-thousand-foot granite peaks into foothills fit for an afternoon hike.

Pretty darned unrealistic.

She'd talked to Jenny, warning her about trying to transform her husband-to-be. Thea had been engaged herself once before and had hoped that her nurturing love would ease an arrogant, ambitious M.D. into a more sensitive human being. Talk about an impossible dream!

But Jenny was in love, and women in love fooled themselves every day. Twice on Sunday.

Why was the parking so dratted far from the only possible destination up here?

As she neared the rough-hewn stone gondola house, Thea noticed the coat of arms, depicting a single blooming rose—probably to represent the rose in Rosemont—two interlocking crowns and four daggers. She thought about what conceit it took for a computer whiz to invent himself a brand-spanking-new coat of arms, then scolded herself. She might get conceited too, if she ever even saw a million dollars.

She should really cut Gregory Rosemont some slack. After all, Jenny loved him. She unlatched the heavy wooden door and pushed it open. No one else was here. And if possible, the stone house was even colder than the outdoors.

Pushing up her parka sleeve, she glanced at her wristwatch. She'd made good time from Denver, considering that she'd driven under ten miles an hour on the scary stretch of snow-packed, winding road without even a guardrail. She'd arrived half an hour early. Still, she'd expected to find someone here to greet her. A butler, perhaps.

She deposited her suitcase and garment bag on the stone benches that lined the dreary granite walls. In one corner was a wood-burning stove, unlit. On the opposite wall were metal lockers and an ornately decorated, old-fashioned combination safe.

The fiberglass gondola car seemed modern enough in spite of giant cog-wheel machinery that, to Thea, smacked of a medieval torture device. She eyed the steel cable from which the gondola car was suspended. Was it strong enough to hold the weight of several people? She was not only *not* fond of heights, she was a card-carrying acrophobe.

Evil boy cousins had stranded her in the rafters in her Uncle Harry's barn when Thea was only five, while her brothers had laughed till they hurled—and she'd never, ever gotten over it. She was good at pretending she had— so far as she knew, no one had ever guessed what a chicken she was—but she couldn't fool herself.

She absolutely expected the gondola ride to be the worst part of her weekend. For Jenny, she would do it.

She left her luggage and went outdoors again, barely making tracks across the crusted, deep-packed snow, angling for the best view of the castle to distract herself from the only possible approach. She hadn't dared try to get a glimpse of the castle from the road. The driving had consumed her white-knuckled attention.

Above the snowplowed parking area carved out of the surrounding forest, she peered across the deep, wide chasm. Through gathering storm clouds, she saw thick stone towers rising on either end of a large main structure. Gothic battlements strangely complemented the Moorish-style arched windows and gables from yet another era. The delightfully eclectic, bizarre architecture bespoke a fascinating history. Jenny inevitably went into raptures describing the castle.

Another vehicle finally pulled into the parking lot below the gondola house. From her vantage point, Thea stared curiously at the four-wheel-drive van. The wedding party was supposed to be small, but Jenny had been dropping gleeful hints about some of the other invited guests. Thea even suspected an attempt at matchmaking. She wasn't really looking for a boyfriend, but a weekend in a castle might be the perfect time and place for a wonderful romantic assignation.

A tryst.

Thea shook her head at herself, careening from pillar to post, dread and certain panic over the gondola to flights of romantic fantasy.

Strangers to her, an attractive couple of about her own age emerged from the van. Then, the rear door slid open, and a third passenger climbed out. A man. A tall, broad-shouldered man.

Spence Cannon.

A shiver gripped her...was it an acute, terrible loneliness? Recognition? Or only the cold?

She hadn't laid eyes on the man who'd once asked her to marry him in over five years. She clapped her chattering teeth tightly together. He looked good. Fine, really...fine. Annoyingly so, she snapped at herself. His sun-streaked hair fell rakishly across his forehead. From this distance, she couldn't see his deep-set blue eyes at all, but she knew that his expression would be cool and outrageously condescending. She'd thought, all those eons ago when she still believed she was going to conquer the world herself, that the combination of cool and condescending was sexy, an invitation, a dare.

She'd fooled herself every day she and Spence were together. Twice on Sunday. And that was a conservative estimate.

She turned back toward the Castle and glared. *Damn you, Jenny.* How could Jenny think Thea *ever* wanted to see Spence again? Whatever they'd shared, even if she'd called it love, had been cold, dead ashes for a long time, swept under a carpet and ground to infinitesimal dust. Her pride would never allow their relationship to be rekindled, even if her sanity went on holiday.

She tried to tell herself that the memory of their breakup didn't hurt anymore, but it obviously did. Pain like a bolt of lightning stabbed somewhere near the center of her forehead. Almost blinded, she recoiled, retreating into the shadow of the trees, hiding herself like a scared rabbit.

A momentary urge seized her to leave this desolate mountaintop. To gather up her grotesque bridesmaid dress and run, not walk, back to the safety of her Denver townhouse and her two cats.

Coward! She'd been looking forward to this long weekend, and she wouldn't let Spence ruin it. She could handle him. She could be strong. She'd done it once. Five years ago, *she'd* been the one to call off their engagement and return his diamond ring. Very tough, very brave, utterly lonely. She'd sat home alone, night after night, staring at the telephone like one of her boy-smitten middle-schoolers, praying for the boy to call. Futilely waiting on the reconciliation call that never came.

She could be strong.

She peeked out from behind a tree trunk. Damn you, Spence. Why did he have to look so good?

TODAY WOULD BE either the best or the worst day of Spence Cannon's life. He hated the uncertainty.

"Come on!" his friend Emily called out. "Let's take a good look at this place."

Spence really couldn't have cared less about the so-called castle. His decision to accept Jenny's wedding invitation was based entirely on the fact that he knew Thea Sarazin would be there. He wanted another chance with her.

"Look at the gondola house! With a coat of arms, no less. That's fairly pretentious!" Emily charged up the path with the agility of a mountain goat, then she whirled and embraced her new husband, Jordan Shane. "Doesn't it make you think of knights in shining armor and princesses and jousts?"

"Looks cold," Jordan said.

"That's the fun part." Her voice lowered to a purr. "We'll share bodily warmth to keep warm."

Spence joined them. "Give it a rest, Emily. All this newlywed joy is making me hyperglycemic."

"What's wrong with you?"

Thea's car, he thought, glancing back at the only other vehicle in the snowplowed lot. That had to be Thea's car. He was distracted, all right. He couldn't explain the combination of excitement and dread he felt about seeing her again. Being with her.

It had been over five years since he'd heard her calm, clear voice. Or reduced calm-and-clear to a throaty cry of pleasure. Or seen her heart-shaped face, or traced its shape with his lips. But he remembered, vividly, the startling depths in her hazel eyes and the silky texture of her chestnut hair falling through his fingers.

So many nights since, he'd wakened with the scent of her musky perfume lingering in the dark around him. In dreams, he knew the indescribable softness of her inner thigh, the sweet fullness of her breasts, the taste of her lush ripe lips. And then, those lips would speak, and she'd tell him she never wanted to see him again. Never.

No compromise.

Not ever.

His friend, Emily, joined him on the path. "You look sad, Spence. Want to talk about it?"

"Thea is the one who broke up with me," he muttered. "I'm the one who should expect an apology. Right?"

"It depends. Why did she end the relationship?"

He shrugged. "She thought I betrayed her."

"With another woman?"

"Hell, no. I'd never do anything like that."

"What was it?" Emily asked. "What did you do?"

"It's complicated." He didn't like talking about relationships, facing the fact that he'd made a mistake and put his career ahead of Thea's needs. Had he been in the wrong? Possibly. Was he sorry? Definitely. "I want her back."

He shoved open the door to the gondola house. Would she be inside, waiting for him? Would she forgive him? The interior of the stone house was about as cold and empty as her heart the last time they were together, but there on the stone bench he saw her luggage.

He dropped his overnight bag on the flagstone floor. Nothing about the place boded well, save Thea's luggage.

Emily and Jordan spilled inside behind him. "Too bad we're not invited to the wedding. I wonder if we can hitch a ride up to the top, just for a treat," she said. "I'd love to see the castle."

"Doubtful." Her husband Jordan studied the cogs of the gondola machinery. "Gregory Rosemont makes the late Howard Hughes look like a party animal. Even that's a stretch. Everyone's heard of Howard Hughes. Rosemont has come out of nowhere."

"But Jordan, you have something in common," Emily protested. "He's a computer guy, like you."

"All the more reason for him to be secretive," Jordan said. "Rosemont might think I was here to steal his ideas."

"Not you, Jordan."

As she melted into her husband's arms again, Spence exited the stone house. Of course, he felt glad that Emily and Jordan had found each other and fallen in love. After what they'd been through with Jordan being unjustly accused of murder and on the run, they deserved some happiness. But their bliss underlined his own solitary existence as a general practitioner in the small mountain town of Cascadia, a far less fashionable outpost than nearby Aspen.

After four years, the locals had pretty much given up on finding him a mate. He'd taken on the role of the kindly, bachelor doc who worked weekends with the Cascadia Search-and-Rescue unit. Searching for Thea, only now seeing small footprints in the crusted snow, he looked up toward the top of a snowy ridge. And there he saw her framed in an icy landscape with dark storm clouds rising behind her.

She'd cut her long hair into a straight, chin-length bob. Her burgundy parka matched her boots and gloves. As always, she looked organized and controlled. Only after he'd gotten to know her had Spence discovered the wild woman who lived inside, an impetuous creature who loved laughter and excitement. His body, having a memory of its own, was already responding to the vision of Thea.

Energized, his inhibitions leaking out with each breath he took, he hiked toward her, fully intending to grab hold of her and kiss the frown off her mouth. He was near enough to see a glimmer of vulnerability in her beautiful hazel eyes. She wanted him as much as he wanted her.

And then she spoke. "You look older, Spence."

His instincts urged him on. *Go ahead. Embrace her. Kiss her.* "You cut your hair."

"It's not the only thing different about me."

He tried to ignore the warning note in her voice. He wanted to touch her, to trace the line of her chin, to brush his thumb across the surface of her lips. "You're still beautiful."

"But older, now. Wiser."

"Wise enough to forgive?" His hand raised, reaching toward her, needing the contact.

"No." She clasped his bare hand in her gloved fingers and gave a firm, business-like shake. Quickly, she released and stepped back. "Spence, why did you come here?"

He felt his heart thud. He reminded her that he and Jenny had been friends long before he even met Thea. "And she invited me."

"Because she thought we'd get back together." Her voice quavered, but she said, "Jenny was wrong."

"Was she?"

"Kiss and make up," Thea said, "is not an option."

Before he could respond, she stepped around him and proceeded toward the gondola house where she politely introduced herself to Emily and Jordan. Spence stood rooted in the snow, staring after her. In the center of his chest, his heart clenched like an iron fist. His lungs ceased operation. A few words from Thea had driven him to the brink of myocardial infarction.

Breathe, you idiot! He sucked down an ice-cold breath, tasting impending snowfall in the air. This reunion hadn't begun the way he'd hoped. She'd rejected him. Again.

He exhaled a puff of steam. *Kissing is not an option? Like hell!* He'd heard the hesitation in Thea's voice.

Growing warmer inside at the notion of Thea and her sweet, maybe unconscious hesitation, he pretended interest in the isolated castle across the wide chasm. The granite structure appeared to be impregnable, perched above high cliffs. But nothing was unreachable. *You can't hide from me, Thea.* They'd be trapped there for two and a half days. It might take that long for him to change her mind. This time, he wouldn't give her up without a fight.

He turned toward the parking area and watched as a shiny new Ford Explorer swerved across the snow, nearly sideswiping his van. A wild man in a colorful ski outfit and dyed white-blond hair leapt out and gave a loud whoop. "Where's my big sis?" he yelled.

Obviously, this was Travis Trevain, Jenny's brother. He was ranked as a world-class freestyle skier, one of those hot-dog show-offs who flip through the air in screaming pirouettes that couldn't really be considered sport.

Spence took an immediate dislike to Travis. He knew the guy was the only family Jenny had left after her father, a renowned virologist Spence had once worked with, had passed away. Baby brother Travis hadn't attended the funeral seven years ago. He'd been in drug rehab.

His current manic behavior suggested a relapse. Two and a half days with this jerk? Spence was particularly disgusted with the way Travis grabbed everybody, including Thea, in bear hugs. *Especially* Thea.

Stalking down the hill, Spence prepared to stake his claim before Travis decided to make her his weekend conquest. But the blond skier bounded halfway up the hill to greet him with arms flung wide. His red and yellow parka matched with skin-tight ski pants made him look, in Spence's jaded opinion, like a demented snow parrot.

Spence blocked the hug and shook hands instead. "You must be Travis Trevain. I'm Spence Cannon."

"Wow, yeah? I gotta say it, then." Travis socked him on the shoulder, shaking his head in admiration. "I owe you, big-time. Thanks, man."

"For what?"

"You hung in there for Jenny," Travis said. "At the old man's funeral. When she needed a friend."

Spence might have pointed out that what Jenny had really needed was her brother, that Travis's addictive behavior had broken his father's heart. That, even then, even after their father died, especially then, Jenny could have used a brother at her side. But there was no point in rebuke. And Spence was in favor of letting the past be over in more ways than the one that mattered most to him right now—getting Thea to let it go. "Jenny keeps me updated on your career. How's your health?"

"Aces, man." Travis started to launch into the marvels of his conditioning.

Spence was rescued from *that* conversation by his friend Jordan, who called up to him. "Hey Spence! Sorry, Travis, but I need Spence to check something in the van."

"No prob." He clapped Spence on the back. "We got a whole weekend to be buds."

Don't hold your breath, hot dog. Spence strode downhill and then fell into step beside Jordan.

As they reached the parking area, Jordan asked, "How are you doing?"

"Fine." Spence spat the word. Thea was talking to Emily up near the gondola house. He wanted to know what Emily was saying about him.

"Your jaw's clenched, my friend. The vein in your forehead is pumping," Jordan observed. "Emily says it's hypertension."

Emily was a nurse, specifically trained in emergency medicine, and Spence respected her ability enough that he planned to leave his practice in her hands during this long weekend. At the moment, however, he didn't want Emily's diagnosis.

"I'm fine," he repeated. He knew where this conversation was headed and he was wishing real hard right now that he had never confided in Jordan and Emily at all. They both knew Spence had a lot of hopes invested in this weekend.

Jordan's dark, intense gaze focused on the surrounding forest as if he were intent upon counting the trees. Emily's husband didn't do a lot of unnecessary chatting. "A while back, you and I had a talk about soulmates. You know the one—for every man, there's one perfect match."

Sneaking a look at Emily and Thea chatting away, Spence wondered what force in the universe it was that always sent your words of well-intentioned advice boomeranging right back at you. "Nothing's perfect."

"No, but some things come close." Jordan kept counting trees. "You never said. Why did you and Thea break up in the first place?"

"It was my fault," Spence said. He'd been an ass, putting his career ahead of Thea, ignoring her needs. He'd been a fool. "I never claimed to be a sensitive guy. I'm a doctor."

"Like the two are mutually exclusive?" Jordan shook his head, apparently dismissing Spence's self-recriminations. "So, are you saying you've changed?"

"Since Thea knew me? Oh, yeah." If Thea gave him half a chance, he believed she'd like the man he'd become—a small-town doc who knew his patients by their first names.

"Well, all I can say is—"

"Shouldn't we at least pretend we're doing something about the van?" Spence interrupted.

"—don't give up." Jordan turned and opened the sliding door on the van, then climbed in. "Let's move this seat."

"Easy for you to say," Spence snarled, about not giving up. He grabbed his end of the bench seat. "If she kicks snow in my face one more time—" He broke off. His rear molars ground together. "I don't need this kind of rejection. There are plenty of willing females in the world."

"But you want Thea."

"God help me, I do."

Chapter Two

The seat removed and reinstalled, Spence backed away and Jordan got out, sliding shut the door behind him as another vehicle chugged into the parking area and yet another one approached on the access road.

A tall, angular man unfolded from behind the steering wheel of a conservative black station wagon. His unsmiling face marked with a prominent, hawkish nose reminded Spence of the early Puritans. This impression was confirmed by the clerical collar encircling the man's skinny neck.

As Spence and Jordan approached, he introduced himself. "Reverend Joshua Handy. Which of you is Gregory Rosemont?"

"Neither." Spence made the introductions.

The reverend appeared impatient. "Jenny told me I'd have a chance to talk with Gregory before the ceremony."

"You've never met him?" Spence asked.

"No." He looked down his long nose. "Where's Jenny?"

"Not here," Spence said. "Not even her car. I'm guessing she and Rosemont have some kind of chauffeur service up to the gondola. They're probably both already up at the castle. Need any help with your luggage?"

Joshua Handy shook his head, and turned back to his hearse-like station wagon. "I'll manage."

Tempted to walk back up the frozen slope and insert himself into the chat Emily and Thea were having, Spence let himself be dragged along with Jordan as the other car pulled into a space near to their own. A tiny dynamo of a woman exited her car. She was overly bundled up for her drive in a puffy parka and a scarf around her throat. Spikes of gray hair poked around the edges of a colorful Norwegian ski cap.

Her wizened features reminded Spence of a troll. Luckily, her beaming mitigated the harshness. "Hello! I'm Doctor Mona Nance."

Spence shook her over-large mitten. "Medical doctor?"

"Psychologist," she said.

Jordan shook her mitten in turn and smirked. "Well, Doctor Mona, you might be real busy this weekend."

BREAKING OFF her conversation with Emily, Thea went back inside the stone gondola house. She carefully kept her distance from Spence as the other guests arrived—Travis the hotshot, Dr. Mona Nance and a dour minister who looked as though he was more prepared for a funeral than a wedding. An unusual group! No one but she and Spence seemed to know each other. She glanced at her wristwatch. It was thirteen minutes past the time designated to depart from the gondola house for the ride to Castle in the Clouds. She thought the wedding party was beginning to show signs of restlessness.

Impatient, Travis repeatedly jabbed the buttons on a cell phone he plucked out of a pocket, trying to reach the castle. He finally snapped the thing closed. "Well, this is a total bummer. I'm not getting through. What's the deal?"

Thea wondered if it was really possible Travis had never had that result in the mountains before.

The Reverend Joshua Handy, meanwhile, was eyeing the gondola machinery that made her nervous too. With long, skeletal fingers, he touched the cogs. "It might be best to take things into our own hands."

A brilliant example of good old Yankee ingenuity? Thea shivered. "What do you mean?"

"Perhaps we're expected to start this thing ourselves."

"I think *not*." She was nervous enough about riding in the gondola without adding reckless incompetence to the mix.

"We should wait," Dr. Mona Nance counseled. "I'm sure we'll receive instructions."

"Don't need a lesson book," Travis said. "You just yank the lever. Like turning on a light bulb. You get it, Doctor Shrink?"

The wizened little psychologist stepped in front of him. Her small face turned up. Her head tilted back. "Because of my stature, I find that term particularly offensive."

"Shrink?"

"Precisely."

The tone of her voice held such authority that even an insensitive oaf like Travis was cowed. "Sorry, ma'am."

Backing off, he and the reverend discussed the possibility of starting the gondola, and Thea's gaze slipped toward Spence. Long legs stretched out in front of him, he sat on one of the stone benches beside his two friends, Emily and Jordan.

A nice couple, Thea thought, who seemed utterly loyal to Spence. Emily just glowed talking about him, expounding for Thea on what a wonderful doctor he was, brilliant, thoughtful, reverent, not to mention an expert in search-and-rescue who had saved countless lives. Thea thought the lives he had saved probably could be counted, but she wasn't surprised. She'd never doubted Spence's competence.

Still, she found it somewhat hard to believe that he'd reined in his world-conquering ambitions and settled for working in a small town. Was it possible that he had changed? That he'd become even a little less arrogant and self-involved?

She tried, on the sly, to assess the differences wrought in five years. His features had become more chiseled with strong jawline and high cheekbones. Fine lines crisscrossed his forehead and radiated from the corners of his breathtaking blue eyes. She wished she could see below the surface, to know if the changes in Spence ran more than skin deep.

Dr. Mona approached and perched on the bench beside Thea. The psychologist's tiny little legs were so short that her feet didn't touch the stone floor. "How do you know Jenny?" she asked pleasantly.

"We work together at the middle school. I teach English and American History."

"Sixth, seventh and eighth graders," Dr. Mona said. "A difficult age. I'm always curious. How do you handle classroom discipline with that age group?"

"Like a lion tamer. With a whip and a chair," Thea joked. She felt Spence's attention on her. "On good days, I enjoy the challenge."

"And on bad days?"

"It's a struggle," she admitted. "What about you, Doctor? Are you a friend of Jenny's family?"

"Actually, Jenny is my client," Dr. Mona said. "I know her quite well."

Though Thea hadn't known her friend was in therapy, it wasn't exactly a revelation. Teaching in an inner-city middle school made for a fairly high-stress occupation, especially after Columbine. It had been in the press recently that teachers in the Denver area suffered significantly more from stress than the already high levels documented nationwide.

Very likely, Thea thought, Jenny had discussed her fiancé with her therapist as well. Dr. Mona's professional opinion would be very interesting. "What do you make of Gregory Rosemont?"

"Mysterious, isn't he?" Doctor Mona commented noncommittally.

"Very. What concerns me, though," Thea admitted, "is that Jenny thinks he'll come out of his shell after they're married. You know, become more sociable." Thea paused. "Do you think that's possible?"

"I believe people can change or modify their behavior." Her cheeks rounded as she grinned. "Otherwise, my work is a sham."

Thea glanced toward Spence. "What does it take to change?"

"Most of all," Dr. Mona said, "a willingness." She patted Thea's knee, and resorted to every therapist's escape hatch. "What do you think, dear?"

Straying from Jenny's issues with Gregory Rosemont, Thea thought that even if Spence had changed, she wasn't sure she could forgive him. Five years ago, he had shredded her self-esteem and handed it back to her like so much confetti on a silver platter.

"Somebody's coming," Travis announced as he flung open the door of the gondola house and charged into the snow.

The others straggled outside behind him. During the few minutes they'd been in the gondola house, the storm clouds had thickened. A bitter chill shimmered in the air.

A stocky, middle-aged man huffed and puffed his way up the path toward the gondola house.

"Hey, dude," Travis bellowed, "you're late if you're here to take us up to the castle."

The man paused, red-faced from his exertions. Before he spoke, he planted both feet and corrected his posture. His shoulders squared beneath his black parka. He assumed an attitude of dignity. "Please accept my apologies for the delay."

The ruddy man carefully removed his knit cap and smoothed the thinning strands of his black hair. "I am the Rosemont butler. My name is Lawrence. May I suggest that before we proceed with further introductions, we step inside?"

Back inside the gondola house, Thea found herself standing beside Spence. If she made a point of moving away, he might think she feared contact. Did she? Was she afraid of him? Quickly, she polled her emotions. First and foremost, she felt antsy. Nervous to be around him. Angry that he looked so fine. More angry that the simmering rage over what he'd done to her five years ago, rage she'd been certain would not cool no matter what, seemed to have cooled in spite of her.

No matter, she assured herself, distracted by Travis's whining, she would never forgive Spence, even if...or when the old rage turned stone-cold.

"May I have your attention," Lawrence said. He pulled out a cell phone. "Anyone else got one of these?"

Everyone nodded, even wizened little Doctor Mona.

"How about computers? Any palm-tops? Laptops?"

The Reverend Joshua Handy bleated. "Is there a point to all this? I need my computer—"

"Sorry," Lawrence interrupted, "but before we make the ascent to Castle in the Clouds, Mr. Rosemont has requested that all computers, pagers, cell phones and other electronic devices be left behind.''

"Why?" Spence demanded.

"The heating and electrical systems in the castle are run by highly sophisticated electronics which might be severely disrupted by interference." He shrugged as if to make light of the need to divest. "You'll find there is no cellular service available in any case."

"No way," Travis protested, though he'd already proved what Lawrence said was true, trying to dial up the castle. "I need to be in contact with my people."

Lawrence replied, "There are, of course, computers and telephones in the castle which will be available for your use."

"I don't like it," Travis said.

"Terribly sorry, but I must insist." Lawrence had caught his breath. He strutted toward the corner of the room and stood beside the large metal safe. "I'm certain you will all be pleasantly enough occupied for the weekend and by the wedding that you won't even miss your own devices. Please do give me all electronic items, and I will secure them here for you to retrieve when you leave the castle."

Grumbling, the wedding guests divested themselves of pocket planners and cell phones. The reverend even unzipped his suitcase and gave up the laptop he had brought along.

Thea stepped back beside Emily and Jordan. "Seems weird," she said.

Emily looked to her new husband, "You're the computer genius. What do you think?"

"I doubt a cell phone could mess up Rosemont's electronics, but you never know."

"What about the computer thing?" Thea asked.

"Paranoia," Jordan said. "A guy like Rosemont might think one of you is a spy, planning to download his programs."

A spy? Paranoia? Seeds of foreboding took root in Thea's fertile imagination. She'd known that Rosemont was eccentric, but locking up the cell phones seemed obsessive. "What happens if the phones in the house break down?"

"Unlikely." Dr. Mona was beside her once again. "Rosemont's attention to detail seems to border on the compulsive. He'll have back-up systems for his back-ups."

The tiny psychologist seemed almost pleased by this turn of events. Thea had the idea that Dr. Mona viewed this wedding as a research project on aberrant neuroses. Speaking of which…

Thea glanced toward the fiberglass gondola car. The moment of departure was rapidly approaching, and she wasn't looking forward to traveling, suspended by a thin steel cable above a thousand-foot plummet into the forbidding, nearly arctic landscape. Surely, that was an exaggeration. The chasm wasn't a thousand feet. Nor was the cable excessively slender. Did it matter? If they fell, the crash would certainly be fatal.

"Nervous?" Emily asked.

"I don't like heights." With a glance at Dr. Mona, Thea hurriedly added, "I'm not acrophobic." But even though she could ride the chair lift to go skiing, as she carefully explained to Dr. Mona, Thea knew she was not telling the truth. "It makes me a little tense."

Spence joined them. "It's okay, Thea."

"What's that supposed to mean?" She hadn't meant to snap, but she didn't want to appear weak in front of him. "I'm not scared."

"You'll be fine."

"I know." To prove her courage, she grabbed her suitcase and the garment bag and went to stand, first in line, to board the gondola car.

As soon as the soles of her boots touched the skid-proof flooring, her knees turned to rubber. There were windows all around the ten-person car, which seemed much like a minibus, except that it would be suspended in mid-air.

"Hurry up," Travis called out.

Concentrating with all her might, Thea stumbled to one of the bench seats and collapsed. The molded plastic seat was so slick that she might have slid onto the floor if her muscles hadn't suddenly tensed. She shuddered into a full-body spasm. The ratcheting noise of the machinery deafened her. Was this thing safe? When was the last inspection?

Thea clutched the garment bag against her body. She was probably wrinkling the frothy bridesmaid dress, but she didn't care. Through blurred vision, she sensed Spence's approach. If he made a snotty comment, she'd kill him.

He sat beside her. "Can I hold the garment bag for you?"

"No." If they fell, she could use the dress as a parachute.

"Is everyone ready?" Lawrence asked.

Her lips pinched together, fighting the urge to scream. What if they fell? Whether it was a thousand feet or five hundred or five thousand, what did it matter? These might be the last people she ever saw in her whole life. The thunder of her heartbeat would be the last sound she ever—

They swooped away from the stone house, suspended from a thread and climbing. Don't look down!

But she didn't even have to look down. An awful sensation, of the earth dropping away, her stomach falling, her heart racing, rushed over her. Frantically groping, Thea clutched Spence's hand.

And before she knew what she was doing, her face was buried against his shoulder. This was wrong, all wrong. And yet, in her heart, she knew if Spence hadn't been beside her, she'd have found herself in the throes of a full-blown panic attack.

In her heart, she wondered what Spence had to do with it.

JORDAN AND EMILY stood beside the stone house, waving at the gondola as it climbed slowly across the precipitous chasm toward the castle which was entirely hidden by dark January clouds. Jordan pulled Emily closer, protecting her from a chill that wasn't entirely due to the weather.

"There's something about this wedding," he said, "that makes me uneasy."

"Leaving the cell phones behind seemed odd. And why was the butler late?" She shrugged. "Maybe we're the ones who are paranoid, imagining a threat at every turn."

After the fugitive hunt that had brought them together, Jordan wouldn't be surprised if he and Emily were overly sensitive to danger. Especially when Spence was involved. If it hadn't been for the good doctor's help, Jordan would probably be in jail on death row. "Spence will be okay."

She frowned. "I'm sure you're right. I hope things work out for him and Thea. I liked her."

"Me, too." Jordan turned away from the gondola. "Let's go."

She dug the toe of her boot into the snow, scanning the dark, threatening skies. "You're right. We should try to beat the storm back to Cascadia."

He nodded. Jordan hated the snow, but he loved sitting in front of a roaring fire with his beautiful new wife.

Emily tracked the progress of the gondola car moving through space toward the Castle in the Clouds. "Did you notice how scared Thea was to get on that thing?"

Jordan shrugged. "Some people are. What's really worrying you? If there's a problem, Spence will call."

"And then what? Take a look at that place. It's a search-and-rescue nightmare. Jagged cliffs on every side. The only way out in an emergency would be helicopter rescue."

"Hold on," he said, teasing her gently. "Earlier, you said the castle reminded you of princesses and jousts."

Emily shivered hard in the blistering cold. "That was before I remembered that dragons also live in castles."

THE SLOWLY ASCENDING gondola car shuddered in the swirling mountain winds, but Spence was unconcerned about the surrounding glacial landscape. The scope of his universe had shrunk to a bell jar. Starting with the moment Thea's forehead touched his shoulder, his consciousness focused entirely upon her. He actually enjoyed the feel of her slender fingers clutching his hand in a white-knuckled death grip of terror. Her fear of heights—something he had never suspected in her—had worked to his advantage.

Spence held himself very still, not wanting to disturb this moment. He knew better than to whisper reassurances that she might take as condescension. Nor did he reach across her body to fully embrace her. His job was simply to be there for her, solid as a rock, trustworthy. Sooner or later, she'd wake up and realize that he was basically a good guy.

Maybe it would be sooner. After all, she'd instinctively turned to him when she was scared, which might mean that on a visceral, almost cellular level, she still trusted him. Or it might mean nothing more than that she would've grabbed anybody sitting beside her in the gondola car. Spence didn't care. He was grateful for this hint of their former intimacy. Careful not to disturb her, he inhaled the clean fragrance of her soft chestnut-brown hair. Through the layers of their parkas and turtlenecks, he felt the subtle outline of her slender body.

In a strangled whisper, she asked, "How much farther?"

"Ten minutes."

He wanted to tell her it wasn't so bad, but he was feeling a little queasy himself. Like a giant yo-yo, deprived of gravity's solace, the gondola bounced in space, hundreds of feet above towering ice splinters. In this hostile environment, the tall conifers marched up the mountainside like a snow-encrusted army guarding the Castle in the Clouds.

At the front of the gondola, Lawrence the butler stood before a simple control panel. The reverend and Dr. Mona were seated, staring and mesmerized by the spectacular view. Only Travis was in motion, ducking down to peer from the windows on one side, then the other.

"Hey, Larry," Travis said, "how did this castle get built, anyway?"

"I prefer to be called Lawrence," the butler said.

"Okay, Law-rence," Travis drawled. "How'd they build this place?"

"I assume you are referring to the apparent impossibility of transporting building materials to such an extremely isolated location."

"Well, yeah," Travis muttered as if it were the most obvious thing in the world.

With a shrug of his round shoulders, Lawrence explained, "The opposite wall of this peak was a marble quarry. In the late 1800s, some of the finest marble in the world was quarried here, then cut and polished by artisans who came from Italy. A narrow-gauge railroad transported the stones which were used in monuments throughout North America."

"So?" Travis said. "Are you saying that the rear approach to the castle isn't so steep?"

"Quite the contrary." Lawrence continued, "In seeking the most excellent veins of marble, the walls were literally shaved back into steep cliffs."

"Interesting," Dr. Mona said. "The castle appears to be the domain of someone seeking total isolation, but that wasn't the case."

"Not at all," Lawrence said. "Though the first owner was known to be a cutthroat entrepreneur, he built this castle to please his wife, a proper Bostonian lady who insisted that the quarry be shut down on Sunday, the day of rest."

The reverend murmured his approval.

Lawrence added, "There's a chapel in the castle."

Spence felt Thea's grip on his hand begin to relax as she listened to the history of the Castle in the Clouds. Though he was glad her fear had begun to abate, he hoped she wouldn't pull away from him. He wanted the connection with her, no matter how tenuous.

"And yet," Lawrence said, "no one would mistake the castle for a cathedral. The bridal suite—which you can see from here—at the top of the north tower where the light is lit, features some rather decadent statuary."

The stern-faced reverend inhaled a disapproving sniff through his long red nose. "The castle's isolation is an appropriate homily." As if pronouncing the locale an indictment against an ill-fated wedding and a groom he had yet to meet, Joshua Hardy intoned, "It was greed that caused them to chisel away at the wall of the mountain, leaving themselves stranded and alone."

Chapter Three

"Dude," Travis shuddered, "that sounds like a sermon."

"That would be the definition of a homily," the reverend said curtly. "An example to edify the flock."

"Sheep?"

"Listen here, Mr. Trevain." The reverend pointed a warning with his skeletal index finger. "I don't appreciate your attitude. I'm here at the request of your sister to bless the holy sacrament of her marriage, and I will not be taunted."

Travis rolled his eyes and flung himself down onto a seat, sending a tremor through the gondola car.

Thea gasped and burrowed more deeply against Spence's shoulder. For her benefit he asked, "Lawrence, is this gondola safe?"

"Yes, indeed. The cable is tested to hold two thousand, two hundred pounds."

"So we have nothing to worry about."

Lawrence swiveled his bald head toward Spence and frowned. "I suppose the machinery could stall."

Not a pleasant image. Spence sure as hell didn't want to be left dangling between two precipices. From his search-and-rescue training, he supposed they'd have to be removed from the car via helicopter in a dangerous, complex procedure involving harnesses. "The stalling thing? Has that ever happened before?"

"Not that I know of," Lawrence said. "But I haven't been in Mr. Rosemont's employ for very long."

"And you probably won't be working for him long," Travis said sulkily.

"I beg your pardon?" Lawrence glared at Travis like an owl sizing up a canary. His tone implied more threat than apology, which seemed uncharacteristic for a butler whose primary duty was proper protocol and tact. Spence glimpsed the black leather of a shoulder holster beneath Lawrence's parka. The butler was armed. Why? What did he expect to find at the castle?

Lawrence turned back to his controls, and they jostled higher and higher in silence. An unmistakable air of tension crackled through the gondola car. Only the diminutive psychologist, Dr. Mona, seemed immune. "I'd like to hear more about the castle's history," she said. "What happened to the quarry?"

"In the 1920s, a fire destroyed the workers' town," Lawrence recited as if he'd memorized the pertinent data. "Then there was a disastrous flood that wiped out much of the quarry operation and the roads. The original owner and his wife moved back east. The narrow-gauge tracks were hauled away as scrap metal during the war. It wasn't until the 1960s that the castle had a full-time occupant. He added the gondola which—I hasten to assure you—has been scrupulously maintained."

As if on cue, they took a sudden jolt. Once again, Thea tensed.

Quietly, Spence said to her, "We're almost there. Only a few more minutes."

The castle disappeared from view behind the trees. They neared the summit and a gondola house which appeared to be an exact match for the one they'd left behind on the opposite slope. As the fiberglass car ratcheted forward and docked with a thud, the stone walls of the gondola house closed around them, protecting them from the fierce winds and threat of snow.

"Made it," Spence said.

Thea yanked her hand away from his and bolted for the exit. Single-minded, she pressed her fingertips against the glass. As soon as Lawrence had the sliding door open, Thea leapt through. For a moment, Spence thought she was going to kiss the wooden planks of the floor beside the gondola car. But Thea had already begun to recover her poise. She inhaled huge gulps of the thin mountain air. Fighting the shudders that vibrated her shoulders, she denied her panic. Her voice quavered as she announced to the others, "That wasn't so bad."

Through the gondola window, Spence saw Dr. Mona pat Thea's forearm. "You did very well," the doctor said. "It's important to face your fears."

"Fears?" Thea laughed semi-hysterically. "No fear. That's what my kids say at school. No fear."

Spence tucked his own suitcase under his arm and gathered up Thea's luggage before exiting the gondola behind Reverend Josh and Travis. Silently, Spence wondered what other fears the weekend might hold in store for them.

As soon as he stepped outside the gondola, Thea grabbed the garment bag. "I'll take that." Her tone was overly bright. Her smile too wide. "I wouldn't want anything to happen to the bridesmaid dress."

He nodded. Though he didn't want to throw her back into terror, he already missed the closeness of her clinging to him for support.

"By the way," she said, "thanks."

"For what?"

Her eyes roamed wildly, showing too much white and avoiding his gaze. "I didn't mean to grab you."

"It's okay. I liked it."

She stiffened. Staring directly at him, she snapped, "Are you saying that you enjoyed the fact that I was scared out of my skull?"

"I was glad you trusted me enough to hold my hand."

"Don't flatter yourself. It was only a reflex."

As soon as she spoke, Thea realized how ungracious her comment sounded. She didn't want to pick a fight with Spence. This was a wedding, supposedly a pleasant occasion, and she was well-prepared to stifle her own emotions rather than ruin the weekend for Jenny and her reclusive bridegroom.

Forcing what she hoped was a polite smile, Thea added, "But thanks anyway."

"You're welcome."

Sometime during this weekend—sometime soon—she had to set down ground rules of behavior with Spence. The best solution was probably to ignore each other as much as possible. But how would she manage that? How could she ignore someone who was so solid and sexy and outrageously masculine?

When she'd clung to him like a drowning woman hanging on a buoy, a sneaky awareness had crept through her panic. She'd felt the strength in his grasp. Leaning against his shoulder wakened unwanted memories of previous intimacy.

She was saved from further contemplation by a loud "harrumph" from Lawrence who stood at the door to the gondola house trying to get an answer from the house on an intercom or radio of some sort. Obviously annoyed, he informed them, "There seems to be an unfortunate miscommunication. No one answers at the castle."

"Well that's just hunky-dory," Travis snapped. "What do we do now?"

Frowning, Lawrence said, "I had expected to be met by a full contingent of staff, including a porter, but no one appears to be responding to our arrival. Ladies and gentlemen, would you mind carrying your own luggage?"

"No problem," Thea said. Travis put on a sulk, but as her tension faded, she was actually glad for something physical and taxing to do. Whatever urge had compelled her to clamp onto Spence was past.

She fell into the single-file line as they hiked up a snow-packed, sanded path winding through the trees. Thea was next to last, and Spence brought up the rear. She could hear his footfalls behind her. She was aware of his measured breathing. He must be in good shape; he wasn't huffing at all on this steep incline.

Of course, he'd be in excellent physical condition. She reminded herself that Spence Cannon was, perhaps, the most self-centered man on the planet. He would take care of himself.

The trees thinned. Suddenly, the castle came into full view. Magnificent! Thea halted and stared up at the walls of chiseled granite blocks that formed nooks and shadowed crannies, dark and mysterious as the storm clouds overhead. Nearest the path was a sculpted octagonal tower. The arched windows on the top story of the tower were lit from inside.

"That's got to be the bridal suite," Spence said. "The room with the sexy statues."

"Jenny must be up there." But why hadn't she come down to greet them? Thea shook off a prickly sense of apprehension. More than likely, Jenny hadn't heard their arrival. Or she was busy with her trousseau. After all, she'd pulled this wedding together in a matter of weeks.

There must be dozens of last-minute details. "I should've come up here earlier to help her. It's my job as a maid of honor."

"I'm sure Jenny has everything under control," Dr. Mona offered, showing no sign of exertion either. "She's quite a capable young woman."

"But look at this place! It's huge. How could anybody manage?"

"With a staff of servants, dear," Dr. Mona advised, tongue-in-cheek.

But surely, even with maids and a cook, the responsibility of taking care of a castle was daunting. It was so large that Thea couldn't even clearly see the matching tower on the far end. The center section rose four stories high with a peaked Tudor-style roof above a stone Gothic entranceway. The mismatched architectural theme also included castellated battlements to mark the parapets and a minaret-style gatekeeper's house by the front doorway. Some of the windows were arched, others were square. The mishmash of designs might have come from flipping through a Lifestyles of the Eccentric Rich and Famous catalog and choosing something from each page. "I wonder if the original structure was added to."

"It seems likely," Dr. Mona said. "Parts of it look Romanesque. Others are definitely Tudor."

"I don't care for the gargoyles," the reverend said.

There was no chance to question Lawrence about the design. He was far ahead, chugging steadily up the hill toward an entrance behind the octagonal tower. Travis stayed close behind him, apparently unimpressed by his first up-close-and-personal view of the castle.

As they came closer to the entrance, the outdoor lights blazed to life, illuminating the stone walls.

"Wow!" Spotlights shining up from the ground gave

the illusion that the massive structure was magically float-ing above the snow-covered cliffs.

"Must be somebody home," Spence said, "to turn on the lights."

"Of course," Thea said. Yet, an aura of stillness clung to the granite walls as if the castle were an empty stage waiting for the players to enter and speak their lines.

Lawrence unlocked and opened a humble door beside a loading dock, and Travis bellowed, "Jenny! Get your booty down here, sis!"

Her booty? Thea forced a grin, trying to be tolerant. The slangy attitude of Jenny's brother reminded her of her eighth-grade students. Though Travis had to be in his late twenties, he seemed like a kid—irresponsible and not a little bit wild.

Thea hiked the last steps to the side entrance and stepped inside a long coatroom with no windows. At the far end a ski rack housed several pairs of skis and boots in a various sizes. Along the adjoining paneled wall, wooden pegs served as hooks between several closet doors. There were even lockers. It all seemed odd to her, like a chalet at some ski resort.

Through an open door, she heard Lawrence exclaiming, "Utterly unacceptable!"

Thea, Spence, Mona and the reverend dropped their lug-gage and went toward the sound of Lawrence's voice into a huge kitchen. Stainless-steel appliances shone amidst an array of marble countertops and butcher blocks. A giant hanging rack displayed copper pots and kettles. Though Thea wasn't much of a cook, the kitchen impressed her.

"No one is here." Lawrence emphatically stated the obvious. "No chef. No waitpersons. No one."

Mona pulled open the door to a double-wide refrigerator

which was packed with food. "At least there seems to be ample provisions."

Disdainfully, Lawrence sneered, "I certainly hope I won't be expected to prepare the meals."

"Where's Travis?" Spence asked.

Lawrence pointed toward a door at the far corner of the kitchen. "That's the servants' stairwell up to the bridal suite. He went to look for Jenny."

"I think I'll join them," Thea said. She really couldn't wait to see Jenny, and it seemed like the next logical thing to do. "I'm sure Jenny can tell us where the rest of the staff is hiding."

Without invitation, Spence followed her into a narrow wooden stairwell that ascended in a sharp zigzag pattern. Every few feet, a single bare lightbulb, attached to the wall and encased in a wire cage, cast their shadows against stone and mortar walls.

"Watch your step," Spence advised. "These stairs are worn unevenly."

"Apparently," she said, trying to focus her attentions elsewhere, and not on the fact that she was quite alone with Spence, "the lord of the castle didn't believe in spending much money on servants."

He looked upward. "I don't see how they carried trays up this staircase."

"Dumbwaiter," she said. Her voice echoed in the vertical passageway. "There has to be a dumbwaiter."

Their conversation seemed innocent enough, but Thea felt a growing sense of apprehension partially caused by her sudden seclusion with Spence and partially because Jenny's failure to appear felt ominous.

"I can't imagine Jenny wasn't waiting for us. She knew when we'd be gathered below, when we'd get here. Do you think there's something wrong? Something..." she hesitated without warning on the stair and swallowed hard. "I don't know…not quite right about all this?"

Spence had to step back down to avoid overtaking her. "Travis must have found his sister, don't you think? Otherwise, he'd be yelling his head off."

Thea straightened. "I'm sure you're right." She was worrying needlessly, still trembling with aftershocks from her panic attack in the gondola car.

They paused on a small landing outside a closed door. "This is only the second floor," Spence said. "I think we need to go one higher."

Enclosed by solid stone walls, they were completely isolated from the others. Spence was surely right that Travis had found Jenny, and there wasn't going to be a better time than this for a private conversation.

She faced Spence. Until now, she hadn't noticed that he'd shed his parka. His teal-blue turtleneck emphasized the blue in his eyes and outlined the breadth of his shoulders. "Spence, we need to talk."

Even in the dim light, she saw his frown. Like most men, Spence had never been fond of relationship discussions—not that they had a relationship anymore. She opened her mouth and took a bite out of the silence. "This is probably the most important weekend of Jenny's life—"

"Agreed," he said. His eyes bore into hers.

Her chin went up. "I don't want to do anything to make it unpleasant for her."

"Of course not. So?"

"So, you and I need to set some boundaries with each other."

"Such as?"

"Let's start with the basic premise that I'm not prepared to forgive and forget, Spence. There is absolutely no way we'll ever again be involved. Not ever." Though she'd kept her voice quiet, a resonating echo stirred the air, underscoring the finality of her words. "Is that understood?"

"I understand. Perfectly," he added. "I just don't believe you."

She scowled. "Do you think I can't resist you?"

"No," he responded quickly. "But I don't accept the concept of 'never.' It's simple biology, Thea. All living things are constantly changing, transforming. We get better or we get worse, but we seldom stay the same."

If he'd been anyone else, she would have applauded his observation. As a teacher of adolescents, she had to believe in the potential of human development. But the man who stood before her wasn't one of her difficult students. He was her former fiancé, the individual who had humiliated her and single-handedly shattered important professional goals. Vital goals. She drew on a vast reservoir of bitterness for lost opportunities before speaking. "Trust me, Spence. My attitude toward you is rock-solid, and—"

"But," he interrupted, "in an hour, you might feel different."

"Different*ly.*"

"Yes." As if she had agreed she might, he nodded.

She wanted to stamp her foot. She crossed her arms over her breasts. "I'm serious, Spence."

He planted a hand on the stone-and-mortar wall high above her. "I know you are, Thea."

"I'm not going to debate life science with you—"

"That's a start."

"—or philosophy or anything else. In fact—"

He gave her a lazy grin.

"Will you stop it, Spence!" This discussion wasn't going the way she'd hoped. He was so near to her in this cold vault of a stone staircase that she could feel his heat.

She tossed her chin-length bob and tried another tactic. "Let's just agree on two things. We won't squabble. And there will be no unnecessary touching. No kissing. Nothing."

"Well, that's hardly fair, Thea, after you spent the gondola ride groping me. You know—"

"I was *not* groping! I—"

"Okay, grabbing." The corner of his mouth lifted in a half smile. His arrogance was devastating. "Okay," he relented, "call it holding on. I just think I ought to have the chance to return that favor."

His blue eyes warmed as he gazed confidently into her face, and she felt herself responding involuntarily, wanting to smile back at him. For an instant, she was tempted to open her arms wide and invite him to come closer. But no! Common sense prevailed. "Don't even think about it, Spence."

"I've got a few conditions of my own," he said.

"So long as we don't squabble and you—"

"Number one—we stay in the present and not dwell on the past."

She gave him a look. "I don't know what you mean."

"Yes, you do. I can see the wheels turning in that sweet, stubborn little head of yours, dredging up every unhappy memory, every accusation we ever threw at each other, every—"

"All right," she cut him off. "We'll stick to the present." Did he think that somehow altered *her* conditions?

"And not dwell in the past. That's the important part, Thea."

Grudgingly, she nodded. "Fair enough."

"Number two—we both keep our minds open."

Thea said, "I've never been close-minded. How could you even accuse me of—"

"Number three..."

He obliterated the distance between them in a single step. His unexpected approach threw her off-balance. The surrounding walls seemed to shrink tightly around her. She felt trapped as much by the intensity of her suppressed emotions as by him—but there should be no mistake. She was trapped in his arms.

When his hands glided around her shoulders, she should have pushed him away. Hadn't he listened to a word she'd been saying?

She didn't want him.

He revolted her.

But none of that, clearly, was true, because her arms went around him as if he hadn't been gone all these years. Her fingers reveled in the feel of his hard muscles beneath the soft cotton of his turtleneck.

A part of her smirked. *What was she doing?* This was insanity. She'd forgotten all about her missing friend, and the conditions she had set out were being trampled. But her head tilted back and her objections died in her throat, vanishing into the thin musty air as she met his dazzling gaze. She realized that all she really wanted was the feel of Spence Cannon's shoulders beneath her fingers.

She wanted the taste of his lips against hers.

Reading her mind from long experience, Spence complied. The hard pressure of his mouth satisfied a longing she'd fought to deny and then to ignore when her denial mechanisms failed her.

Her heartbeat quickened. An all-consuming passion exploded in the very core of her being, heightening numbed sensation to a tantalizing, trembling, voracious desire.

More.

She wanted more. She wanted a hundred more kisses. She wanted to touch his body, his bare-naked flesh. And more than that! She yearned for his caresses, the feel of his hands on her breasts, her thighs, she wanted his lips, the touch of his tongue to the dimples in the small of her back.

In a distant corner of her mind, the part that smirked, Thea knew she was dangerously close to making a big mistake, opening herself to all sorts of emotional pain. Sex with Spence, desire, had never been an issue, never a problem—except that it was so good, so desperately good that it had overwhelmed real problems for too long.

Against the aching thrill of his hand caressing her breast beneath her parka and the heat of his breath on her neck, she knew she had to stop him. Had to stifle her own sensual impulses before they destroyed her. There was a reason she'd asked him not to touch her. When he touched her, she lost track of the fact that he didn't respect her at all, or at least he hadn't—and his behavior in every other way had proved it, if only she'd been looking.

With the shred of willpower left her, she tore herself away from him.

He didn't force her to stay in his embrace. Nor had he forced the kiss. Thea had had ample time to object, and she hadn't warned him away. She'd asked him not to touch her, but when he came near enough, she'd allowed it. Craved it. And she really couldn't blame him for her own lapse in good judgment. He had offered, and she had wantonly and unwisely accepted.

In a ragged voice, she vowed, "That can't happen again."

"Thea—"

But his impassioned plea, whatever he had been going to say, was interrupted from the top of the narrow staircase by a shout. It was Travis, calling his sister's name. "Jenny! What's the hap, woman? Where are you?"

Thea spun away from Spence and flew up through the stairwell on shaky legs. There was no handrail and she braced herself against the rough stones and crumbling mortar.

Standing at the door leading to the third floor, Thea gathered her composure, taking steady breaths to calm the ridiculous fluttering in her chest. She tore off her parka, hoping to ease the intense heat that flushed her body.

The third-floor landing was lit by wall sconces and a high chandelier. In contrast to the dank gloom of the servant's staircase, the decor was bright and clean with white-on-beige wallpaper above polished wood wainscoting. An octagonal Persian-style rug covered the wood floor. Travis—in his red and yellow ski clothes—looked too modern and out-of-place.

"Jenny's not here," he said gesturing to the three wide-open doors as if Thea were responsible. "I looked everywhere."

Thea headed toward the center doors as Spence came up behind her. "Is this the bridal suite?"

"Don't you believe me? Didn't I just say, *she's not here?* Didn't I just—"

"Travis, calm down, okay? This is a very large castle." She felt like she was talking to one of her obstreperous students. She was struck, somehow, in this lighting, by Travis's unruly platinum-hued hair, and the fact that his brows were so dark by comparison. He'd bleached his hair, bowing to some ultra-hip image of himself as king-of-the-world ski racer. *Hip* probably wasn't even the right word. But he was still Jenny's baby brother, and he was probably very upset not to have found her. "Jenny's here somewhere, Travis. She's got to be. Don't worry. I'm sure we'll find her."

"But this was the only room where the lights were on," he said.

"That's true," Thea said. "But someone also had to turn on the outside lights when we approached."

"Not necessarily." Spence said. "The lights could be on a timer. More likely, they're motion sensitive."

She cut Spence a look. The thought had occurred to her as well, but to keep Travis under wraps she'd been trying to take a positive outlook on the situation. But maybe more than to reassure Travis, she needed to quiet her own forebodings.

Didn't she have enough worries after that earth-shaking kiss on the staircase?

"Let's take another look around. Maybe Jenny left a note or a trail of bread crumbs or something."

"Yeah, maybe she and Rosemont are getting it—"

"Maybe," Thea cut him off, "Jenny and Rosemont are off watching a movie in some fantastic entertainment room with a sound system so wonderful that they haven't heard us troop in."

"Freaky Pollyanna," Travis muttered, but the suggestion of something that cool looked like it might occupy his nearly vacant head for a while.

Thea opened the doors to the bridal suite. It was everything Lawrence had promised and more—a fantasy in pinks, reds and ripe purples that would almost certainly mortify the puritanical sensibilities of Reverend Joshua Handy. Thea's gaze came to rest on a life-sized incandescent marble sculpture of lovers so entwined it looked as if they had come straight out of the pages of the *Kama Sutra.*

Several smaller versions of couplings and threesomes stood scattered about. Spooky, unseeing marble eyes leered or rolled back in expressions of stone ecstasy.

Beneath the windows was an opulent pink-veined marble bathtub with Jacuzzi jets. Opposite was the largest bed Thea had ever seen. This place was obviously a sex palace.

Thea could not imagine Jenny in this room. It went beyond opulent right straight to decadent, making her feel embarrassed with Spence so near and their kissing so recent. She swallowed hard. "Interesting."

"Yeah," Travis agreed. "I can't believe my prissy-pants big sister would even walk in here, much less sleep in the same room with these dudes."

"They're not all dudes," Spence observed wryly.

Travis opened the mirrored closet door. "But look. Here's Jenny's stuff."

Ignoring the marble orgy, fending off her own growing alarm that Jenny wasn't right here to show off the castle, Thea went to the walk-in closet. She recognized a few of Jenny's blouses and sweaters. Centered on the rack, hanging all by itself, was a black silk garment bag. A bit of white lace was visible above the top of the zipper. The bridal gown!

Jenny had described her wedding dress in detail, but Thea hadn't yet seen this handmade creation with satin, imported lace and real pearls embroidered on the sleeves. Surely, it wouldn't hurt to take a quick peek.

She unzipped the bag and pulled apart each side to reveal the dress her friend had chosen for her fantasy wedding.

But a terrible gasp tore out of Thea's throat. In the center of the bodice was the dark red stain of dried blood.

Chapter Four

Spence was a medical doctor, certified in search-and-rescue emergency medical procedures, and while he'd interned at Colorado University Medical Center in Denver, he'd spent months in the ER, where he repaired bone-deep gashes, probed for bullets and had once delivered twins. The sight of blood shouldn't have affected him.

But when he saw the stain on Jenny's wedding gown, and yanked the gown from the garment bag, his gut wrenched. The filmy white fabric burned in his hands.

From the moment he'd first seen the castle, he'd sensed something was wrong, and other things only kept piling on to confirm his instincts. The remote location. The butler's shoulder holster. The bizarre request to leave behind all cell phones, which were useless anyway without cellular service in the area.

Then, not only the absence of staff and servants, but Jenny's failure to appear at all. Spence couldn't even excuse Rosemont, who might be expected to keep to himself were it not the weekend of his wedding.

Now this. The bloodstain on Jenny's bridal gown caused all the vague threads to draw together, like blood fibrin congealing. They were all caught up and in danger—perhaps mortal danger.

What had happened to Jenny?

Both Thea and Travis looked toward him as if they expected Spence to have an answer, but there was no rational explanation. It didn't take the training or standard operating procedures of the search-and-rescue unit to state the obvious. "We should call the police."

"Right," Thea said, her features drawn tight in anxiety for Jenny. She darted across the room and picked up the bedside telephone and stabbed out 911. But when she listened for an answer and apparently got no response, her alarm notched higher. She shook the receiver, tapped the plunger button. Her gaze darted frantically around the room, bouncing off the obscene marble statuary. She met his gaze with her eyes wide. "The phone's dead."

"What the hell is this scene?" Travis yelled. "If that bastard hurt my sister, I'll kill him. Swear to God, I'll tear his heart out with my bare—"

"That's enough!" Spence commanded. "You won't help Jenny by falling apart. We have to find your sister."

Travis sank onto a plush purple chaise longue. Leaning forward, he ground the heels of his hands into his eye sockets. "It's my fault. I should've taken better care of her."

For the first time, his voice held a surprising ring of sincerity. Though Travis was a brash, self-centered jerk, he might actually care about his sister.

Spence hoped that was the case. If Rosemont turned out to be a bust, and it sure as hell was starting to look that way, Jenny was going to need her brother's support.

But where was she? Was she all right? Spence looked

down at the gown in his hands and inspected the dried bloodstain, which was the approximate size of a postcard but irregular in shape. There were splatters. The fabric had not been torn.

"This stain didn't come from a wound." He turned the bodice inside out. "You see? There's no rip. And there's less blood on the inside than the outside."

"What does that mean?" Thea asked.

"Someone poured this blood onto the dress."

"But why?"

"It might be a threat," he surmised. "Maybe we were meant to find this dress."

She took his idea one step farther. "If someone wanted us to find the dress, it means the threat is directed at us. The wedding party."

"Bull." Travis bolted from the chaise and got right up in her face. "This isn't about you, babe. It's all about my sister."

"Back off," Spence warned.

"You know what, dude?" Travis whirled and confronted him. "Who died and left you boss?" With a stiff index finger, he poked at Spence's chest. "Why you? Huh?"

Lightning fast, Spence clamped the younger man's wrist in a vise-like grip. "Could be because between us, I'm the grown-up."

"Yeah, good old Spence. Manly man." Through clenched teeth, Travis said, "You were at my old man's funeral. Jenny said you were such a comfort. Said she couldn't have made it without you. Well you know what? That should have been me."

"You're right." Spence hadn't usurped the job of com--

forting Jenny. She had no one else; her brother was absent, tucked away in a rehab center, hiding from his grief. "You should have been there, Travis."

"You don't know anything about me." Travis wrenched away from him. Like a petulant, spoiled brat, he cradled his wrist.

Spence turned toward Thea. Moments ago, he'd held her in his arms. He'd kissed her. That idyllic interlude seemed far gone, erased by the intrusion of real threats. Of danger. "Let's go downstairs and tell the others. We'll search the castle and find Jenny and then we're out of here."

Thea was already on her way out the door. "Let's go."

Leaving the gown in the bridal suite, they descended the narrow staircase into the kitchen.

Lawrence sat on a high stool fiddling with some kind of hand-held electronic game. Dr. Mona had arranged fresh fruit in gleaming silver bowl and sat peeling apples and pears. "Did you find Jenny?" she enthused, then shrank into herself at Thea's grim expression.

"No. We didn't."

While Spence outlined their discovery of the blood-stained dress and his plan to search the castle, he noticed the psychologist observing him closely with her bright black eyes. Occasionally, she nodded. Her expert opinion might be useful. "Mona, I'd like to hear what you think about all this."

"Blood on the wedding gown," she said. Her small, wizened face twisted in a frown. "Highly symbolic, isn't it? Almost archetypal."

"Psychobabble," Travis said with a groan. "Can we get started with the search?"

Ignoring him, Spence said, "What else, Mona?"

"It's a theatrical gesture, well-planned." She scratched the back of her head, ruffling her short gray hair. "I'm reminded of those murder mystery weekends when several people gather to solve a fake crime."

"Fake?" Spence could only pray that Dr. Mona was correct. "Are you suggesting this might be an elaborate joke?"

"I don't know. I seriously doubt that Jenny would prepare such a complicated scenario—and why a murder mystery on the weekend of her wedding? To what purpose?"

"What about Rosemont?" Spence asked.

"I've never met Gregory Rosemont," Mona said. "I suppose he might be enacting some unknown agenda and perhaps convinced Jenny to play along."

"We're wasting time," Reverend Joshua intoned. "Much as I hate to agree with Travis, I believe we should begin our search without further delay."

Spence turned toward the butler, who shut down his game and tucked it in the inside pocket of his jacket. "Lawrence, is there a floor plan of this place?"

"Not that I am aware of."

As he stepped forward, Lawrence buttoned his black wool blazer. The jacket fitted so well that Spence hardly noticed the slight bulge of the shoulder holster. Lawrence had obviously taken the time to move the holster and weapon to wear it even indoors. The question arose again. Why was the so-called butler armed? "Come with me, Lawrence. I want to ask you about the lighting system."

"Certainly."

The butler followed Spence into the coatroom. Before

Spence could close the door, Thea slipped through. She closed the door. "Excuse me," she said. "I had a question for Lawrence."

"Yes, ma'am?" He inclined his head toward her.

Deftly, she reached toward him, unfastened the button on his blazer and flipped it aside. "Why do you have a gun?"

Spence winced. Subtlety had never been one of Thea's attributes.

"In addition to my duties as a butler," Lawrence said, "I occasionally act as a bodyguard. I am licensed to carry a concealed weapon."

"Is Rosemont expecting trouble?" Spence asked.

"He did not see fit to confide his suspicions," Lawrence answered, dismissing the subject. "Did you have a question about the lights?"

"They came on when we approached the outer door, but there wasn't anybody here. Who turned them on?"

"All the lights in the house are motion sensitive. You'll find that's true throughout the premises. When you enter a room, the lights will come on. Ten minutes after you leave, they automatically extinguish—unless you've pressed the bypass switch. The gas fireplaces work in a similar manner. Quite modern and efficient."

Spence wasn't impressed. "Like the state-of-the-art phone system that doesn't work?"

Lawrence looked truly surprised. "The phones aren't working? Are you sure?"

Thea nodded. "I tried to phone the police from the bridal suite. I didn't even get a dial tone."

"Well," Lawrence balked. "All technology has a few glitches."

"Are there computers in the house?" Spence asked.

"Well, of course, there are computers," Lawrence answered disdainfully. "Mr. Rosemont made his fortune from Web sites."

"Is his Internet access through the phone lines?"

"I couldn't really say." Lawrence scratched his head.

Unwitting, Thea touched Spence's arm. "What are you thinking?"

"I'm *hoping* that Rosemont has installed cable or a dish for the newest satellite access. We can reach the police that way—but if he operates on phone modem, we're out of luck."

"We can take a look," Lawrence offered. "I assume you will know what you're looking for?"

"Yes."

"Very well." Lawrence led the way back into the kitchen. "Ladies and gentlemen, please follow me."

Spence fell into step beside Thea. They held back from the rest of the herd. In a low voice, he said, "In the future, you might want to think twice before confronting a man with a gun."

"I found out what we needed to know, didn't I?"

"All we learned was what the butler was willing to tell us. Not much, Thea."

She rolled her eyes. "Were you planning to interrogate him? Please, Spence. Don't get all macho on me. You have a good plan. Let's just follow it—find Jenny and then get out of here."

Though Thea wasn't looking forward to another ride on the gondola, she knew they had to escape and that was their only way out.

As they walked through the arched serving area to the

dining room, brilliant lights flashed to life. Twenty high-backed chairs ranged around a long table which was covered with a damask and lace table cloth. Pink roses made a lovely centerpiece. Fresh roses! They looked almost dewy, as if they'd just been picked from a garden.

While Dr. Mona had been reminded of a murder mystery weekend, Thea thought of the sinister castle in "Beauty and the Beast" where unseen servants performed all the work and the visitors hardly realized they were pampered prisoners. "Spence, do you think this is a trick or some kind of a joke?"

He grimaced. "Let's hope so."

Lawrence announced, "We are now entering the Grand Drawing Room. This is where the wedding ceremony is to be held."

Four light fixtures reflected against the gold-painted ceiling. A gas-powered fire flared in the massive stone fireplace, fronted with green-veined marble tiles. The furnishings were antique, mostly hunter green, mostly Queen Anne style with high-backed chairs.

A whispery voice floated, disembodied, through the air. "Please be seated."

The wedding party shared a single gasp. Each of them glanced nervously at the others.

"Please," the voice repeated. "Everyone find a seat."

Thea found herself looking toward Spence. Arrogant as all hell, the man made a natural leader. At the moment, she wanted someone to tell her what to do.

"Let's do it," he ordered, looking about the room for speakers. "Must be an audio tape," he said. "Possibly activated like the lights as we came into the room."

"Are you sitting?" the disembodied voice asked.

"Radical," Travis mocked, all nervous, angry energy. He planted his hands on his narrow hips and shouted to the proverbial rafters, "Where is my sister, you bastard?"

"Travis, for heaven's sake, shut up and listen," Thea urged, troubled by his expression, his haughty attitude of entitlement which not only set off alarms inside her that she couldn't quite pinpoint, but would almost certainly enrage Rosemont. "Maybe we'll learn something if you knock it off."

Travis glared at her, but, with the exception of Lawrence who stood posed in front of the mantle, they each found a spot, Thea beside Spence on a brocade sofa. She whispered, "This is too weird, Spence—"

The mysterious voice interrupted her. "I am your host, Gregory Rosemont. Welcome to Castle in the Clouds."

There was a pause, as if to allow them to respond. No one spoke, though Travis looked as if he was eating ground glass to keep quiet.

"The world is such a lonely place," the voice of Rosemont continued, "and yet, it's been said that we're all connected. Each of us knows someone who knows someone who knows someone. Within six degrees of separation, each of us may be connected to every other person on the planet by those we share in common. All of you, for instance, know Jenny, but not necessarily each other."

No one seemed confused by Rosemont's reference to the infamous "six degrees of separation." Thea supposed everyone had heard of the theory by now. And as far as Thea could figure, she and Spence were the only members of the wedding party who were previously acquainted.

"Each of you also knew one other special individual—

a sensitive but tortured soul. Each of you, in your own cruel way, wronged this person.

"This weekend is for reparations. This weekend is your *last* chance to repent," Rosemont said. "You have forty-eight hours to admit to your crimes and betrayals. At that time, a helicopter will arrive to transport the survivors down from the mountain. If you refuse to face the wrongs you have done, you will die."

Thea shuddered. A terrible bitterness rang in the disembodied voice of Gregory Rosemont. He wasn't proposing a parlor game. The stakes in the contest he had arranged were life and death.

"Jenny will not be included in your fate," Rosemont said. "She is blameless and will come to no harm for her role as the nexus between all of you. You need not concern yourselves with her safety."

Travis bounded to his feet. "Prove it! Come on, Rosemont, prove that Jenny's okay."

"Goodbye," the disembodied voice whispered, unresponsive to Travis's demand. "For now."

Reverend Joshua stood. The tendons in his scrawny neck strained as he looked upward, addressing their unseen host. "I won't be a part of this. No man has the divine right to judge another."

"Who are you talking to, you freak!" Travis demanded, as if it weren't obvious that they'd been listening to a pre-recorded litany. "He's not here, man. Didn't you just hear him say bye-bye?"

The reverend refused to acknowledge Travis. Reverend Joshua's narrow shoulders hunched. The corners of his eyes twitched, and he seemed caught in his own fearful reverie.

Thea wondered if the reverend had already guessed the identity of the person mentioned by Rosemont. "Reverend," she said, "do you know what tortured soul he's talking about?"

"I don't know." For some unfathomable reason, the reverend still wore his galoshes, and he stumbled toward the door. "Lawrence, I demand to be taken back down the mountain. Immediately."

"What about Jenny?" Thea said. "We can't leave her here with this madman."

"I won't stay," the reverend said. "You can't force me to stay."

Tiny Dr. Mona popped up beside him. "I have to agree with Reverend Joshua. If we start playing Mr. Rosemont's game, we implicitly give our consent to the consequences."

"Bunch of cowards," Travis snarled. "What consequences? Where's Jenny? There's your stupid consequences. My sister is missing, and I'm not leaving till we find her." He clapped Thea on the shoulder. "You and me, babe. We'll stay."

Thea jerked away. "Travis, if you touch me again I will cripple you."

"Oooh, baby," Travis began mocking her, right up until he sensed an imminent dismantling by Spence. Travis backed off. Way off. "C'mon, you guys! If we divide up the castle, we can find her fast."

Thea found herself agreeing, at least in principle, with Travis. They couldn't leave Jenny here until they'd exhausted every possibility of finding her. On the other hand, she felt intuitively that they shouldn't split up. In every scary movie she'd ever seen, the trouble came when the victims started wandering off by themselves. She trusted her own instincts, but again, she found herself looking to Spence. "What are you thinking?"

Spence hurriedly dispensed with either option until they could follow through on their original plan, which Rosemont's tape had forestalled. "For the moment, we'll stay together while I try to contact the police. Agreed?"

Some grumbling went on, but in a few moments they'd all given their consent, even the reverend. Thea finally conceded in her own mind that Spence's arrogance wasn't a fatal flaw at all. At least in this situation, what looked like arrogance was, in truth, real leadership, getting consensus from a scared and wrangling bunch. Spence turned toward Lawrence. "Show me the computer."

"Very well, sir."

The butler led the way across the marble-floored entryway with a towering Venetian-style chandelier sprinkling light on several tall, green plants. The ornate banister on the main staircase was carved from dark cherrywood, the stair steps from the purest white marble. Thea could imagine what Jenny would have looked like, walking gracefully down the stairs in her wedding gown, holding her bouquet. This should have been a splendid weekend, a triumph for a thirty-four-year-old woman who deserved a chance—just once in her life—to be a princess.

A light sigh escaped her lips, and Spence was quick to respond. His hand touched her elbow, gently guiding her. Quietly, he asked, "Are you okay?"

"I've been better," she whispered back.

"We'll get out of this, Thea. I promise."

"Don't make promises you aren't sure you can keep."

He nodded. "I'll get you out of this or die trying."

Those alternatives weren't exactly comforting, but she had to give him points for honesty.

The library, lined with bookshelves, was solid and masculine with heavy, leather-upholstered furniture. Thea noticed the faint, lingering scent of pipe-smoke, as if someone had only recently left off studying at the polished oak desk.

The computer monitor was an opaque eye in the dark room, staring blankly from a hutch behind the desk.

When Spence sat at the keyboard and moved the mouse, the Rosemont coat-of-arms flashed onto the screen. A single rose, the interlocking crowns, the four daggers.

"The symbolism is so painfully obvious," Dr. Mona observed. "A rose for the person whom Rosemont believes was wronged. The crowns for the marriage ceremony. Daggers for us."

"But there are six of us," Thea pointed out. "Me and Spence, you and the reverend and Travis, and Lawrence."

"I hardly think I'm included," Lawrence said.

"No?" Thea asked. But why, really, was he carrying a gun? "Maybe you can tell us. Is Rosemont a practical joker? Is he going to jump out and yell surprise and let the wedding begin?"

"I couldn't say."

"You must have some idea what sort of man he is," Thea persisted.

Lawrence frowned. "I've never actually met him. All of our communications have been via telephone, fax and e-mail. On my two visits to the castle, Jenny showed me around and told me the wedding plans."

"If I had to guess—never having actually met Gregory Rosemont myself—I would say," Dr. Mona volunteered, "that the man exhibits all the signs and symptoms of OCD."

"Obsessive-compulsive disorder?" Reverend Joshua queried with dismay.

The troll-like little psychologist nodded. "Obsession, you see, is a mental state. Rosemont is obviously fixated on revenge. Look at the lengths he has gone to in order to arrange this weekend. 'Compulsive' describes the behavior. His refusal to allow any photos of himself to be taken is an example."

"Yeah," Travis added, "like making us cough up our cell phones."

"Precisely," Dr. Mona went on while Spence worked at the computer. "OCDs are often highly intelligent. They build complicated, elaborate schemes to fulfill their fantasies. They are generally introverted and lack even rudimentary social skills. They cannot take no for an answer. I may be completely off-base, here, but all we've seen up to now certainly fits the profile."

"Great," Travis complained, stretching the word out to eight or nine syllables.

From behind the computer, Spence cursed. An Access Denied message blinked on the screen. "I can't get into the system. Are any of you computer specialists?"

"I've a bit of experience," Reverend Joshua said. "Let me try."

Spence moved aside and the good reverend took the hot seat. Facing the computer, he wiped the back of one hand across his forehead. Though the temperature in the castle seemed to be a well-regulated sixty-eight degrees, the reverend's face shone with sweat. His long skeletal fingers trembled as he plucked at the keyboard.

He was obviously fearful, and that seemed odd to Thea. Wouldn't a man of God be the least nervous of all in a situation like this? Unless he really *wasn't* a man of God. There were only four daggers. If Lawrence was right about himself not being counted in Rosemont's revenge scenarios, there was an extra person. A ringer?

Reverend Joshua tried a couple of sophisticated hacker-looking ploys. Each ended with the same message: Access Denied.

"We're locked out," he said. "We have no way of communicating with the outside world except to leave this evil place."

SLATE-GRAY SKIES erased the dusky stars. Spence looked up into the ink-black clouds that rumbled over the castle, spitting hard sleet bullets. It was going to be a hell of a storm.

In spite of ongoing disagreements, he'd managed to herd everyone into the coatroom where they put on their parkas, hats, scarves and boots. Now they were on the path to the gondola house. He couldn't get Thea off this godforsaken mountain soon enough.

"I'm not leaving," Travis said for the ten-thousandth time. "I don't know why I should walk down to the gondola with the rest of you."

"Until we have our bearings," Spence said, "we need to stay together as a group. As I told you before, it's basic search-and-rescue procedure. The last thing I need, Travis, is for you to go off by yourself and get lost or hurt. Then I'd have to waste time and energy looking for you."

His only real concern for Travis was an abstract urge, based on the Hippocratic oath he had taken as a doctor, to protect human life, even a specimen as obnoxious as Travis. Spence was far more worried about Jenny and about what might happen to Thea. He wanted her safely away from this castle. Though she wasn't going to like riding the gondola again, he had to convince her to go back with the reverend and Dr. Mona.

As the others went inside the gondola house, he pulled her aside. The light from the gondola house shone on her thick lashes. Her cheeks were reddened by the cold. Her skin looked moist and fresh. A wisp of her dark hair whipped across her eyes. He tucked it back inside the hood of her burgundy parka.

"You should go, Thea," he said.

"You're not leaving." Her head cocked. Her voice challenged.

"Somebody has to stay here with Travis."

"Maybe, but you're really staying here because you're worried about Jenny. Just like I am." She glanced back toward the castle. "I can't abandon her."

"You always were stubborn."

"Thank you," she said.

"That wasn't a compliment."

"I know you prefer women who know their place, who are content to stand behind their men and bask in reflected glory. That's not who I am. Even if you've forgotten the details, Spence, I think you should remember that much."

"I haven't forgotten." Five years ago, they'd butted heads. Spence had won the battle, but he'd lost Thea. "This is different. Whether or not Rosemont is crazy, he's one dangerous SOB."

"I understand. I'm willing to take the risk. We should

just put Dr. Mona and Reverend Joshua on the gondola and—''

''You don't even know what the risk is, Thea!'' he interrupted. *She* might be willing to throw herself in harm's way. Spence wasn't. She was a schoolteacher, not trained in handling danger. ''Rosemont isn't somebody you can back down with a stern reprimand and a slap on the wrist with a ruler.''

Anger glittered in her eyes, but her voice remained calm. ''For your information, Spence, rulers are historical artifacts. Teaching in an inner-city middle school isn't the world's safest profession. I've confiscated weapons from kids on drugs who were twice my size. I've taken karate, self-defense classes and I've been trained on handguns. If I were you, I'd rather have me protecting your back than Travis.''

''Not a good example,'' he said. ''I'd rather have a tree frog back me up than have to count on Travis.''

Thea's lips twisted in a half-grin. ''Ribbet.''

''What?''

''The sound of the tree frog. Ribbet, ribbet.''

He didn't want to smile back at her, but Spence couldn't help himself. She was too damned cute, too damned smart, and the woman was going to get her way. ''You're a pain in the butt, Thea Sarazin.''

She reached up and lightly patted his cheek with her mittened hand. ''Thanks, again.''

''That wasn't supposed to be a compliment, either,'' Spence muttered as he followed Thea into the gondola house. The Reverend Joshua and Travis were snarling at each other while Mona tried to mediate. Lawrence stood by the giant cogwheel controls, observing with a bemused expression.

Spence slammed the wood door, and everyone went quiet.

"Why haven't you boarded?" Spence asked.

"I need to bring the car around to the opposite side," Lawrence explained. "Shall I proceed?"

"Yes," Spence said. "Do it now."

Lawrence flipped a lever, and the fiberglass car inched forward with a screech of cold metal gears as it chugged around the half-circle, lining up for a descent down the mountain. When the car was suspended above open space, Lawrence pulled the lever again.

A fierce crack echoed in the stone house.

"My God!" Lawrence leapt backwards. Flailing his arms, he fell against the reverend.

"What's wrong?" Spence demanded.

The answer came with horrifying immediacy.

The steel cord holding the gondola car snapped. Grating violently, it whipped through the cogwheel machinery.

Screeching along the loose steel cable, the car groaned and dropped twenty feet straight down. The rear lodged against a jagged rock, teetering and grinding against snow and ice and frozen granite. Then, overbalanced, the car careened, end over end, plummeting down the side of the cliff and out of sight.

Paralyzed, awaiting the final muted crash of the gondola car, Spence remembered Rosemont's promise of a chopper to ferry the "survivors" back to civilization.

He didn't have to wonder if the cable had snapped

ahead of schedule. He had no doubt. Rosemont had intended anyone who chose to run from his deadly game to die in the spectacular crash of the gondola car.

They were trapped.

Chapter Five

The last echo of the crash reverberated in her ears. Thea's fear of the gondola had come to pass. As the car fell, she felt the nightmare sensation of falling herself, falling, falling in a jagged, unstoppable plunge through space with the wind screaming past her ears. Then, it was over with a terrible, squealing thud.

Her senses were heightened, but her fear seemed contained. She'd managed to ride chairlifts at the ski resorts with her eyes closed and her muscles clenched, but there always came the end, the top of the line, when she could alight and find everything was fine after all.

Perfectly fine.

No fears.

She peered over the edge where the gondola car had disappeared, surely crushed like an aluminum can beneath the heavy foot of gravity.

Travis stood beside her, staring down. "Oh, man. What a rush."

A satisfied grin curved his mouth, as if he'd been craving more excitement and was momentarily fulfilled. Beneath his bleached, spiky hair, his eyes gleamed with a strange wildness. Thea had the uncomfortable feeling that he might give her a little shove over the edge for no other reason than to watch her body splatter against the fang-like rocks.

"Looks like you got your wish, Travis," she said, prudently stepping back. "We're all staying here at the castle. We're stuck."

"Somebody could ski down," he said.

"That's an almost vertical descent. Do you really think you could make it?"

"I know I could make it. I compete internationally, babe. You can count on watching me 'up close and personal' at the next Olympics in freestyle. And I've done extreme skiing, too."

Thea thought it was worth a shot. She waved to Spence. The reverend had slumped against the rear stone wall of the gondola house with his eyes closed. Spence checked the reverend's vitals, then left him in the hands of Dr. Mona and Lawrence and strode toward them. His expression was grave. Again, she was grateful for his solid, reassuring presence. He made a good protector. With his wide shoulders, he appeared to be in nearly as good a physical condition as Travis the Olympian. Additionally, Spence had something the bleached-blond skier might never attain—a little maturity.

"Is the reverend all right?" Thea asked.

"He fainted."

"No joke?" Travis chuckled.

"It's not a laughing matter," Spence said coldly. "His pulse is weak and thready. He might very well have a heart condition."

"Or he might very well be scared out of his skull," Travis mimicked with an unsympathetic sneer. "Listen, man. I was just telling the babe here—"

"Don't call me that," Thea snapped, tiring of correcting

Travis's behavior around her. "I have a name. Thea. Use it."

"Most babes like it when I—"

"Well, I don't," she said. Turning to Spence, she explained, "Travis thinks he might be able to ski down the mountain for help."

"It's nearly dark," Spence said doubtfully, checking the evil-looking clouds in the gathering dusk. "There's a blizzard on the way."

"Which is exactly why I need to go now. You got a better plan?" Travis asked.

"I thought you wanted to stay here and search for your sister."

"You guys are trapped here," Travis said. "You can find her, but I'm the only one who could make it down."

"It might work," Thea said. "I'd feel a lot better if Travis gets through to contact the police or a search-and-rescue unit."

Spence considered for a moment. "There might be an emergency flare in the house that you could use for light. Let's check out the slope behind the castle. It might not be as treacherous as the forward approach."

With Dr. Mona and the butler helping Reverend Joshua back to the castle, Thea and Spence followed Travis along another narrow path which hadn't been recently sanded.

Their boots crunched on crusted snow. When they moved beyond the glow of lights from the castle it was still possible to see across to the ragged peaks of the next mountain. The wind gusted, stirring the intense cold. Snowflakes stung her cheeks. Travis had disappeared over a rise. She felt dangerously alone. "Spence?"

"I'm right behind you."

She reached out and touched the rough bark of a tree trunk with her mitten. As she looked ahead of them and to the north, all the other trees, conifers with high limbs, seemed in the slanting light remaining in the day to be reaching down at her like claws. But the snowpack beneath the trees wasn't as deep, so it was easier to move from tree to tree.

Travis had bounded ahead and was nowhere in sight.

Needing the reassurance of another human voice in the vast silence, she said, "It's starting to snow."

"Are you cold?"

"Freezing."

She wished she'd gone back inside with Mona and the reverend. A chunk of snow dislodged from a branch and splattered on her hood. The damp cold slipped inside her parka and shivered down her spine. Inside her boots, her toes were numb.

Though a drop-off loomed just ahead, unless it gave way to a sheer cliff face, Travis would have an easier time of it heading downhill from this aspect.

Thea edged forward as the darkness deepened, threatening to consume them. It seemed too early to be night, only a little after six o'clock, but all of a sudden, she could only see a few feet in front of her face. Her arm swung wide, groping for the next tree. But there was nothing in front of her. A biting wind tore through her body and chilled her soul. Tentatively, she inched forward. Her foot slipped. She sensed the abyss. Sudden vertigo. Balance gone. She was going down. "Spence!"

His strong arms wrapped around her. He pulled her close against her chest, restraining her.

They stood at the brink of a precipice concealed by the deep shadows of darker clouds. She peered down, unable to see to the bottom, relieved that she'd been spared that vision. Her heart raced.

Spence eased her backward. "Come on, Thea."

"I'm trying." But her legs were stiff. She'd come to the very edge of disaster. If she'd taken one more step...

They were back in the trees. Safe again, for now.

"We need to go back," Spence said. He raised his voice, "Travis!"

"Over here!"

"Go back to the castle," Spence yelled.

"On my way, man."

When Spence loosened his grasp, a wave of panic washed over her. Thea groped, latching onto the snowy branch of a tree, hurling herself toward the trunk. Quickly, the fear ebbed.

She was hugging a tree, feeling a little silly but unwilling to stand on her own in the disorienting darkness where the depths could creep up and claim her. *Don't be stupid, Thea. You're safe now.* The mountainside wasn't going to sneak up and grab her.

Clearing her throat, she spoke in a slightly shaky voice, "Did you see where we were?"

"Yeah."

Her voice squeaked. "At the edge of the damn world."

"My fault," he said. "I should've gone first."

"I'm glad you didn't," she said, peeling her arms away from the tree. "If you'd been on the edge, I wouldn't have had the muscle to pull you back."

He made a murmuring noise, deep in his throat. Still touching the tree trunk with her mitten, grounding herself, she tried to see through the dark. Spence's face was a pale shadow. She couldn't even guess at his expression. "Did you say something?"

"No. But..." He came closer to her, ducking beneath branches that seemed tall enough for an ordinary man to walk under. "It almost sounds as if you care what happens to me."

"Of course, I care." Sure, there had been a time—right after they broke up—when she wished he was dead, but not really deceased. "I don't want you to—"

"You don't want to lose me," he said with a hint of triumph in his voice.

Damn him! Tears sprang to her eyes. Every time she started to feel closer to him, he made a smug, macho, assuming comment, as if they were in some kind of competition and he was winning. His arrogance might manifest as leadership with the others, but she found it as overwhelming as ever. Why wouldn't he accept her rejections?

He took her chin in his bare fingers. She could blame it on the extreme cold, but she didn't have the nerve or the wits or even the desire to slap his hand away.

"Admit it, Thea," he commanded.

"Fine." She swallowed hard, stuck in her memory with the feel of his arms as he kept her from going over that precipice. "I don't want to lose you."

"I knew it."

"You see?" she shrilled through her chattering teeth in a dark so deep she couldn't see the glint of any light off his eyes. "Can't you even hear how arrogant that sounds? *I knew it,*" she imitated his tone. "Sounds a lot like *I* don't know my own mind. Well, I do, Spence. I know what I want. I don't have much choice about it right now. Until we get off this mountain," she said, "I'm stuck with you. We have to work together. But—"

"After that?"

She let go of the tree and glared up at him, though she knew he couldn't see her expression any more than she could see his. "You just saved my life. Thank you very much. I'm truly grateful neither one of us fell off the edge of the world. But for now, let's quit playing footsie and figure out how we're going to survive the night."

"Well, that's another subject, Thea." Nothing in his tone indicated that he had taken this protest seriously either. "I want you to stay close to me tonight."

"Don't you ever stop? I don't want to hear any more sexual innuendo or—"

"I'm serious," he cut her off angrily. "I'll tell you what. If I'm making sexual innuendoes, I'll let you know. If I'm making a pass at you, sweetheart, I won't have to let you know, because neither one of us will be talking. Until then, you can safely assume it's your damned safety I'm talking about."

"What about it?"

"Rosemont just sent us a pretty clear message with the gondola cable snapping. He's serious, Thea, and he's probably a little more miffed now than he was an hour ago."

She swallowed. Her whole body writhed, as much from the sudden terrifying insight Spence forced on her as from the cold. Whoever refused to play Rosemont's game had been meant to die in that crash.

"People are going to die, Thea. I want you with me. The danger isn't any less inside." He started to go on, then took her by the elbow. "If we stay out here any longer, we're going to be dealing with frostbite next."

He led the way back through the forest, and she followed in his footsteps, taking small leaps to match his stride. When they came out of the trees, the snowfall had begun in earnest. Loose blobs of icy sleet pelted them as they hiked back to the sanded path. Travis joined them from out of the darkness there.

"This sucks," he complained. "No way can I go now."

Spence agreed. "Even if you could make it to base in one piece, you wouldn't survive the sub-zero conditions."

"When you're right, you're right, man." Travis shivered. "Maybe tomorrow."

If they lasted that long. Thea trudged into the circle of light illuminating the towering granite walls. Though the weather out here was miserable, she wasn't looking forward to what might be waiting inside the castle.

In the coatroom, they discarded wet parkas. Thea tried to think of some way to get rid of Travis, but he made some comment about hitting up the wine cellar posthaste and ducked inside without noticing at all that she was hanging back.

Spence had clearly read her intentions, and plugged in a small electric space heater. She drew near and crouched down beside the heater, near enough to Spence to speak softly.

"What did you mean about there being as much danger inside the castle as out?"

He sat on his haunches, rubbing his chilled hands together near the heating coils, and looked over at her. "You were the one who pointed out the discrepancy between the four daggers on the Rosemont coat of arms and the six of us in the wedding party. Suppose we assume the daggers indicate how many of us will die if we fail Rosemont's little test. Suppose we don't count Lawrence. There are still five of us, and I'm guessing that means there's somebody in our little group who's working with Rosemont."

Thea nodded. "I'd thought of that. I'm with you so far."

Spence clasped his hands. "One of the men might even be Rosemont himself."

"Still with you," she said. "There aren't any photos of him. He could be the reverend or Travis or even Lawrence."

"We can't count Dr. Mona out," Spence said. "All we know is what she's told us. She claims to be Jenny's therapist, but we have no way of knowing whether she's telling the truth or not. What if she's in cahoots with Rose-mont? Who better that a psychologist to be conspiring with a psychopath?''

''Spence, by that logic—'' Thea broke off. She'd been about to suggest that by his logic the rest of the wedding party might conclude that, working with sick people, having easy access to controlled substances, perhaps Spence was conspiring with Rosemont to keep Jenny knocked out or drugged to keep her hidden away. The thought of Jenny like that dismayed her.

Spence looked hard at her. ''What is it?''

She shook her head and shrugged as if she could shake off the thought and have it be untrue and impossible, but he insisted. She told him what she'd been thinking. How he could be colluding, or at least, how the others might believe it that Spence was a villain.

He searched her eyes to see if she believed it. ''That assumption would be wrong, wouldn't it?''

''Yes.'' Her own voice seemed breathless to her. She didn't believe it, and Spence knew it, and knew that she was as concerned about him, in her way, as he was about her. These close quarters, enforced by absolutely no way left to escape, were going to make for tensions and suspicions that made them all dangerous even to each other.

''All I'm saying, Thea, is that we can't afford not to be suspicious of everybody.''

She nodded again, and, staring into the brilliant red heating coils, held her hands up to the heater. ''Have you thought about what Rosemont said on the tape? About the sensitive, tortured soul?''

''Not much.''

Nor had she. Of course, there had been people in her life that she'd offended, but Thea could think of no one she'd purposely harmed. Except, possibly, Spence. ''Do you think we should? That we should go along with Rose-mont, or at least pretend to go along until Travis can get out and call for rescue?''

"We're going to have to create an appearance of co-operating at least." He paused, and reached for Thea's hands, taking them into his own when she failed to resist. She couldn't find one intention in her soul to pull away.

She couldn't take her eyes off them either, their two pairs of hands together, his so large and masculine, far more roughened by his search-and-rescue work than most doctors', hers, smaller, paler, so delicate-seeming in con-trast.

"Thea, do I have your promise that you'll stick by my side, no matter what happens?"

In sickness and in health, she thought, so foolishly taken by their hands together in just the manner of a couple reciting their vows. *For better, for worse.*

Thea nodded. And knew that she was in very deep trou-ble indeed, no matter what became of this wedding party.

THEY ENTERED the kitchen, where Thea was pleasantly surprised to find that Reverend Joshua wasn't completely worthless. He stood before one of the stovetops, stirring a pot of something that smelled like melted butter with a tang of wine.

"Stroganoff," he said glumly. "As long as we're forced to stay here, we should keep up our strength."

Mona had assembled a leafy green salad in a huge wooden bowl which Lawrence lifted from the countertop and carried toward the door to the serving area.

"Where are you going?" Spence asked.

"I presume we will be dining at the table," the butler said without breaking stride. "In the dining room."

Another scent tickled Thea's nostrils. "Coffee. You

made coffee.'' Caffeine, straight up, was what she needed. That and a good dose of a reality check. When, *when exactly* between repeating for Spence her litany of rejection and the instant that he took her hands into his, when was it that he'd managed to slip by the brick wall of her better judgment?

"Shall I pour you a cup?" Mona asked.

"Yes, please."

And her own failure to withdraw wasn't all that was so odd. The normalcy of their dinner preparations seemed completely out of touch with reality. Jenny was still missing, and they were all acting as if they had each somehow detached from Rosemont's threats and the accidental crash of the gondola—that was no accident.

Mona placed the coffee mug in Thea's hands and asked, "Would you like anything in your coffee? A bit of amaretto? Whiskey, perhaps?"

"One drop of liquor and I'll go right to sleep," Thea said, cradling the warm ceramic mug in her cold fingers. "Which isn't an altogether bad idea, except that I'm afraid I might wake up dead." Not to mention that Jenny might do the same.

The reverend banged his spoon against the side of the pot. "Excuse me, Thea. We have decided not to speak of our situation. Mona and I have agreed. We will not be drawn into Rosemont's sick game."

"That's one approach," Thea said. The ostrich approach. She exchanged glances with Spence, who had also accepted a mug of coffee and had added an ounce or so of whiskey to it. "Do you think if we ignore the threats, they'll go away?"

"Perhaps," he answered curtly.

"Well, Reverend, the only problem with burying your head in the sand is that it leaves your butt unprotected."

"No doubt, man." Travis had already drunk himself halfway through a bottle of chablis.

With eloquent and disdainful silence, the reverend turned back to the pot on the stove, apparently shunning any discussion of his vulnerable rear end.

While Mona stirred noodles into a pot of boiling water, Thea sipped the hot fragrant brew. A soothing warmth spread through her body. In spite of the infusion of caffeine, she realized that she was very tired. It wasn't even eight o'clock, but she'd been up since dawn, driving from Denver.

During this high-stress day, she'd suffered one devastating shock after another, starting with her first confrontation with Spence. She'd endured the gondola ride only to witness it crashing, exactly as she'd feared. And just in the last hour, she'd nearly slipped off the edge of a world and then plummeted instead off another sort of precipice altogether when Spence Cannon had scooped her hands into his.

"Do you want to freshen up?" Mona asked her.

Thea nodded. Might that help? "I'd love to change out of these wet boots."

"Grab your suitcase and come with me."

Spence objected. "Not a good plan. We need to stay together."

"Don't worry," Mona said. "I'll take Thea upstairs to the bedroom and stay with her."

Thea met Spence's eyes. He exhaled sharply and nodded. "Don't be long."

"We won't." Toting her suitcase and her garment bag, Thea followed the small, gray-haired woman up the narrow servants' stair to the second floor. Mona led the way to a large bedroom that was part of the central castle, not part of the towers. Neither as opulent nor as decadent as the bridal suite, the style was homey French provincial with pastel-blue wallpaper and white fleurs-de-lis. In addition to a king-sized four-poster bed and an armoire, there were a table and two chairs.

Thea focused on the bed. Staggering forward, she dropped the suitcase and collapsed facedown on top of the blue-and-white patterned comforter. The mattress felt like heaven.

"I'm tired too," Mona said. "This is a lot of excitement for an old dame like me."

Thea flipped to her back. Her eyelids slammed shut, and the bedroom disappeared behind a velvety black curtain. But she didn't dare go to sleep. "We still have to search for Jenny. And figure out some way to get out of here."

"The voice on the tape—Gregory Rosemont, one must assume—said that Jenny was all right," Mona said. "I'm inclined to believe him."

"Why?"

"This weekend has been planned with compulsive attention to detail. Rosemont won't deviate from his original plan. He has no intention of physically harming Jenny, I believe." With a frown, she added, "I'm afraid it goes without saying that Jenny will be emotionally devastated if this turns out to be Rosemont's sole purpose in bringing us together."

Poor Jenny! The whirlwind courtship and the wedding plans had been nothing more than fragments of a madman's scheme. Already half-asleep, Thea wondered if Rosemont had taken Jenny to bed. She'd talked all around the subject of her sex life, but then she was not any more graphic or descriptive than Thea had ever been.

With a groan, she forced herself to sit up on the bed and lean down to unlace her supposedly waterproof hiking boots with the thick, sensible soles. She glanced at Mona who perched on one of the chairs beside the table. Her legs were crossed at the ankles, and her feet didn't reach the floor. "The reverend said you agreed with him?" Thea asked. "About ignoring Rosemont's instructions. Is that true?"

"It makes for a professional dilemma," Dr. Mona responded. "Rosemont indicated that there was someone from the past whom we had all failed in some way. Possibly, this person was my client, and I can't ethically discuss people I've treated."

Thea didn't point out that unless they did as Rosemont said, they might all be killed—a fact that, in her opinion must certainly outweigh professional ethics. Instead, she concentrated on pulling off her boots. Her wet socks were plastered to her feet. "I suppose Reverend Joshua feels the same way?"

"Naturally," Mona said. "As a minister, parishioners come to him with personal problems which he cannot divulge, similar to a priest in the confessional."

With her socks off, Thea wiggled her toes. Then she pulled her feet up underneath her, hoping to warm them. "If neither of you are willing to compare notes, at least, then it will be impossible to come up with the identity of Rosemont's mystery person."

"Perhaps not," Mona said. "You and Spence might be able to come up with a few names. You seem to have a history."

"We were engaged," Thea said.

"When was that?"

"Five years ago."

Dr. Mona nodded slightly, encouraging Thea to continue with her story. "Would you like to talk about it?"

Thea hadn't discussed her breakup with a therapist. Though she had nothing against psychologists and had often worked with counselors in the schools, she hadn't wanted to share this pain that cut so close to the bone. Possibly, she feared a therapist might tell her she'd been a victim of foolish pride.

"Five years ago," she repeated. "Spence had just completed his residency at University of Colorado Medical Center in Denver. It was the moment we had been waiting for. We planned to get married and start our life together."

"You loved him?"

"What red-blooded female wouldn't love Spence? He's gorgeous. Broad shoulders. Blue eyes. A smile that could melt granite. Plus, he was a doctor."

Mona said, "But did you love him?"

"Yes." More than his handsome face and great body, Thea loved his idealism. He'd gone into medicine for the noblest of reasons—to help other people, to be a healer. "Spence is one of those people who throws himself into a task and carries it through no matter what. He's dedicated, incredibly hardworking. Maybe a workaholic, I don't know."

Everything had fallen apart when he joined a rich practice, which had changed him in a way that adding an M.D. to his signature never had. "He got puffed up with his own self-importance. Instead of being concerned with his patients, he was totally focused on his brilliant career. He was asked to join this committee and that review board until he hardly had time for patients, never mind me."

Mona nodded sagely. "It must have been quite a busy time for him."

"Oh, yeah. He was making the right connections and kissing up to his mentors. Our relationship took a distant second place." But Thea didn't believe she'd been impatient at all. She was willing to wait until Spence settled down. She tried to concentrate on her own career. "I was

working with a group of teachers, social workers and ther-
apists on an ADD project to be implemented in the public
schools. We needed the backing of the hospital review
board for funding.''

"Ah, politics," Dr. Mona murmured.

Thea barely heard her, mired as she was in the memory
of betrayal. She'd had such high hopes. And she'd fallen
so low. "Spence cast the deciding vote against us. Against
me! He'd been pressured by one of his high-and-mighty
mentors to turn us down.''

"What happened?" Mona asked.

"What do you think? Without the support of the hospital board, we were toast. The project fell apart. I felt like
it was my fault." The bitter taste of humiliation still lingered in her mouth. "I was so furious at him. And it didn't
help that I was also going through a personal crisis. My
roommate had committed suicide just a few weeks before.''

Mona's eyes narrowed. "I'm so sorry. That must have
been terribly hard for you.''

"Spence had zero sympathy. He told me to move on
with my life. He said I was dwelling too much on the
suicide. He even reminded me that he dealt with life and
death every single day. Whatever happened in my life or
to my goals was utterly unimportant to him.''

Retelling the old story churned up a lot of conflicting
emotions. By ending their engagement, she had affirmed
her own self-worth. I am woman. Hear me roar. But any
sense of triumph was tarnished with bitter regret. She'd
lost him.

"So you didn't really want the relationship to be over,"
Mona said.

"I wanted the man I fell in love with. Not the man he
had become.''

When Dr. Mona offered no response, Thea looked toward her. "Well? What do you think? Did I throw away my one and only chance at a happy relationship?"

Mona's small, wizened face was calm, almost serene. Her age and her attitude combined to make her seem very wise. "Thea, you're a strong, intelligent woman with a healthy self-image. You demand respect. You'd never settle for a man who wasn't your equal. And yet, such a man—a man like Spence—will challenge you for the very reason you are attracted to him."

"Which is?"

"You are equally strong, equally stubborn," Mona said. "For any relationship to work, there must be compromise. Unfortunately, neither of you will back down."

Ouch! Thea had to acknowledge the unflattering reality. She had never been good at compromise. "Could Spence and I work things out?"

Mona shook her head. "I'm not a fortune-teller, Thea."

No, Thea thought, Mona was a more Yoda-like figure, even resembling in her physical appearance the Star Wars Jedi Master. She'd described Thea and Spence's relationship as a riddle: each seeking a mate to match an uncommon strength of character. But the forceful personalities involved would always be doomed to fight tooth and nail.

Thea sighed. "And I thought all I wanted was to get married and live happily ever after."

"Happiness doesn't necessarily come with marriage."

Thanks, Yoda. Again, Thea thought of Jenny and what a debacle was being made of her wedding weekend. There was only one rational conclusion to be drawn: Relationships suck. And Thea had to stop Spence cold, now, or suffer the inevitable consequences.

Chapter Six

When the wedding party—minus the bride and groom—took their places around the dining-room table, Spence could see that Thea had changed her attitude along with her clothes. She wore black penny loafers, gray wool slacks and a red sweater set with a strand of pearls. She looked all buttoned-down and preppy, which gave him the urge to mess with her shiny chestnut hair, smear her lipstick and glide his hands under that tidy little sweater. Then she shot him a warning glare that sliced to the bone. Her message was real clear. She didn't want to be anywhere near him.

Spence didn't understand. Before they'd come back into the castle, he'd thought they were both on the same page—willing to trust each other and work together. He thought he'd had her clear promise. He thought he'd seen some small bow to feelings for him rekindled. But now, her brows arched disdainfully above her chilly hazel eyes and her lips hiked in a snarl when she deigned to speak to him. She avoided sitting beside him at the dining-room table, instead choosing a spot between the reverend and Travis.

Opposite her, Spence leaned across his china plate and silver setting. Tentatively, he tried to make contact. ''Thea?''

Her lips formed a silent response. "Drop dead."

What did she think? That he'd curl up and die? That he'd come to pieces—*ah-jeez!*—what had he done this time?

"Reverend," Thea said. For him, she had a sweet smile. "This Stroganoff is delicious. Where did you learn to cook?"

"I'm self-taught. As a bachelor, I had to figure out how to feed myself."

"Really? I'd think the ladies of your church would be delighted to keep you knee-deep in casseroles."

"I wasn't always a man of God," he said. "I came to the church rather late in life."

"What was your line of work before?" Spence asked. Since he obviously wasn't going to make headway with Thea, they should get started on solving Rosemont's puzzle. If the reverend would open up and talk, he might reveal some clue about a mysterious person he might have wronged.

"If you don't mind," the reverend said, "I'd rather not discuss anything about my past."

"Don't worry," Spence said. "Nobody here is going to tell the tabloids about your wild, heathen youth."

"I was neither wild nor heathen."

But he had reacted immediately when, on tape, Rosemont had spoken of someone whom each of them had wronged. The reverend had an idea, and Spence was determined to get at it. "So? What was your job?"

The reverend deliberately set down his fork and prayerfully laced his long fingers. "I know what you're attempting to do, Dr. Cannon. You're trying to trick me into telling some dark secret from my past."

"Is there a dark secret?"

"As I told you before, I refuse to give one moment's

credence to Rosemont's accusations." His gaze flitted around the dining room as if he were searching for something or someone. "No man will cast the first stone. Judgment will be left to the Lord."

"Who are you talking to?" Travis looked up from his plate and snickered. "Rosemont ain't hiding behind the curtains, man."

"But he might be," Dr. Mona piped up. She seemed far less interested in the food on her plate than on the vintage bottle of burgundy that had taken up residence beside her crystal water glass. "Rosemont might be anywhere."

"How do you figure?" Spence asked her.

"His message suggested that he would watch us and see if we repented. Therefore, I must conclude that he's somewhere in the castle. Watching."

Good point, Spence thought, if it hadn't been so obvious. This place could easily be honeycombed with secret passageways and hiding places for a watcher. And the tech-minded Rosemont could as easily have put into place hidden cameras and transmitters virtually anywhere. How else would he know what they were doing?

Mona said, "He wants to watch us squirm."

And Spence wanted to know if Mona was helping him. Taking a sip of his own wine, Spence forced himself not to glance around the room, searching for the telltale gleam of camera lenses. He wouldn't give Rosemont the satisfaction of seeming so jumpy.

"If he's really spying on us," Thea said, "we need to be careful about what we say and do."

"Rosemont can watch this," Travis said, making an obscene gesture. "That's for you, creep."

Spence banged his empty wine goblet with a spoon. "We're a little off track here. Reverend, you were about to reveal a bit more of yourself. The point, of course, is to determine whom we might all have known in common. Whom we might all have unwittingly harmed in some way.''

He held up a hand to forestall complaints and renewed objections by the reverend and Dr. Mona. ''We saw a demonstration of Rosemont's commitment to this little project with the gondola. Would either of you rather die than admit you may have failed a client?''

Joshua Handy clamped his jaw shut rebelliously. Dr. Mona gave a troubled sigh.

Spence took their silence for assent, however reluctant, and looked for several long seconds at Thea. Long enough to make her look away first. ''Since Thea and I knew each other prior to this little soirée, and our lives last intersected five years ago, why don't we think in that time frame. Reverend, you said you came late to the ministry. What were you doing five years ago?''

''I have said it before and I will say it again,'' the reverend said tonelessly. ''I will not sit here and be judged by some madman who—''

''—will then kill you?'' Travis interrupted cheerlessly. ''Way to go, Reverend. Offer yourself up as the sacrificial lamb. Maybe the rest of us will be off the hook.''

Spence shot Travis a quick glance. It was always such a toss-up, which way Travis would show up. Most of the time, he remembered his sister first and called anyone a coward who wasn't willing to help find her. Other times, he could land these cynical knockout jabs as if he couldn't care less.

But Travis had reinforced Spence's point, reminding all the reluctant members of the wedding party that they could die. That Rosemont wasn't kidding. Maybe, given a little time to themselves with the reminder, each of them would think really hard about dying versus trying to make amends.

Spence glanced past the ornate silver candlesticks toward Thea. She'd made it real clear that she had a problem with him, and he wanted to hear why. He needed an excuse to get her alone.

"After dinner," Spence said, "we'll search for Jenny."

"But why?" Mona asked. "Rosemont said she wouldn't be in physical danger."

"I know." Spence spoke more curtly than he intended. "But I have a problem taking the word of a madman for gospel, Mona. I'm worried about Jenny. If Rosemont had allowed her to leave, she would've stopped all of us from coming here." Again, Spence looked toward Thea. The possibility had occurred to her first that Jenny had been drugged or knocked out, since nothing else could adequately explain her failure to show up. "She's locked away someplace in the castle, and we've got to find her."

"Locked up?" Travis said. "Dude, she's not supposed to be hurt."

Back to unruly-little-brother Travis, Spence thought. "I didn't say she was hurt. I said locked up. She could be held captive without being hurt."

"Rosemont might have some Beauty and the Beast fantasy going," Thea explained. "The Beast took care of Beauty. She was surrounded by perfect luxury, but she couldn't leave."

Somehow, Spence doubted their story would have a fairy-tale ending.

After they'd finished, Lawrence cleared the table and retreated to the kitchen, muttering that a butler shouldn't have to wash dishes.

"I'll help with the clean-up," Mona volunteered as she

rose unsteadily to her feet. She'd polished off at least four glasses of wine.

"The rest of us will search," Spence said. "Nobody should be alone at any time. We'll stay in pairs. Reverend and Travis. Thea and I."

Thea lifted her chin. "I'd rather go with the reverend."

Spence finished his wine, set the glass on the table and stood. No way was she going to avoid him. "What's the matter, Thea? Are you afraid to be alone with me?"

"Of course not."

"Then, let's go." He nodded to Travis. "You and the reverend stay in the middle section of the castle. Thea and I will take the far tower. If you get in trouble, start yelling and we'll find you."

The reverend cleared his throat. "I really don't wish to participate."

"This is a search-and-rescue mission, Reverend. We're looking for Jenny. I assume she goes to your church."

"Yes, but—"

"Think of her as a lamb gone astray. It's your job to find her."

He frowned. His long nose twitched. "I suppose you're right."

Spence checked his wristwatch. "Let's give it half an hour. Meet back here at ten o'clock."

MOVING STIFFLY at his side, Thea followed Spence through the Grand Drawing Room, where the lights lit and the fireplace flared as they passed, to the far side where there was an arched hallway.

As if needing to break into the silence she maintained between them, he commented, "We won't search these rooms. This is still the center section." Not a very inspired interruption. Thea just looked at him, reminding herself that she had to stop the incursion he'd already begun to make into her emotional territory.

As they proceeded, he scanned the ceilings and walls, looking for surveillance cameras. So far as Thea could tell, he spotted no telltale signs of Rosemont spying on them, but the ornate decor provided countless nooks and crannies—endless possibilities, caches for hidden cameras. Rosemont could be watching them right now. He could be listening to every word.

At the end of the hall, Spence pushed open a set of double doors. If the architecture on this end of the castle matched the other, the tower itself would rise three stories and attach to a longer, larger central structure.

The first floor seemed to conform to the pattern. She followed Spence into a vast, high-ceilinged room with a polished expanse of marble floor. The furniture was pushed back against pale gold walls. At the far end sat a grand piano.

"A ballroom," he said.

"A piano," she murmured. She had intended to maintain her stony silence, but unwittingly breathing the word, *piano*. She dragged her eyes off it and surveyed the ornately framed mirrors on the walls and the three sets of French doors that allowed heat to escape at a fearsome rate, making this room colder than anywhere else in the house. The overhead chandeliers could have been stalactites rather than crystal. But when she'd taken everything else in, her gaze went back to the piano.

In his condo, Spence had kept an old upright.

He crossed the floor, his footfalls echoing, and went to the grand piano. Her mouth watered. Her heart thudded. The first time she had ever been inside his place, Spence had reproduced pretty darn well the character Goose's rendition of "You've Lost That Lovin' Feelin'"—straight out of *Top Gun.*

That night, she'd fallen in love with him. He inspired laughs and lust in her in the same fell swoop.

He flipped the lid open and played a few scales before he hammered out the opening chords to Beethoven's Fifth. "This thing is in perfect tune."

"You'd know," she remarked disparagingly. He had a good ear. It would have been nice if he had the same discrimination in emotional tones.

He pulled out the bench, sat and plucked out the beginning to "Moonlight Sonata." His fingers stumbled a couple of times, but he kept playing, warming to the rich resonance of the Steinway.

Thea breathed deeply and exhaled. "Spence, we don't have time for this. We have to find Jenny."

He looked up at her but his fingers went right on stroking music out of the keys. "Five minutes is not going to make a difference one way or another." He switched to a Scott Joplin ragtime tune.

"It might," she insisted.

"I want to know what's gotten into you. Why the attitude? Why the cold shoulder?"

"Five minutes—" She broke off. Her chin went up. She wanted him to stop the jaunty ragtime because it would make whatever she said light and frothy and inconsequential. But he segued from one to another, now "Raindrops Keep Falling on My Head," and she knew he wasn't going to stop.

She raised her voice to be heard over the music. "Five minutes is not going to change anything between us. It's not going to work, so if you want some theme music here, why don't you try 'Fifty Ways to Leave Your Lover'? You know, as in 'Hit the Road, Jack'?"

"Cute. But if it's Simon and Garfunkel you want, I prefer 'Shadows Touching Shadows' Hands,' you know?'' But he moved on instead to "Some Enchanted Evening," ignoring her sneer at the blatantly romantic selection, and then "Misty."

Transfixed in some way she didn't want to think about, she was mesmerized by very specific, very intimate memories Spence evoked with only a few bars of all the songs he'd ever played for her. She couldn't think of a way to make him stop.

It should have been obvious to her. It should have occurred to her that all she had to do was to leave, to continue searching for Jenny on her own. He would be back at her side in a New York minute because he didn't want her wandering off alone, making herself vulnerable to an attack by the madman Gregory Rosemont.

And in a few hours, she would think of it, but now, at just the moment she might have thought of it, he began to play "Strangers in the Night."

Spence always slept in the nude, and when he couldn't sleep, he got up and played that way. She would awaken and follow him out to the old upright, and climb across him, straddle him, taking him inside herself while he played and nuzzled her breasts with his lips and tongue. They weren't strangers in the night for long.

The castle ballroom filled with melody. The chandeliers seemed to glow more brightly as they caught the resonance and trembled. His singing voice wasn't anywhere near the caliber of Sinatra, so he hummed. "When somebody loves you…"

They had loved each other, all the way. In all ways. She'd thought for always, too. But about the time Spence had joined a private practice, he'd stopped playing the piano. She should have seen the end in sight.

They'd been good together. He wanted to believe it could happen again.

She was afraid to believe it. She wouldn't set herself up again. His hands fell still. A cold quiet fell around them. "What's wrong, Thea? Tell me what's wrong."

She meant to suggest that the timing was all wrong, that they had to go find Jenny, and even after that...but what came out of her was all about what had happened five years ago. "After I broke off the engagement, why didn't you call me?"

"Because you told me not to." He looked baffled by her question, and frowned. "I respected your decision."

"You were relieved," she said.

He winced. She could see that the truth hurt, and that he wasn't going to deny it.

He took a deep breath. "I thought we'd grown in different directions. I thought you weren't trying anymore to see what I needed."

"Poised to take off like a shooting star into some high administrative position?" She hated her sarcasm. She only got that way when she felt vulnerable and threatened, and Spence knew it. "I didn't even *want* to know what you needed."

"Our breakup was mutual," he conceded. "It wasn't until later that I realized how much I missed you."

"When?" she demanded.

"Six months." Within six months after Thea had ended their engagement, he'd been working in ER, his area of expertise. But one night, consumed with his administrative responsibilities and all that his advancement had entailed, he'd turned the care of a seven-year-old girl over to a resident and failed to check up on whether his orders had been followed and with what outcome. The little girl had almost died. His nearly fatal inattention had reminded him of why he'd gone into medicine—to help and to heal. Which had reminded him of Thea, which had made him confront, for the first time, what he'd lost.

He told her the story. "If I had called you at that point," he said, "would you have forgiven me?"

"I don't know." The piano, looming between them, made her ask. "Did you start playing the piano again?"

He closed the cover over the keys. "What do you mean?"

"You quit, you know. About the time that you joined the high-rent physicians group. You really didn't seem to care about your patients anymore, and you surely didn't give a damn about my project with the ADD kids."

"Thea—all I can say is that I've changed. I won't deny what you're saying, but I'm not going to fight a losing battle with you, either. If you don't want to look at who I am *now,* then I guess we've got nothing to talk about."

"So that's it? Not even an apology for scuttling my ADD proposal?"

"I am sorry, Thea, but—"

"But nothing!" she cut him off, every bit as angry as she had been five years ago. "I was hurt and humiliated, and when you voted down my funding, you were telling me in no uncertain terms that my dreams didn't matter."

"You're wrong—"

"No, I am not! You say you've changed, Spence, but you won't even acknowledge that what you did…oh, forget it!

"I'm glad you never called."

His jaw tightened. "So am I."

Her chin wavered. She was going to lose him all over again. "I refuse to care about you, Spence Cannon, because you are not even going to make it off this rock alive—not if you can't even admit that what you did hurt me. Rosemont will see to that!''

Spence reddened and clapped his mouth shut. She thought she'd finally made a dent in his impervious macho arrogant thinking, but he stalked off and shoved open the doors at the far end of the ballroom.

She followed because she had to. He'd crossed over into a serving kitchen with ovens from which to serve hot canapés, counter space and a wet bar. There wasn't room in here to turn around, much less for Jenny to be here.

When he turned to leave, Thea blocked his way. ''Am I wrong, Spence?'' she demanded.

''Yes. And you've got a lot of nerve bringing Rosemont's nasty little game of Truth or Consequences into this. Your funding proposal had real flaws, Thea, and my vote had nothing to do with sending you some kind of message that I didn't care about you and your dreams. I was a jerk, but I can see now that I've wasted the past five years thinking about you, regretting the way I handled myself, trying to be the kind of man I thought you could care about.''

''Tell me, Spence. What kind of man have you become?''

''I'm a family practitioner in a little mountain town, Cascadia. Not far from Aspen in terms of miles, but it's in a different economic stratosphere. The people who live in Cascadia are the ones who work in Aspen. The waitresses, the bellhops, the ski-lift operators. They're good people.''

''And what would they say about you?''

He shrugged. ''What does it matter? You wouldn't believe them anyway.''

''That's not true. I believed your friend Emily when

she told me how devoted you are to Cascadia Search-and-Rescue, how the whole town—"

"Emily's PR is probably exaggerated."

"She said you let the local Girl Scout troop meet at your place."

"They're Brownies," he said gruffly. "You know, the little ones. But they aren't skipping around in my front room. There's a big room on the back of my house that used to be a garage. It's where SAR keeps their equipment."

"And you're telling me that you regret the past five years?"

He hesitated. She recognized that he was strung out between conflicting emotions, anger at her, maybe, and a need to explain. "I'm lonely, Thea," he blurted. "But I'm not going to stand around here and be gutted like a trout over what happened five years ago." He stepped past her into the hallway. Against one wall was a curved staircase. The other side offered more closed doors. "We'll finish this floor first," he said, putting an end to the discussion, "then we'll go upstairs."

"Wait, Spence. I want to tell you—"

"We don't have time." He checked his wristwatch. "It's less than fifteen minutes before we meet Travis and the reverend."

"We'll talk later," she said.

"Sure."

But she wasn't so sure he would engage with her again at all on the subject of his feelings, or hers, or what this weekend meant to them both. More confused than ever, swinging desperately from wanting to arrive at an understanding with him and forcing herself to abandon any hope, she felt an uncomfortable tightness fill her heart.

DETERMINED TO SET ASIDE everything but finding Jenny, moving purposefully, she searched the rooms on one side of the unadorned hall while Spence took the other side. This seemed to be a storage area with no windows and solid granite walls. Behind unlocked doors, the rooms were unremarkable and mostly empty. Lonely. She closed a door with a soft click and glanced over her shoulder toward Spence.

He happened to be looking in her direction at the same time, and their eyes met. She was the first to look away, and her resolve crumbled. Searching through empty rooms couldn't occupy all her thoughts, and she found herself going over it all again. She couldn't believe Spence had admitted to being lonely. Was it possible that he'd changed, that a germ of sensitivity had infected his utterly arrogant soul?

A private smile touched her lips as she imagined the demanding, macho Spence Cannon playing host to a giggly group of Brownies. But why should she be surprised? He'd always liked kids. For a while, she knew, he'd even considered pediatrics as a specialty.

The end of the hallway intersected with a well-lit corridor, carpeted and wallpapered. Spence pushed open a set of frosted-glass doors to reveal a glass room two stories high. The panes were rimmed with icy frost.

"The solarium?" Thea guessed. Unlike the rest of the house, this greenhouse area had not been tended. Dead foliage clumped in thorny masses of gray and black. Withered fronds clung to several tall, dead palm trees. Marble urns overflowed with dried ivy. Humble gardening flats held pots of hard earth. Everything was dead.

The gardening tools lay scattered in disarray on a long countertop. Clippers. Trowels. Sharp-edged shears. Amid bags of potting soil and fertilizer were containers of liquid plant food and insecticides, marked with skull and cross-bones. Thea shivered. It was freezing in here.

"Let's see what it's doing outside," Spence said. "I'm going to turn off the light."

He flicked off the switch. The dark closed around them. Shadows of dead, gnarled, disfigured trees and plants silhouetted against the tall, ice-encircled windows. Lights from outside the castle illuminated a fierce, heavy snowstorm. A blizzard. The greenhouse panes rattled with the force of the keening wind.

"I feel like we're trapped inside one of those glass balls that you turn upside down to make it snow," Thea said. The cold seeped through her body, and hopelessness through her heart. There was no escape from this castle. "We're not going to get out of here."

"The hell we're not."

"Rosemont set this up so cleverly," she said. "We have no way of sending for help. We all told everyone we'd be gone for three days." She looked out again at the blindingly thick snow being hurled about in massive waves. "It almost seems like he arranged the weather."

"Rosemont can't control the snow."

But she feared the storm wouldn't end quickly enough. Rosemont had promised death if they failed to meet his insane demands. "We've got to do what he says, Spence. We've got to get the others to sit down and talk about their pasts. There's no hope if we can't figure out the identity of the person Rosemont claims we wronged."

"I think the reverend knows," Spence said.

"So do I. He reacted so quickly when he heard the tape, as if he had a guilty secret. And he was desperate to get away from here. He'll talk."

"Let's find Jenny first. Then we'll deal with the reverend."

When they left the macabre solarium and went back into the lighted hallway, Thea felt a little safer, a little more in control. Though her feelings for Spence kept rising to the forefront of her mind, they needed to concentrate on the present danger.

It seemed useless to meander through this labyrinthine structure, searching. They had to be smarter. "Maybe we're being too methodical here," she said. "Going from room to room like this."

"This is how it's done, Thea. Exactly like this. Imagine a grid—"

"When you're on a real search-and-rescue mission—I bow to your expertise." But in a classroom full of adolescents, she had learned to think three steps ahead of them. To anticipate trouble long before it had a chance to pop out. "It's like choosing where you're going to begin your grid, Spence. I think we can cut to the chase if we think like Rosemont—if we can figure out where he'd keep Jenny hidden."

"What are you thinking? A secret room?"

"Too cutesy," she said. "He's toying with us, no doubt, but he is also an obsessive-compulsive personality, if Dr. Mona is right."

"Okay," he said. His fist unconsciously clenched, ready to take a swing at their invisible tormentor. "Where does an obsessive-compulsive personality hide Jenny?"

"In the tape, he referred to her as the nexus between us. Maybe she's somewhere in the middle of the castle, trapped like a fly in a spider's web."

Spence muttered, "I wish we had a blueprint of this place so we could see where all these hallways connect—but if she's in the central portion, the reverend and Travis will find her." He paused. "I'm thinking the towers would better fit Rosemont's purposes. He'd need to keep Jenny somewhere secluded so we couldn't hear her make noise. Do you think there's a dungeon in this place?"

Thea hoped not. She hated to think of her friend locked in some bizarre medieval prison. But Spence's observation about the towers made sense. "If he's truly obsessive, Rosemont has a deep-seated need to keep everything ordered, all precise and tidy. Even…symmetrical."

Spence nodded. "And?"

She paced around a bit. "Check this out. We expected to find Jenny in the bridal suite, the highest room in the castle. The tidy opposite to that would be a basement or a sub-basement."

"But the bridal suite isn't the only highest room," Spence pointed out. "There's another tower. This tower."

"The opposite…"

"…is here. In the top room."

His conclusion sounded right to her. Thea glanced at her wristwatch. "We have just enough time to check there before we go back to meet the others."

They returned to the hall outside the ballroom, racing past the rooms they'd already searched, and Thea felt encouraged for the first time. She allowed no doubt as she darted behind Spence's three-step pace up the curving stone stairway.

At the second floor, the lights flashed on, clearly illuminating a tidy corridor and closed doors. "More bedrooms," she said. "And bathrooms."

"One more floor," Spence said.

She chased behind him. Her hopes rising with every stair she climbed. Up here, isolated, she was certain they'd find Jenny. Her bloodstained wedding gown in the bridal suite should have been a clue. The fantasy of being a bride had been murdered. Jenny was nothing more than a tool used by Rosemont to lure the rest of them. He would hide her as far away from a bride's legitimate place as possible, while maintaining some essential symmetry.

The staircase led to a circular third-floor landing with another stair descending on the opposite side. There were three closed doors.

Spence approached the door to their left. "This door would correspond to the layout of the bridal suite."

He twisted the knob and shoved open the door. Inside was a sterile white room. The windows were hidden behind a wall of white brocaded curtains. And Jenny lay silent and still on a collapsible gurney. An IV dripped into her arm.

Mortified that her idle premonition of finding Jenny drugged had come true, Thea flashed on a screen image of a corpse awaiting identification. She ran to her side, grasped her hand. The flesh felt warm. "Jenny! Jenny, wake up!"

Her friend's color seemed drained, but she wasn't dead, not a corpse at all. Jenny stirred slightly, but her eyelids stayed closed. She'd been arranged under the white blankets with her arms at her sides. She wore a white flannel gown. Her long brown hair hung in two perfectly even plaits on either side of her face. A smile curved her lips as if she were having a pleasant dream.

"Let me see her, Thea," Spence said.

Helplessly, Thea moved back. She'd never been more grateful that Spence was a doctor. "What's wrong with her?"

He checked her pupils, then tested various reflexes, pinching and running his thumbnail along Jenny's flesh. He tested her fingers, her hands and feet, and clapped loudly beside her ear. Twice he pressed deeply at the beds of her fingernails. It seemed to Thea that Jenny should have reacted more.

"You were right," Spence said, grimacing. "She's been drugged. Her pupils aren't reacting as quickly as I'd like…" He lifted Jenny's hand. "Her pulse feels strong. Steady."

"Is it in the IV?" Thea asked. "Shouldn't we disconnect it?"

"Not yet," Spence said, eyeing the bag of fluid, checking the bulb for drip rate. "I don't know if that's the drug delivery system or if it's only saline to keep her from dehydrating."

He stepped away from the bed and looked around. "We need to move her to a place where we can monitor her. I'll check around for unopened IV fluids. You—"

But Thea was already on her way to the door. "I'll get the others to help."

"Wait! Thea!" He turned from Jenny and caught Thea's wrist.

"We can't just leave her here, Spence," Thea said. "And we can't move her by ourselves. What if Rosemont moved her before we got back?"

"If the two of us can't move her, Rosemont can't either. Look. I'm not saying you shouldn't go for help. I'm probably better off alone up here than you would be. Just be aware that this may be part of Rosemont's plan—to get each of us alone. Go quickly. Don't stop for anything, and don't put up with any delays."

Thea nodded. "I'll be right back."

"If you get into trouble, yell your head off."

She stepped onto the third-floor landing. In her mind, she retraced her steps to the center of the castle. Down two flights of curving stair. A short corridor. Enter the ballroom. Cross the ballroom. Another hallway. Then, she was home free in the Grand Drawing Room.

She descended the stairs quickly and shouted back up. "I'm okay, Spence."

His response echoed against the granite walls. "Be careful."

"Don't worry about that," she muttered. Thea had no intention of becoming Rosemont's next victim. Her gaze scanned the windowless walls. Earlier, when they'd searched, there hadn't seemed to be so many shadows.

She walked at a steady pace, glancing over her shoulder. The nape of her neck prickled as if someone was watching, observing, waiting. She was ready to run. If someone came at her from the rear, she'd hear footsteps against the flagstones.

She entered the ballroom, lit by chandeliers. No one could hide in this vast open space.

As she reached the very center of the room, the lights went out. The faint sound of piano music trembled through the darkness—"Misty."

AT SPENCE'S Cascadia home, where they were staying for the weekend, Emily and Jordan snuggled before the fireplace. She topped off a glass of wine and gazed into the flames, watching the fiery dance of blue and yellow flames, inhaling the heady fragrance of her wine and the burning piñon pine.

Though technically on call for local medical emergencies, Emily didn't expect to be summoned. On a weekend like this, buried under a blizzard, most people would stay home and keep warm. "I wonder how Spence is doing in the castle."

Jordan cuddled her closer. "They're fine."

"Do you think Thea will take him back? I'd love for Spence to finally hook up with the woman of his dreams."

"Me, too."

Emily couldn't imagine a more romantic setting. A secluded and probably luxurious castle in the clouds. There
would be servants to wait upon them, lots of wining and
dining. Yet a shiver went through her. She had a nebulous,
sinking sensation whenever she thought of Spence up
there. "I hope nothing bad happens. Staging a rescue to
that place would be nearly impossible."

"What could happen?" Jordan leaned down and kissed
her forehead. She tilted her head back, inviting him to kiss
her lips. He was right. There was nothing to worry about.
"They'll live happily ever after."

"Like us."

Jordan pulled her closer, and she sighed. There was
nothing better than a snowy night, a warm fire and a glass
of wine. Her stab of apprehension vanished as she melted
into Jordan's arms.

Chapter Seven

The sudden darkness in the ballroom splashed like a cold wave over Thea, momentarily blinding her and disorienting her senses. Her arms groped empty air. Her loafers slipped on the polished marble dance floor.

Ghostly piano music softly assaulted her ears as if emanating from the walls. "Misty." The tone and cadence were exactly as Spence had played the song, but somehow the poignant chords held a certain threat.

Seeking light, Thea squinted toward the faint snowy reflection through the French doors. They were closed, sealed against the weather.

And still, she heard "Misty." Who was playing? Whirling, she confronted the darkest corner of the ballroom where she could see the graceful outline of the grand piano. Who was there?

The air stirred. She glimpsed a movement to her left and turned. In the dim light, she saw wide, staring eyes set in a bone-white face—the face of fear. Her own face. She saw herself reflected in a ballroom mirror, one of many mirrors.

As her eyes grew more accustomed to the dark, she became aware of other reflections, full-face and profile, a shadowy platoon. She chided herself. *Get a grip, Thea. You'll scare yourself to death.*

Cautiously, she neared the Steinway, almost expecting to see some phantom in half mask swirling his cape.

But no one was there. No hand touched the ivory keys.

"Thea." It was the whispery voice of Rosemont. "You've been a naughty girl."

She stiffened. Her glance shot around the room. Her name seemed to come at her from all directions. Surround-sound terror. This, she thought was no tape. Rosemont was speaking to her specifically. She clenched her fists. "Where are you?"

"You were instructed, were you not? I told you to search your mind, to find the person you wronged with your heartless indifference."

She listened hard, trying to figure out where the voice was coming from, but the ballroom acoustics made it impossible to determine. Rosemont must be speaking through a sound-system microphone wired to speakers concealed in the elaborate decor.

"Who is this person you're talking about?" she demanded. "I can't think of anyone I've wronged."

"Think harder!"

She jumped at his command and hated herself for being skittish. Nervous sweat trickled down her spine in spite of the chill in this room. Her stomach knotted. Telling herself to be strong, she straightened her shoulders. She had to stand up to this bully. He enjoyed seeing her fear, her trembling, her helpless confusion.

"Thea," he whispered.

It sounded as if he was close behind her, on her heels, whispering like a serpent straight into her soul. She darted forward, pivoted. Her foot slipped on the polished marble, and she fell to her hands and knees. A sharp cry escaped her lips.

She scrambled to her feet, refusing to cower. He was sick and his little game, wrong. She yelled to the four corners of the ceiling. "I've done nothing I'm ashamed of. Do you hear me? Nothing."

"Only half correct," the disembodied voice accused. "You did nothing when there was much you could have done. You turned your back. You walked away. You always walk away, Thea. And that is shameful."

The soft music teased her recent memory of her conversation with Spence. She'd walked away from him, too. She could have made the phone call to Spence, and stopped her own dithering, mopey behavior. She could have forgiven him, pursued the most important relationship in her life. Who was to say that they couldn't have worked out their problems if she hadn't cut him off? Or forbidden him to call her, ever again.

In fact, though she had refused to examine the possibility in all this time, he might have had a point about troublesome defects in her grant proposal.

Instead, she'd taken his vote personally, turned her back and hidden herself away. Why?

Was she afraid of confrontation?

Would she rather be right than to have what she truly wanted?

She swallowed hard and lashed out at Rosemont. "You don't know me."

"On the contrary. I've watched you from a distance for a long time. I know you very well."

The music ended with a soft click, and she realized that he'd taped and replayed Spence's music for background, to haunt her, to goad her. If he'd recorded Spence's impromptu recital while they were in the ballroom, he'd also been listening to their private conversation.

Oh Lord, what had she said? What personal secrets had she betrayed? "You have no right or reason to spy on me."

"My reason is revenge," he said, so softly that it sounded nearly musical, almost sweet. "And you, Thea, will shepherd the others to their confessions of cruel disregard, or all their tragic fates will be on your head."

"You're insane!" she cried. "You can't be serious—"

"A shame, Thea, if you believe I will not hold you accountable for all." His voice echoed eerily. "Shame, shame, shame."

Thea shivered violently as the silence deepened around her. She felt more a pawn that ever before. She clapped a hand over her mouth to stifle the slightest cry. She didn't want to give Rosemont the satisfaction, or herself the space to fall apart.

She couldn't understand what he was up to. If Rosemont had wanted, he could have hidden Jenny away so far that they would never find her. He could have put her on a video monitor none of them could ignore. Instead, he put her where she was sure to be found.

All of which left Thea with only one rational explanation—Rosemont had intended that Jenny be found. That she and Spence had clashed over the piano had simply provided the madman more grist for the mill.

And now, he intended to hold her responsible for forcing the admissions of cruelty and harm from the rest of the wedding party.

She determined to set that aside and follow through with help for Spence in rescuing Jenny. She headed for the door that led back to the center section of the house. Placing one foot in front of the other, she walked carefully through the silent ballroom. The tap of each footstep sounded louder than a gunshot. It occurred to her that she might be walking straight into Rosemont's arms, right into a trap. Where was he? Shivers of apprehension raised goose bumps on her skin. She breathed the cold air in tense tortured gasps.

As she reached for the golden doorknob, he spoke again. "Thea. If you fail, you will die."

"Go to hell."

She flung open the door and bolted into the brightly lit corridor that led to the Grand Drawing Room. Doors were closed on either side, and she moved past them quickly, fearing the unseen peril that might lie behind these glorious facades. Rosemont could be hiding anywhere. He could leap out at any second.

"Mona!" she shouted. She needed to find the others, to confront solid, real human beings. "Travis!" Why wouldn't they answer? Where were they? She hastened her steps as she realized again that there truly was no escape. The castle was a labyrinth of danger, and Rosemont was completely in control.

A tall figure appeared in her peripheral vision. She flattened her back against the wall, too panicked to scream. Her heart clanged against her ribcage like warning bells.

He stepped into the light. It was only the Reverend Joshua Handy.

"Are you all right?" he asked.

Her breath trembled. When he reached toward her with his long skeletal fingers, she recoiled. "Fine," she squeaked. "Reverend, where are the others?"

"Travis and I split up to cover more area. I haven't seen Mona or Lawrence since we left the table."

Idiots! But she and Spence had split in the end, too, and

Rosemont had gotten to her. "Did you see anything? Hear anything?"

His long nose twitched, and he gave a disdainful sniff as if he could smell her fear. "Nothing."

Travis bounded down the hallway toward them. "Dudes, this place is totally amazing. There's a video room on the second floor that's too—"

"Travis, have you gone completely wiggedy-whack?" Thea cried. One minute he behaved as if he were on some treasure hunt and the next he was completely psycho about Jenny's welfare. With her middle-schoolers, she expected short attention spans, but Travis's self-absorption was over the top, and it bugged her. "Pay attention! We found Jenny, and we need help moving her."

Beneath his cockscomb of bleached hair, Travis's forehead crumpled in an uncharacteristic frown. "Is she okay? Is my sister okay?"

"Yes." Thea could only stare at him, fighting a sense of misplaced déjà vu. What was it about him that pushed her buttons? "Spence thinks she's been drugged."

Travis shook his head. "Drugged as in stoned? Or drugged as in—"

"Unconscious," Thea said. "She's lying on a gurney, hooked up to an IV."

"Well, that's just great," Travis lashed out as if it were all Thea's fault. His lower lip quivered. "She's all the damn family I got left." More cursing forced through his clenched teeth. "Why is this crap falling on me? Why?"

"Snap out of it, Travis," she ordered. Even her thirteen-year-olds knew better than to blame the messenger. She'd never confronted a situation remotely like this. "Travis, listen to me. We have to move quickly. We—"

"What should we do?" the reverend asked, wringing his hands.

The two men—so opposite in appearance and demeanor—looked to her for instructions. She didn't want to lead the chorus in this unfamiliar refrain, but she had to get help back to Spence. She'd probably already taken twice as long as he would expect. "Come with me. We need to move Jenny." She urged them to move it. "We have to stay together. Nobody—and I mean nobody—wanders off by themselves."

Though she hated to enter the ballroom again, it was the most direct route. Head down, Thea shoved open the double doors. The lights had been restored, and she marched across the brightly lit room of marble, gold and sparkling mirrors, leading the way. She guided the two men through the other door to the servant's stairwell serving this tower.

When they reached the upper landing, Spence stood waiting. He was wearing his doctor face. Serious yet encouraging, he gave the impression that he was in charge. Thea had never been so relieved to pass the torch. He took Travis in hand before he could fly off the handle. "Jenny's going to be all right," Spence said. "We'll need to monitor her condition, but she'll come around. A few minutes ago she awoke long enough to get up and use the bathroom."

Spence stepped aside to let Travis and the reverend enter the tower bedroom, describing Jenny's few semiconscious moments. She hadn't responded to him at all, or given him any sense that she understood her condition. "She'd have torn the IV right out of her wrist if I hadn't been here."

"What'd you do, man?" Travis demanded.

Spence showed them where the needle at the end of the tubing on the IV bag fitted into what he called a "venous catheter," which was taped to Jenny's wrist. There were two rubber ports for either the IV or injections by hypodermic needles. "The saline drips in here, and any other medication can be injected right into the rubber port." He'd had to pull the needle dripping saline into Jenny's vein when she got up.

Spence pivoted and reached toward Thea. Thank goodness! she thought, more than ready to lean on him, to collapse into his arms, to accept his comfort. She no longer had the strength to stand alone.

But Spence pulled her outside the room to the landing and only held her wrist, checking her pulse, watching her closely. He drew her just outside the door onto the third-floor landing. "What happened, Thea?"

"How do you know something happened?"

"You're pale, trembling and breathing hard. You were gone too long." He cradled her cheek with his other hand, and she felt the radiant kilowatts of his attention. He lightly stroked her hair, calming her. "Take a couple of deep breaths and tell me what frightened you."

She did as the doctor ordered. Breathing steadily, Thea felt the warmth return to her body. She wasn't sure whether her fear had merely run its course or if Spence's manner had quelled her panic. She explained what had happened with the lights going out in the ballroom, the recording of his piano playing and the voice of Rosemont. "It was creepy, Spence. Only your playing was recorded. Rosemont was responding to what I said."

Spence grimaced. "What did he want?"

She bit her lip. "He put it all on my head. He said I should shepherd the others to their confessions or all their…I don't remember exactly. All their oh…" She remembered then. "Their 'tragic fates,' he said, would be on my head."

He exhaled sharply, whispering now. "My God, he's crazy like a fox."

"Spence!" she protested. "Why would you say that? What am I supposed to do, dole out homework assignments to everyone in the wedding party? Write a theme on the subject of 'Who I Wronged on My Summer Vacation'?"

He leaned very close to her, and spoke below a whisper right into her ear to insure Rosemont would not also hear him. "Thea, *think.* The point is that Rosemont is pitting us against each other."

She understood. Still, she shook her head and spoke as softly into his ear. "Are we supposed to let him think it's working? He's a lunatic, Spence. He'll kill us all anyway."

"He's in control," Spence admitted. "He's obviously hiding somewhere here. He's got the place bugged, and you can bet he's armed, but what he really wants is our confessions." Cheek to cheek with Spence, so near she could feel the prickle of his whiskers, she couldn't see the expression in his eyes. "Let's get Jenny moved to the opposite wing. Then, we'll come up with another plan."

Together, they went back into the tower room where Reverend Joshua hovered over the gurney, hands folded in prayer.

Travis paced in front of the windows, bursting with stifled energy. "Is she going to be okay, doc?" he demanded as soon as Spence drew near.

"I don't have any reason to think she won't be all right. We'll have to wait until whatever drug she's been given clears her system."

Thea noticed that Spence had not reconnected the IV bag. "Did you decide the saline contained the drug?"

Spence shook his head. "I suppose it's possible—but

the drug is probably being administered through the buffalo cap." He pointed to Jenny's wrist, where the tiny tube taped to her skin entered her vein. "As soon as we get her moved, I'll hang saline again. A fresh bag."

"What is she on, man?"

"There's no way of knowing for sure. It could be a morphine derivative, could be any one of a dozen drugs we use for conscious sedation. People describe it as an amnesia drug. If that's what it is, it allows Jenny to wake up long enough to go to the bathroom, for instance, but not much more. Whatever it is, it's not a lethal dose."

"How do you know?" Travis demanded with that imperious tone again.

Spence spoke soothingly to Travis, as, Thea supposed, he would to any concerned family member. "Because she's still alive."

The implication was that Rosemont intended to keep Jenny in a state of suspended consciousness from which she would awake with few ill effects. But he also must have anticipated that they would find her and care for her. "How soon do you think the drug will wear off?" Thea asked. "By morning?"

She watched Spence measuring his answer. If the drug cleared her system and Jenny awoke, what then? What would she tell them? They couldn't be sure about Jenny's role in this weekend. She hadn't been injured—no cuts or bruises, no evidence of a struggle. Had she been drugged while she slept? Had Rosemont already broken her heart and then been forced to drug her to keep her quiet?

In the end, Spence avoided saying much of anything substantive to Travis and Reverend Joshua—both of whom Spence regarded as suspicious characters. He gave them the standard doctor spiel—that it would depend on Jenny's own metabolism. "Meanwhile, we'll keep a close watch over her and make sure Rosemont doesn't get the chance to dose her again.''

Travis fumed. ''I am going to kick some butt. Who does that bastard think he is anyway?'' He reached into an inside pocket of the quilted red ski vest he'd been wearing since they first saw him. He produced a flat, silver automatic pistol. Very small, probably a .22 caliber.

''Why are you carrying?'' Spence asked sharply.

''I got enemies, man. I'm one of the best freestyle skiers in the world. There's guys out there who want to bust my kneecaps. I know what I'm doing—''

''Is the safety on?'' Spence demanded.

''At the moment. But—''

''Keep it that way.''

''—answer me this, man. Who died and left you boss?''

Spence ignored the juvenile outburst and handed out assignments. ''I'll carry Jenny. Travis, you break down the gurney and tote it along. Reverend, the medical supplies, if you will.'' Spence nodded to a carton containing various sealed bags of saline, tubing and syringes. ''Thea, you lead the way. Open the doors.''

Spence directed Thea down the staircase to the second floor. They hadn't searched this level, but he hoped it went straight across to the opposite tower. ''We'll go this way. I'd rather bring Jenny straight across to the bedrooms on the second floor.''

''Fine with me,'' she said. ''I'm not anxious to waltz through the ballroom again.''

While they walked past closed doors, Spence easily carrying Jenny's dead weight, he asked Thea in low undertones what she knew about Jenny's medical history and habits.

Thea stared at him a moment before pushing on. ''Nothing about her history, except that if Dr. Mona really is her therapist, maybe Jenny is on anti-depressants." She frowned. "Why do you want to know? What are you thinking?"

"Gauging from her reflexes, I think it is only a conscious sedation med that Rosemont is using on Jenny—but she's a little too deeply sedated." He shifted Jenny's weight in his arms. "I'm worried about drug interactions Rosemont may not have taken into account. Conscious sedation on top of recreational drugs could be dangerous."

"She's not a user, if that's what you're asking." Heading in the direction of the other tower, Thea pushed through a door that opened onto the common area of several suites of rooms. To her left she saw the media room that had sent Travis into spasms of delight.

"You're sure?" Spence asked. "You know, Travis missed his father's funeral because he was in a drug rehab program. Travis's habit makes me think twice about Jenny. Addictive behavior tends to run in families."

"Like brother, like sister?" Without breaking stride, she rolled her eyes. "Aren't you being a teensy bit judgmental?"

"It's simple genetics," he said. "I'm not condemning Jenny or Travis. Like alcoholism, their addictive tendency might be in the DNA."

"Well, I know for sure that Jenny doesn't use recreational drugs. At school, we have the D.A.R.E. program to get kids off drugs, and Jenny told me she couldn't understand why people would think drugs were fun. Still..."

"What?"

"When I told Travis that his sister had been drugged, he asked if she was stoned."

They descended two steps, crossed a landing with a staircase leading down, and ascended two more, staying on the second floor. Thea said, "Would other prescription drugs worry you?"

"Possibly." Spence paused to look around. Travis and the reverend straggled up behind them, huffing and puffing with their awkward loads. "Okay, we're here. These are the second-floor bedrooms in the tower above the kitchen."

Thea pointed to a closed door on her left. "This is the bedroom I'm sharing with Dr. Mona."

"Try the door on the right," Spence told her.

She opened a door and stepped into a suite of rooms consisting of a comfortable sitting room with a fireplace, and beyond that, another bedroom. The lights came up as she walked in. The bedroom had been decorated to serve as a children's nursery. There were a couple of double beds, a crib and rocking chair, and a massive play area furnished with a sort of indoor jungle gym and life-sized stuffed animals, including a giraffe that stood at least seven feet tall among a zoo-like collection.

Thea watched Spence sizing up the suite of rooms as he held Jenny's limp form. All the doors could be shut off against Rosemont, and there was plenty of room left to set up the gurney. Spence told Travis to raise the gurney into place.

"I don't know why you just don't put her on a real bed," Travis complained, though he lifted the gurney and locked it.

Spence rolled his eyes, but he exercised a tolerance Thea found amazing. "The IV pole is attached to the gurney, Travis. And just in case I have to perform an emergency procedure, I'll need Jenny at a height I can work at."

Travis backed away and Spence placed Jenny on the

gurney. "Thea, would you get an unopened bag of saline and new tubing?"

She found the bag, encased in sealed plastic, on top of the box the reverend had carried, along with a box of tubing. She tore open the packaging and handed the bag to Spence. He spiked the saline and attached an enclosed needle, then plunged the needle into the rubber buffalo cap. Thea snatched up a roll of white silk tape, and he secured the needle in place.

"You and the reverend stay with Jenny while Thea and I go find Mona and Lawrence," Spence said to Travis. "We'll all hole up in this suite of rooms for the night."

For once, neither the reverend nor Travis complained. Spence guided Thea out the door toward the servant stairwell.

The last time he'd been alone with Thea in this space, Spence had kissed her. Though it had been only a few hours ago, he felt as if an eternity had passed. In the meantime, they'd bounced all over the emotional spectrum. They'd argued. They'd made up, united in danger. They'd been repelled and attracted. Halfway down he said to her, "Thea, wait."

She turned and backed up against the rough brick wall, putting as much space between them as possible. She gave him a look. "Don't even think about a kiss, Spence."

He met her eyes. "I can't help what I'm thinking," he said.

"Nor can I." A wry smile twisted her generous lips, but her hazel eyes warned him away. "Was there something else?"

"We need to get the others talking about who it is Rosemont wants to avenge," he said. "I'm thinking if you confide in Mona that Rosemont is now holding you accountable for all of us, she'll step up and help."

Thea nodded. "I'll try."

"And another thing. You're the only person here I can trust. When we settle down for the night, I want you to stay close to me. As a back-up."

Doing what he asked would put her in close quarters with Spence, and the idea of that made her pulse skitter. Still, she nodded again. "Okay," she said.

It went without saying that he'd do the same for her. He'd protect her, make sure nothing bad happened. "You need to trust me, too."

Her lips parted. She seemed ready to give that simple assurance of mutual confidence. Then her eyes flashed. He knew her well enough to realize that she was replaying the past, dredging up old fears. *Damn* her stubborn memory.

"You promised not to do that, Thea." His voice was low and urgent, compelling. He moved in on her and she stood her ground.

"Not to do what?"

"Keep the past between us."

She had. Her pulse hammered at her throat, in her ears. He made her both more honest and less certain than ever that she'd had a right to cut him off without hope of ever resolving their differences. And standing so near her, so handsome, so earnest, so male, he made her want him.

He took her chin in his hand, and just as before, she knew what was coming. She had a split second in which to decide, and then he closed off the possibility of retreat. He cupped her nape with his other hand and drew her nearer. His handsome, intent face descended to hers, and for long moments, the caress of his lips on hers closed off all possibility of an emotional retreat either. He touched his tongue to hers, igniting a storm of desire.

She put her arms around him, pressed her body to his,

and entwined her leg with his. Heat roared inside her, physical need fused with emotional.

"Ah, Thea." He wrapped her in his arms and filled his hand with her bottom, drawing her so tightly to him she felt his powerful arousal at her belly. Desire streamed through her blood like a shot straight into her veins of the most powerful aphrodisiac known to man.

A nearly hysterical banging echoed up the stairs, jerking them both back to the reality of their situation. Spence let her go, and backed away. She wanted to scream.

He dragged a hand through his hair, then backhanded his wet mouth. "Thea…"

She crossed her arms tightly over her breasts, tight against her throbbing nipples. She had lost it completely, lost her reticence, all her self-righteous anger, gone hot and damp as she hadn't in all their years apart. "Spence."

The banging started up again. Glancing down the stairs, he swallowed. She hugged herself tighter. "Stick close to me, okay?" he murmured.

She nodded. His voice was ragged. She couldn't find hers.

He plunged down the stairs two at a time. She followed.

At the foot of the servants' stairwell the raucous noise and banging they'd heard from above increased. The clamor was coming from the kitchen. Loud crashes and gales of laughter. What the hell was going on? Spence opened the door.

In the kitchen, Dr. Mona and Lawrence the butler sat side-by-side on a butcher-block table under the circular hanging rack of copper-bottomed pots. Each of them held a long-handled ladle in one hand and a glass of wine in the other.

Mona raised her glass in greeting. "Listen to this."

She whacked the bottom of a hanging pot, producing a

clang. Then Lawrence banged out four hits on another pan. Then Mona made two more clangs and giggled. "Did you get it?"

Thea looked at Spence. Her body still hummed. Vibrated. "Sorry, no."

"Lemme do it again," Mona slurred. "Ready, Lawrence?"

"You betcha."

This time, Mona sang along with her banging. "Shave and a haircut. Two bits."

"Swell," Spence said.

Mona chortled. "I never told you? I used to play the glockenspiel."

Spence and Thea exchanged a glance. Under his breath, he said, "At least, somebody's having a good time."

MONA BEGAN CLUCKING at her own misbehavior, paying not the least attention. Spence asked Lawrence if he had another gun in addition to the one in his shoulder holster. "At your ankle, maybe?"

Lawrence put down his ladle. "I do. Why?"

"Give it to Thea."

Lawrence started to protest, then seeing Spence's look, reached down, pulled up his pant leg and pulled out his backup weapon. He handed it to Spence, who checked the safety and handed it in turn to Thea.

She had no place to put it. She took the gun in her hand and got used to the feel of it as Spence told the half-drunk pair that Jenny had been found, drugged, and brought to the nursery suite upstairs. Tipsy and silly, Mona's eyes grew wide as she clapped a hand over her mouth. "No!"

"Yes. We're setting up a command post there for the night. Starting now."

He returned to the nursery suite with Lawrence, and

Thea linked arms with Mona, escorting her to their shared bedroom on the second floor. The little psychologist was more than a little wobbly but in high spirits as she mumbled slurred renditions of guttural-sounding drinking songs.

Inside the room, Thea put down the gun and locked the door. The room was interior, so that there were no windows nor any drapes to pull. "Are you German, Mona?"

"Yes," she chirped, then waved a finger in the air, "but not Freudian." Hands on hips, she stomped in a surprisingly agile folk dance. "I'm a feminist."

"Good for you."

Spying Lawrence's handgun, Mona gaped open-mouthed. "Doesn't that pistol belong to Lawrence?"

Thea frowned. "Mona, didn't you just see—never mind. Yes it's Lawrence's. Spence thought we should have it."

"Do you know how to shoot that awful thing?"

"Yes." After the tragedy at Columbine High School, she had had to accept the possibility of gun violence in the classroom and prepared herself by taking lessons on handling pistols and rifles. Though she didn't personally own a firearm, she'd fired hundreds of rounds at a practice range. More training, actually, than she had given Spence to believe.

Mona eyed her curiously. "Could you shoot another human being?"

"Given certain circumstances, yes. If someone threatened me or my students, I'd fight."

"But how do you feel?"

Thea sighed. Ever the therapist, even in her drunken state, more Freudian than she admitted. *Yes, but tell me, how do you feel?* "I just pray never to be in that situation."

But she'd spent many a sleepless night staring up at the blank ceiling in her condo, imagining what would happen if a crazed, violent gunman burst into *her* classroom. How would she save the kids? How would she save herself?

Unless she escaped this isolated mountain and the clutches of a certifiable loon, she would never have that worry again.

She had to enlist Mona's help, which was why she'd come to this room with the tipsy woman.

The wizened little psychotherapist had plunked herself down in a chair at the table. With her gnarly fingers, she touched the black metal bore of the pistol. "If only we lived in a world without guns."

"Murderers would still find a way," Thea said.

"It'd be different," she asserted with wine-induced vehemence. "Did you know that lots of people who commit murder really don't intend for someone to die. In fact—"

"That's interesting, Dr. Mona, but we've got to—"

"—they most often lash out in a sudden, uncontrollable rage. Or they want to teach someone a lesson. They want attention. And if they happen to have a gun in their hand…" She withdrew her hand from the weapon. "Guns are too easy to use. Too lethal."

Thea grabbed her opening. "What about Gregory Rosemont? Do you think he just wants our confessions, or does he intend to kill us?"

Mona's narrow shoulders rose and fell. "I don't know him well enough even to guess."

"I'm sure Jenny must have told you all about him." She wasn't sure at all. It was still entirely possible that Mona was not who she claimed to be. But Thea's questions might shed light there too.

Mona's brow raised. "Jenny believes her fiancé is handsome, intelligent, generous and kind. As I've said before,

I've learned not to expect accurate observations from women who look through the eyes of love.''

"But Jenny is usually very perceptive," Thea said. "Very conscious."

"But when we're on antidepressants, we all tend to see things—" Mona clapped a small hand over her mouth. "I shouldn't have said that. Confidentiality, you know."

But Thea wanted her to go further down that path. There were secrets that Mona might reveal. "It must be difficult to listen to other people's problems and not be able to unload all that painful baggage."

"That's why I go to a therapist of my own," Mona said. "And that therapist goes to another and another and—"

"Like Rosemont's six degrees of separation."

"Exactly." Mona bounced out of the chair and went to the bed. "We're all *powerfully* interconnected."

"We are, no doubt." Thea followed her to the bed, thinking how to frame her next question. If Rosemont was listening, she wanted him to believe she was seriously going after the information he wanted, and with a certain finesse. "In fact, we're interconnected enough that I think it *is* possible that we all somehow failed whoever it is Rosemont is so bent on avenging. And the truth is, if we don't confess our sins, we're going to die. Have you thought about who it might be? Do you have any names to suggest?"

"Lots." Fading fast, Mona pulled a pillow out from under the covers. "I'm a decent psychotherapist, but I've failed with some of my clients."

"Like who?"

"No, no, no." She waggled a finger at Thea. "No names. But I will tell you this. Some people blame me for making their problems worse."

Thea needed specifics. "What kind of problems?"

"Marriages that end in divorce. Teenagers who run away from home. Depressions that turn suicidal." She laid her head on the pillow and sighed. "They blame me. Their families blame me."

Thea was losing her connection. Dr. Mona was falling asleep. "Stay with me, Mona! Nobody's asking you to rat out your patients. Was it a breach of ethics to tell us Jenny is a client?"

"Not my fault," Mona murmured, low and uneasy, her eyelids drooping piteously.

"Mona, listen to me!" Thea literally shook the tiny old woman by her shoulders. Should she tell Dr. Mona that her own life was now on the line? Would it make the slightest impact on her to know that Rosemont intended to hold Thea accountable?

But she was fighting a lost battle. Mona had nearly fallen off. "Dr. Mona, if Spence and I come up with a name between us, will you at least confirm the name?"

"Not my fault." Mona's eyes fell shut for the last time. "I always did the best I could."

Chapter Eight

When Spence had first embarked on this weekend wedding party, he'd hoped to hold one woman in his arms: Thea, and only Thea. But he'd had to carry Jenny down from the opposite tower room, and now he found himself carrying the conked-out Dr. Mona Nance in his arms from the tower bedroom to the nursery suite. Without fully waking, Mona reached up and patted his cheek. "You're a good boy, Spencer."

"Thanks." Little old ladies and seven-year-old Brownies adored him. Please God, Thea too.

"Where are we going?" she chirped.

"To the headquarters we set up in the nursery suite." The center of the castle on the second floor. In her drunken stupor, Mona clearly remembered little of what he'd said in the kitchen. Spence reminded her. "We're all going to spend the night there. Together."

A loopy smile curved her features. "Oh, goodie. An orgy."

"Jeez, I hope not." The idea of group sex would be enough to give Reverend Joshua Handy an aneurysm. The tall, gaunt man of the cloth didn't look like he'd ever indulged in pleasures of the flesh. And, if he had, he surely hadn't enjoyed himself.

In the large sitting room, Spence gently placed Mona on one of the matching flowered sofas and tucked a pillow under her head. The others had already staked out their places.

Travis was stretched out on a window seat where he occasionally cupped his hands around his eyes and peered outside, before giving a repetitive weather report. "Still snowing. Real hard."

The reverend crouched in a velvet wingback chair with a footstool covered in needlepoint. He was nearest the blazing fireplace and had pushed up his sleeves. His skinny, almost hairless white arms laced like pipe cleaners across his narrow chest.

Lawrence had made himself comfortable by dragging in a twin-sized mattress and comforter from one of the other bedrooms. He had shed his sports jacket, no longer bothering to hide his shoulder holster and handgun.

Thea emerged from the adjoining bedroom where they'd set up Jenny's gurney.

"How's Jenny doing?" Spence asked her.

"She looks peaceful." She beckoned to him. "Why don't you come here and take a look."

He crossed the room as Travis unnecessarily reported, "It's a damn blizzard out there." The wind could be easily heard through the thick castle walls.

Inside the enormous nursery bedroom there were two double beds with colorful alphabet comforters, matched by a ceiling border of the ABCs. Attached to one wall was a huge chalkboard.

Spence noted that Travis and the reverend had followed instructions and shoved an enormous dresser against the hallway door to prevent Rosemont from sneaking inside— using a key to unlock the outer door. The three-room suite—bedroom, sitting room and bath—should be completely impregnable once the armoire in the sitting room was moved to block that entrance as well.

Spence leaned over Jenny's gurney, which stood beside a waist-high wooden slide in the shape of an elephant. He made a routine check of the IV drip, then of Jenny's vital signs and reflexes. For an instant, there seemed to be movement behind her eyelids. "She's coming around," he said. "Damn, I wish I knew what Rosemont used to drug her."

Thea stroked her friend's chilly hand. "Would it help to induce vomiting or something?"

Spence almost laughed. "Only if she'd ingested the drugs."

Thea bounced the heel of her hand off her own forehead. "I'm an idiot. Don't pay any attention."

Spence's lips turned up. "You're not an idiot."

His smile sent Thea's pulse knocking. There hadn't been a lot of reason to smile.

He gave Jenny one last visual once-over. "The best treatment is to let her sleep it off."

Thea stepped close and whispered, "What are we going to do next?"

"The ball's in your court. You want to try wheedling names out of the motley crew?"

She gave a deep sigh and murmured low. "I can't believe anything I say will make a difference."

He looked steadily at her. "Let's give it a shot. We've got nothing to lose," he encouraged. "Besides, they like you, Thea." He turned away from the bed and gave her his full attention. She still wore the gray slacks and preppy red sweater set but had taken off her pearls. Though worry etched her brow, she looked adorable. "I like you."

She narrowed her eyes. "Are you patronizing me?"

"Nope. I'm applying a simple solution to a complicated problem."

He'd learned a lot about group dynamics working SAR missions. Several rescuers at a time were often called on to head into the mountains to track lost hikers—or respond to an accident, or deal with the often tragic aftermath of an avalanche. Though there was always an appointed leader who coordinated efforts and monitored the walkie-talkie communications, another type of leader inevitably emerged. Someone who monitored the mood of the group.

In the case of SAR missions, that person usually turned out to be his friend, Emily. She seemed to intuitively understand when the rescuers needed a pep talk. When they stalled or faltered in their mission, Emily knew when to be gentle and when to be tough.

Spence suspected that Thea also had that kind of empathy, that talent. "You're more than capable of turning yourself into the emotional leader here. Everyone already picks up on your attitude. Even Travis behaves when you crack the whip."

She grinned. "Gosh, thanks."

If it was compliments she wanted, he'd be more than willing to continue. He'd start with the sheen of her chestnut hair and work his way all the way down to the snug fit of her casual loafers on her slender, arched feet. What lay between, well… But this wasn't the moment to indulge in graphic appreciation—not while they were preparing to spend the night with four other people.

He took her arm and escorted her to the door, offering one last whisper of advice. "Give it a shot. Get them to open up."

"I guess I will, since my life is apparently depending on it." When she glanced up at Spence, he winked. Somehow, they'd lined up on the same team, and she was glad.

Spence accompanied her into the sitting room, now cluttered with too many bodies and luggage here, there and everywhere. She crossed with a determined step to the sofa opposite the one where Mona was stretched out, barely taking up half the length. The little psychologist wouldn't be much help in this discussion.

She took stock of the others. The reverend avoided eye contact. With his arms folded, his body language was not encouraging. Likewise, Travis and Lawrence both seemed stand-offish. And, she reminded herself, they were both armed.

No harm in trying? She hoped not.

"Well," she said with her most cooperation-inspiring tone, "as long as we're all here with nothing else to do, I think we should talk about Rosemont's mystery person."

"I've already made my position clear," the reverend said. "I will not discuss unfounded accusations. Why should I?"

"If we know the identity of this person," she cajoled, "we might get some leverage to negotiate with Rosemont."

"Why negotiate?" the reverend said. "I believe we should stay holed up here, in these three rooms, until Monday. At which time, we will be rescued."

"Rescued?" Thea questioned.

Reverend Joshua looked toward Spence. "The doctor assured me that his friends would return to pick him up on Monday. What were their names… Emily. And Jordan. They will surely notice the ski gondola crash. And we will be rescued by a helicopter."

"That's true," Spence said. "*If* the blizzard stops by Monday. *If* the roads leading in here are passable. *If* a rescue chopper is available. That's a lot of conditions to be met."

"Besides," Thea said, "it's still only Friday night. That means we're trapped here for three nights and two days. A lot could happen."

"Not if we all stay together," the reverend said. "Surely, Rosemont wouldn't attack us all."

"He might," Travis said, still staring out the windows at the snow. He had on earphones now that he must have found in the media room, small ones that fit inside the ear canal, plugged into a Walkman. It was a wonder he could hear them talking as well.

"The guy," Travis went on, "is totally zoned. He could be standing outside the door with a bazooka for all we know."

Thea hadn't wanted to focus on the possibility of physical assault. "Let's at least try talking."

"I'm up for it," Travis said. He unplugged the earphones, left his perch on the window seat and sauntered toward her. He'd changed his skintight ski clothes for the skateboarder style—baggy jeans, T-shirt and zip-up sweatshirt. "A game of Truth or Dare."

From her association with adolescents, Thea was familiar with the game. Not very hopeful, she knew it was at least a start. "All right," she said. "Truth or Dare. Here are the rules. We select a person to start—"

"Me," Travis said, warming to the challenge. "I'll go first."

"Fine," Thea said. "Travis gets to pick whether he will tell the truth and answer one question truthfully, or fulfill a dare which will not involve anything dangerous."

"I've heard of this," Lawrence said, as he moved from his mattress and comforter nest onto the other end of the sofa where Thea sat. "I vote for the game. If for no other reason than to pass the time."

"Okay." Thea slipped off her loafers and tucked her legs under her. "Travis? Truth or Dare?"

"Truth," he said with a cocky smile.

Thea phrased her question carefully. "Will you tell us the names of every person you've ever wronged in your life?"

"What do you mean by wronged? Like…ticked off? Cuz that'd be a boatload." Travis rattled off a series of names mostly Nordic, variations on Sven and Bjorn. "Those are guys I've beaten in freestyle skiing. Big whiners." Then he moved on to the rich and famous. "…and then, there's the Trumps."

"Oh really!" Lawrence scoffed. "I can't imagine how you could possibly be acquainted with all of these extremely well-known people."

"Hey, dude. I'm a world-class skier. I spend a lot of time in Aspen."

"So do I," Spence cracked. "And I've never seen a single Trump."

"'Scuse me, doc. But you're not exactly in my league."

Thea waded in before direct accusations started flying. "Travis, that's the point. None of us know these people—and Rosemont was very clear that we had *all* somehow wronged the same person."

"Hey, I was telling the truth. And this isn't helping my sister, so—"

"Wait." Thea interrupted him again, though it was probably useless. Since Jenny was now safe—at least under Spence's watchful eye, Travis wasn't motivated. "We talked at the dinner table about narrowing the time frame. Spence and I knew each other five years ago. Is there anyone you can think of, any normal workaday person, who you might have wronged five years ago?"

Travis heaved a petulant sigh. "Sorry. No little match

girl in my past." He rubbed the palms of his hands together. "Now, I get to pick somebody else. Lawrence. Truth or Dare?"

"Very well," the butler said, tucking away his electronic game. "Since none of this soul-searching applies to me, I shall choose—"

"Wait a minute, Lawrence," Thea said. "Why don't we assume, just for the game, that you are relevant to our search."

"But I'm not. I only met Miss Trevain for the first time last week when I toured the castle. Therefore, I am exempt."

Thea shook her head. "It doesn't matter when you met Jenny. What matters is whether or not you played a role in harming someone five years ago."

Lawrence broke off eye contact with her and nodded to Travis. "I shall choose a Dare."

"Awright!" Travis said. "Get down on your hands and knees, bark like a dog and lick Mona's face."

Thea expected the butler to object to such demeaning behavior, but instead, Dr. Mona herself popped up, mad as a wet hen. Thea stared at the hyper-alert little Yoda.

"You," she sniffed at Travis, "are the most absurd excuse for a human being—"

"I knew it!" Travis snarled, jumping up, pointing his finger at Mona. "You're phony as a plugged nickel, you old biddy. You've been playing possum this whole time!"

"I beg your pardon," Dr. Mona snapped, awfully alert and articulate for someone who had been out cold in a drunken stupor. "I simply have no use for this Gestalt for the mentally challenged. I was resting—"

"Bull puck." Wild-eyed, Travis wheeled on Thea. "This is a joke. *You're* a joke. You want to know what I think? I think this whole set-up reeks. I think—"

"Travis—" Thea stood and started to rein him in before he came completely unglued, but Spence, watching Travis intently, stopped her. "Let's let him have his say, Thea. Go ahead, Travis. You've got the floor."

"So speaketh the oracle." Travis snarled at Spence. "You're probably the one keeping my sister doped to the gills. Who the hell else knows their way around a hypodermic? And you, Law*rence,* where were you and the troll when we were searching for my sister? Huh?"

He turned on the Reverend Joshua Handy, mocking him for a sanctimonious clone off the shortlist of fallen televangelists. "But Teach, *you're* the cream of the crop. You make me sick." He mimicked some of her earliest remarks, fluttering his eyelashes in disparagement. "'I should have been here for Jenny. I'm the maid of honor.' Well, where the hell were you, huh?"

He stomped off across the room, pivoted and pointed at them all. "I hope old Rosemont toasts the lot of you. Serve you right."

He turned to leave, but Spence's softly voiced question stopped Travis dead in his tracks. Made him turn and listen. "Why don't you turn that razor intellect on yourself, Trav? What's *your* gig? Dumb and dumber or avenging angel?"

Travis blinked. "Your call, freakazoid. I'm outta here. I'm gonna go shoot the breeze with my doped-to-the-gills sister." He disappeared into the bedroom of the nursery suite.

Thea let go a long, shaky breath. "Encores? Anyone? That was brilliant, Spence, letting him shoot off his mouth to his heart's content—"

"Sometimes, Thea" he interrupted her, his voice so low it sent chills through her, "it's better to bleed off steam before the pressure can build to an explosion."

She clapped her mouth shut, then apologized. "I'm sorry. You're right, of course."

Spence shrugged. "Don't worry about it."

She drew in a deep, steadying breath. "Mona. Reverend. Would you please put your heads together in mutual confidentiality and try to come up with a name? Family or friend or foe or client that you might have had in common."

Mona agreed without a peep of protest.

The reverend nodded reluctantly. "I promise you, however, that it will be a pointless endeavor. But first, I would like to know how each of you would answer Travis's charges. For my part, I can assure you that I have nothing in common with those despicable charlatans—"

"Spare us your spiel, Joshua," Dr. Mona interrupted. "You're a true disciple. We get it. But Spence is no more responsible for Jenny's unfortunate condition than the man in the moon. And I'm sure Thea would have arranged to be on hand to be of help had Jenny asked. As for Lawrence," she gave the butler a considerably softened gaze, "let's rise above the cliché. The butler certainly did not do it."

"Nicely put, Dr. Mona," Spence said. "We are all blameless. The trouble is, we're not."

She blinked, very Yoda-like. "Might I suggest we continue with the game? It will give Travis time to cool off, and—"

"Gestalt for the mentally challenged?" Lawrence teased, poker-faced.

"Whatever." She waved her tiny hand. "It may serve to keep us from killing each other before Rosemont gets the opportunity." Flicking her gaze from one to the other of them, Mona gave Lawrence a sweet smile. "It is also remotely possible we will come up with some useful information. Thea, dear. I believe it is my turn. Do you choose Truth or Dare?''

"Truth," Thea answered.

Spence walked across the sitting room to peek in and make sure Travis wasn't making any mischief, then returned to his post by the fireplace. Travis, he said, was just slouching in a chair beside Jenny's gurney with a foot propped up on the rails, keeping time with unheard music through his headphones.

"Very well then," Mona resumed. "Thea. What was the saddest day of your life?"

Thea balked. "I...why don't we at least try to stay on the topic. My saddest day isn't going to get us anywhere—"

"Just go with it, Thea," Mona urged. "It's much like dream work. Perhaps your own saddest moment will trigger an insight into what has plunged Rosemont into such depths of despair that he now holds us hostage to his fantasies of revenge.''

Spence cleared his throat. "Respectfully, Dr. Mona, I think he's moved beyond fantasies."

Lawrence sat nodding sagely. "Mona's point *is* well-taken."

"Blather!" the reverend muttered. The flesh stretched tight over Joshua Handy's skull seemed to mottle. He was either the most fearful man of God, or the angriest.

"What do you say, Thea?" Mona prompted. "What was your saddest day?"

Her gaze tilted up, searching in her mind through her past for the most emotion-ridden moment. The saddest day? Breaking up with Spence had been pretty darn miserable. She remembered a damp depression, weeping and sleeping, but her memories glided backwards to an earlier time.

"I was thirteen. My oldest brother had a huge argument with Mom. He had the worst temper of all of us."

"How many siblings were there?" Mona asked.

"Six. Four boys and two girls."

"Interesting. In such a large family, you must have needed to be very strong and stubborn to gain attention."

"I had a very normal childhood," Thea said, seeing Spence smirk from the corner of her eye. She wasn't being defensive, merely stating a fact. "No abuse. No major weirdness."

"Please continue with your story," Mona said.

"After the argument, my brother stormed out of the house. He took the car." Her voice shook, and she cleared her throat. "He was driving too fast. Lost control. Crashed into a tree."

Unexpected tears welled up behind her eyelids. Even now, after all these years, she felt overwhelming sorrow. "He was in a coma for nearly a day before he died. Sad— my God. It was the saddest day of my life. My heart just shattered into little pieces." Even now tears welled in her eyes.

Mona and Lawrence exchanged meaning-filled looks.

"What?" Thea demanded.

"The loss of a sibling can be a catastrophe. Suppose Rosemont suffered such a loss?"

"That's a useful insight, Mona," Spence said, "but what are we supposed to do with it? How many of us know the siblings of even our closest friends, never mind acquaintances?"

"I'm with Spence," Thea said, feeling the inevitable sense of loss that came when she spoke of her brother begin to subside. "Rosemont may have lost a sibling, but it could have been a spouse, a lover. Or even a parent."

"We are only exploring possibilities," Mona reminded

them. "We have guessed that the occasion of our various failures happened five or more years ago. Now, let's add to that someone who died. Someone peripheral enough to our lives that the name doesn't just leap out at us..." Mona trailed off.

Thea felt a chill descend her spine. This additional criteria had a profound ring of truth about it. What chilled her more, however, was the distress in Joshua Handy's unfocused eyes.

"Reverend—"

He started violently. "What!"

"Have you remembered someone that—"

"Absolutely not," he cried. "Why are you all looking at me? What would satisfy you buzzards? A confession of evil? Do you suppose I alone in the universe have—"

"Take it easy, Reverend," Lawrence placated, "before you give yourself apoplexy."

"I have no recall," the reverend uttered, "of wrong-doing that would inspire this madman to presume to dole out the judgment of the Lord."

Spence traded looks with Thea. "I guess it's my turn. I'll take a Dare. Thea? You want to make it?"

"Sure." Her flesh still feeling a crawl over the reverend's outburst, she drew a deep breath and exhaled. "I dare you to tell us, what's the worst thing you've ever done? That Rosemont might be interested in," she amended, narrowing the scope.

He stared a few moments at his hands. "I guess the worst in my mind is what happened to the Strindberg girl. Amanda was her name." He looked around. "Is the name familiar at all?" No one had any recollection of the name. "Her parents were Rose and Peter." Still, no glimmer or recognition.

"What happened to Amanda, Spence?" Mona asked.

He glanced at Thea, and she knew this must be the name of the little girl who had nearly died in the ER because Spence hadn't followed up soon enough on the resident handling the little girl's deadly infection. "My inattention nearly cost Amanda her life."

The Reverend Handy latched onto the horror of it, as if, Thea thought, Spence was the guilty party among them. "Just because the innocent child did not die does not mean you are absolved of all responsibility," he accused, pointing a bony finger.

Spence just looked at the reverend, who was so vociferous in his own defense that only the Lord had the power to judge. "The point, Reverend," he said evenly, "is that it can't be Amanda that Rosemont is avenging, because none of the rest of you even know the name. We are *all* supposed to have wronged this poor soul." He straightened. "My turn. Reverend, we're up to you. Truth or Dare?"

"I choose Dare," Reverend Joshua said. "And I reserve the right to refuse humiliation."

"No problem." Spence found a pen and a legal-sized tablet in the desk. He carried them to the reverend. "Here's the dare—to follow up on your earlier agreement to write down the names of everyone you've counseled in your ministry and then compare your list with Dr. Mona's."

"How will *we* know," Lawrence asked, "if the reverend supplies any names at all?"

Handy bristled. "Are you questioning my integrity, sir? *You* have not taken a Truth or Dare."

"I'm sure the good reverend will comply," Mona intervened. "Why don't you tell us, Lawrence. Is there anyone in your past whom Rosemont might believe you wronged?"

Lawrence shifted in his chair. "Several years ago a client who had hired me as a bodyguard was murdered in his sleep." He gave a name that, as with Spence, no one recognized. "All right then. That is all I have to suggest."

"Game over," Spence declared. "Mona, Reverend, please write down your lists and compare notes privately."

"With any luck, you will come up with at least one match," Thea said, grateful that Spence had taken the lead and resolved a complicated interaction among them. "What do you say, Mona? Reverend? You could help the rest of us so much. Please, will you do it?"

Reverend Joshua picked up the tablet and walked to Mona's sofa. "I will agree to confer."

"In the meantime," Spence said, "we'll need to take turns watching Jenny. When she comes around, maybe she can provide a few answers herself. I'll take the first shift. The rest of you try to get some sleep." He enlisted Lawrence's help to move the heavy, six-foot-tall armoire into place so that even if the locked door to the suite was opened by Rosemont with a key, he could not gain entrance.

Thea watched Spence's back as he retreated into the adjoining nursery bedroom. Travis ambled out and went back to the window seat. She turned off a few lamps and stretched out on the sofa. Her thoughts flitted for a moment to Spence's courage in admitting to his nearly disastrous inattention to little Amanda Strindberg. He'd discarded his relentless ambition and made a drastic change in his life. She couldn't help thinking that it had all been for the best.

With eyes half-closed, she watched Mona and the reverend scratching out a list of names, conferring in whispers. Exhaustion rolled over her, but she couldn't fall asleep. Not yet. Not until they had a name. A mystery person. Someone who had been wronged.

After nearly an hour, Mona called out to her. "Thea?"

"Yes?" She sat up on the sofa, willing herself to alertness. "Do you have a name?"

"Not a single match."

"Well, of course not." Disappointment rankled inside her. "That would be too easy." She slapped on a look of gratitude that suggested she knew they'd done their best, then pulled her sweater more tightly around her. "I guess we'll have to start over tomorrow."

She wriggled into a comfortable sleeping position and began drifting toward slumber. Tomorrow, things had to get better.

Until then, she would rest and dream, escaping from worry and fear if only for a few moments. Jenny was safe now from further harm. They were all safe here, all the wedding party gathered behind barricaded doors.

Her last conscious thought was of Spence, of the way they once had been, not so much younger. Only five years ago. But not mature. Not so wise. Foolish. And in love.

When she startled awake, he was leaning over her, close enough to kiss, and she was tempted by his nearness. "Is it morning?" she asked.

"Depends upon your definition. Four o'clock." He tucked a blanket around her. "Go back to sleep."

But he must have approached her for a reason. Her brain staggered toward conscious thought. Her gaze fell on the gas flames in the fireplace. All the others were sleeping.

"I should take a turn," she said, sitting upright on the sofa. "You go ahead and get some sleep, Spence. I'll tend to Jenny. Has she come to at all yet?"

"Not really." He laid a finger across his lips. "Hush, Thea. Close your eyes. I can do another hour or two."

"No, I'm awake." She swung her legs around and stood, aware of cricks in her back from sleeping on a sofa.

Though she was far from refreshed, she'd had a lot more rest than Spence. "I'll take over now."

"Fine," he said.

She followed him into the adjoining nursery. Though Jenny still wasn't awake, she no longer lay still as Sleeping Beauty waiting for her Prince Charming. One arm cocked at an angle. Her hair was messy and damp on her forehead. She made a tiny groan and twisted on the hospital bed.

"She's restless. Coming out of it. She must have had one hell of a dose to keep her this far under for so many hours." Spence whispered. "It seems almost cruel to drag her back to reality."

"She went to sleep a bride, and now..." Thea shuddered with disgust. "Rosemont used her. He never loved her."

"Why couldn't she see through him?"

"Women in love are blind," Thea said, "so caught up in the fantasy that they can't see the thorns."

"Is that how it was with us?" he asked.

"I don't know, Spence. After we broke up, I was bitter. I wouldn't let myself remember the good times. It's a shame." She faced him. "Because there were some very, very good times."

She closed the space between them, allowing herself to peer deeply into his tired blue eyes. She took his hand and nodded toward one of the double beds in the nursery. "Lie with me, Spence."

Without speaking, he followed her. He threw back the alphabet comforter and eased under the sheets. She snuggled against him, turning so her back was against his chest.

"Don't go to sleep," he warned.

"I won't." But she felt so comfy and warm, perfectly relaxed.

If Jenny made a noise, Thea was sure she'd hear. Until then, she wrapped herself in a spooning embrace and closed her eyes. Dreams of Spence had become reality. She'd come home to the place she never should have left.

After what seemed like only a few minutes, her eyelids snapped opened. She checked her wristwatch. Five o'clock. She'd been dozing nearly an hour. Concern for Jenny drove her from Spence's arms.

She left the bed and walked toward Jenny. Sound asleep again? But she looked comfortable. Surely, nothing was wrong.

Stepping into the outer room, stretching, Thea surveyed the others. Lawrence was a lump in the corner under the covers. Travis had made his bed on the window seat. The reverend sat upright in his chair with his eyes closed and his mouth open, loudly snoring. And Mona was...

Dear God... *Where was Mona?*

Chapter Nine

She flew to the bathroom off the nursery bedroom, but it was dark inside, and empty. Mona wasn't there, and hadn't moved to a different or more comfortable place to rest inside the bedroom.

More acutely alert than she had been in hours, Thea stood rooted in a growing panic in the darkened bedroom. The sound of Spence's steady breathing competed with the keening wind and the lashing of frozen, brittle snowflakes against the window panes. A set of shadows at the far end of the bedroom deeper than she had noticed before niggled at her attention, but Thea couldn't seem to focus.

Mona... *Dear God.* Had Rosemont gotten into their impregnable suite anyway, and snatched their most easily manhandled member?

Trying to control the tide of panic rising up in her, she gave herself a string of mental commands. Stop dithering. Go check again. Check the sitting room. Check behind the sofa. Leaving behind the quiet sough of Spence's breathing, she moved out of the bedroom and into the sitting room to comply with herself. As soon as she went through the door, she spotted the armoire barricading the outer door lurking at an odd angle to the doorway.

A wedge of space that shouldn't be there. Her heart leapt into her throat.

Space enough for a person to slip out. Or in.

From behind her back, Thea heard the thud of heavy-soled boots hitting the hardwood floor. She turned and saw Travis, sitting up on the window seat. His shoulders hunched. His head drooped down. A shimmer of firelight distorted his features. His eye sockets were dark, vacant holes beneath the spikes of bleached blond hair.

"Whassup?" he growled.

"Mona's not here," Thea said. "Did you help her move the armoire?"

"No." As unconcerned as if he really could not grasp the meaning of Thea's question, Travis turned and peered out the window into the darkness. "It's still coming down. Must be three feet of new snow."

From the corner nearest the fire, she heard a click. Lawrence had wakened with his gun at the ready, braced in both hands and aimed toward her and Travis. He squinted angrily at them and pointed the weapon toward the ceiling. "Sorry."

Reverend Joshua unfolded from his wingback chair and stretched his arms over his head. His skeletal fingers reached for the ceiling. My God, he was tall.

Thea's instincts told her to get away from these three firelit gargoyles. There was something dark and threatening in their manner and appearance. But the meaning of that heavy armoire, angled so incongruently to the door, akimbo as a severely broken bone, arrested her attention again. She edged backward through the door to the adjoining bedroom.

Spence had also risen. She started to say, *Spence, the door...the armoire...Mona...*but he stood beside the hospital bed, taking Jenny's pulse, pulling her eyelids up gently with his thumb to check her pupils in the dark with a penlight. When he glanced up, she saw tension etched deep in the lines of his face. He beckoned her closer. "She's deeper in unconsciousness now than when we found her. Someone got to her, Thea. Someone had to have injected another dose of sedative into the IV line."

"Oh, no!" Thea felt the blood rush out of her head. She was supposed to have been watching over Jenny. Mona... Not wanting to believe it, she looked at him, begged with her eyes for him to clear everything up, to tell her nothing was wrong at all, that she'd only been hallucinating these past five dreaded minutes.

Instead he looked at her and knew she'd dozed.

"Spence, are you saying someone came in here while I was..."

He nodded grimly. "Thea, I'm not blaming you—"

"No, I am." Icy fingers slithered up and down her backbone. Rosemont had been here. In this very room. He'd been only a few feet away from them. He'd drugged Jenny, again. And Mona...

"Dammit, Thea!" Spence swore. "Nobody could have gotten in here. Rosemont isn't a ghost. He can't dematerialize and glide through locked doors." He glanced toward the sitting-room door. "The only possibility is that Rosemont is one of them."

"Oh, my God." Similar suspicions had been creeping at the edge of her thinking. She had no frame of reference for Travis, Lawrence or the reverend. She'd never met them. She had no reason to trust or mistrust them, either, but one of them had to have helped Mona move that armoire. "Spence—Mona is missing."

"*What?*"

"She's gone. Vanished. She's not in the other room.

One of them either helped her move the armoire or moved it themselves and took her away or—''

But Spence, staring off intently into space, waved her silent, and moved to switch on a lamp. Across the room, she saw what he was looking at, what accounted for the deeper shadows her mind hadn't been able to account for—a dark square maw of a hole in the wall where the chalkboard had been removed to reveal a service dumbwaiter.

Spence exhaled sharply. ''There's just enough room for an adult to curl up and climb inside. Rosemont must have used it.''

''But how would he have activated the pulleys, Spence? How was it possible that I didn't hear the chalkboard being removed from the wall?''

''I didn't hear it either, Thea, and being on call all the time, I'm a light sleeper.'' He was trying to assuage her guilt, she knew. ''And with all the fancy electronic cueing around this place, Rosemont could easily have this pulley system on a remote control.''

Grimly, Spence checked out the pulley that functioned to raise and lower the dumbwaiter from floor to floor and back again. To Thea's mounting dismay, it moved as smooth as glass, as silent as a whisper.

They traded looks as the meaning of the dumbwaiter sank in. If any of the men in the sitting room had, in fact, been Rosemont, he wouldn't have had to resort to the dumbwaiter to gain access to the nursery suite.

''We've got to find Mona. Quick.'' Spence checked Jenny again, determined that she was not in any acute distress, and strode toward the door. He didn't like the way things were going at all. ''Come on, Thea.''

''Do you think he's murdered her?''

''I don't know.'' He wasn't ready to borrow trouble or

speculate—Rosemont was content to keep drugging Jenny, but he had promised to kill whoever failed to own up to responsibility for failing whoever it was they'd all wronged. Spence didn't think Rosemont might suddenly be gripped with mercy, but he didn't want to upset Thea or the rest of the wedding party until he knew for sure what had happened to Mona.

In the sitting room, the other three men were all at the windows, peering out at the continuing snowfall and commenting glumly.

Spence wanted to shake them all out of their stuporous denial. "Any of you notice Mona is missing? Or that the armoire is shoved out?"

Lawrence blanched. "I presumed she'd gone down to the kitchen to make coffee! I never even thought...she isn't big enough to have moved—"

"Do any of you know what happened here?" Spence asked, his patience all but evaporated. "Did she speak to any of you during the night? Did you hear someone enter, or hear her cry out, or *see* anyone?"

Blank expressions stared back at him. He really couldn't imagine that one of these morons could be the ingenious Gregory Rosemont. Not unless he was pulling off one hell of an acting job.

"Hey, doc," Travis said. "You got anything for a headache? I'm dying here."

"Me, too," Lawrence said, kneading the space where his nose met his forehead.

"I, too, have a migraine," the reverend reported. His long nose twitched. "And there's a most unpleasant stink in this room."

Lawrence agreed. "Possibly a slight gas leak from the fireplace?"

"No." The reverend lifted his lapel to his nose, inhaled

and made a sour face. "The odor is on my clothing. It's...I'm not...I can't place it. A swimming pool, maybe?"

Spence came closer to him and took a whiff. *Chloroform.* Rosemont had managed to move around without waking them, snatching Mona and ducking out the door behind the armoire. The chemical sedation was an elegant solution, knocking each man into a deeper sleep.

But he and Thea hadn't been drugged. Guiltily, Spence wondered if they had looked too cozy, wrapped in each other's arms as if they didn't have a care in the world. How darkly amused Rosemont must have been.

"You've all had a whiff of chloroform," he said. He quickly described Rosemont's dumbwaiter ploy, but kept silent about Jenny having been drugged again so Travis wouldn't derail. All three were dumbstruck by Rosemont's ease of getting by their fortifications. "Check in the bathroom for aspirin and come back here. Make it quick."

"What's the big hoohah rush?" Travis complained.

Spence gritted his teeth. "We need to find Mona."

"Oh, dear," Lawrence said. His face crumpled in genuine dismay. "Do you think something bad might have happened to her?"

"Is she in danger?" the reverend asked.

"We're all in danger." Spence swallowed hard to keep from snarling at them. He might have lit into them for being such simpleminded dolts that the danger wasn't obvious to them—except that Rosemont had gotten past him and Thea as well. "In future, I don't want to have to remind you that we're in serious danger. Now, move it!"

As soon as the three stooges stumbled into the bathroom in search of aspirin, Thea said, "Spence, I was really starting to believe that Rosemont was one of them... Lawrence knows his way around the castle and he's never given up discounting himself as one of us. He's always playing with that Game Boy or whatever it is. It could be exactly the sort of remote control Rosemont needed to get up here on the dumbwaiter—''

"Except that he was already here."

Thea nodded. "He's too old to be Rosemont anyway. Most Internet entrepreneurs are twenty-somethings, aren't they?" Deeply concerned about Mona, Spence dismissed the subject. "It's a moot point, Thea. But it would sure as the devil have helped us if Jenny hadn't been drugged again. If she could have told us something—''

"Which is exactly why Rosemont needs her unconscious," Thea guessed.

That caused Spence some medical worry. "It's not good for her to be so severely drugged for three days. We can't let this happen again." He paused a moment, massaging his reddened eyeballs. "Didn't Jenny ever describe Rosemont to you?"

"Mostly she talked about the gifts he gave her. She told me every detail about color, clarity and carats of her diamond engagement ring. But no. She'd go all dreamy about how attracted she was to him, but I don't think she ever even said what color his eyes are."

The reverend returned, followed up by Travis and Lawrence. Spence issued orders. Under no circumstances was anyone to wander off by themselves. They were on the buddy system, and it was more important now than ever. He made sure Thea had Lawrence's second pistol.

Because Lawrence was most familiar with the castle, he would accompany Thea and Spence in their search for Mona. Spence directed the reverend and Travis to stay here and watch over Jenny.

"Hey, man." Travis confronted him. "I thought my sister was supposed to be awake by now."

Spence debated with himself again on the wisdom of telling them that Jenny had been injected again and decided against it. "I expected her to come around," Spence said. "She will."

Travis wasn't done complaining. "Yeah, well I don't want to be paired with the rev again. When do I get some coffee?"

"After we find Mona," Spence said. "You might want to work on disabling the dumbwaiter in the nursery bedroom."

"Cool. I'm good at disabling things." Travis replied.

Spence led Thea and Lawrence into the hall where the lights immediately turned on. Spence wasn't optimistic about their search. The second-floor tower bedrooms were silent and vacant. The pre-dawn stillness of the castle magnified the sound of their breathing, the echo of their footsteps. Though the computer-controlled heating system held the temperature at a comfortable level, a draft tickled the nape of his neck, as if they were being observed.

Instead of taking the narrow servants' stair to the kitchen, they returned to the main staircase at the center of the castle. As they descended into the Grand Drawing Room, the lights flashed on. The fireplace flared. Spence noticed a whir, the sound of static.

"Good morning," came the raspy voice of Gregory Rosemont.

Thea jumped closer to Spence and grabbed his arm. "Where is he?"

"It's another tape," Spence said.

Rosemont continued, "I'm disappointed. I told you to remember your cruelty. To atone. And you failed."

Though his voice was disguised, Rosemont's anger resonated through each word.

"I had to show you I'm serious," he said. "This time, Mona pays the price."

Spence watched Lawrence for a reaction. The butler had drawn his pistol, ready for confrontation. His gaze darted around the room. But he didn't seem surprised.

"Doctor Spence Cannon," Rosemont said, "your story about mistreating one of your patients five years ago was exactly what I would expect from you. At least, you admitted your gross incompetence. Dr. Mona Nance was not so honest. She claimed she did her best. Poor fool! She should have done better, should have been more careful in tending her garden."

A static hiss. Then silence.

Spence's blood boiled. Who the hell was this guy? What gave him the right to judge, to spy, to threaten? Rosemont was toying with them, like a cat with a mouse between its paws. And there was no way to escape.

With effort, he reined in his anger. He had to be smart. He had to find a way to out-think Rosemont. "He's feeding us clues." To check his own recall, he urged Thea to try to remember. "Tell me as you recall it, every word Rosemont just said."

"He said he was disappointed." She squeezed her eyes shut as if she could see Rosemont's words on the back of her eyelids. "Mistreating a patient...five years ago...incompetence...Mona was dishonest...she should have tended her garden."

"Tended her garden?" Lawrence shook his head. "It's crazy. What could that mean?"

Thea's eyes opened. "Where would we find a garden?"

"An untended garden," Spence said. "In the solarium."

With Lawrence leading through the labyrinth of hallways, they hurried toward the glass room at the rear of the castle.

At the doorway, Spence hesitated. If Mona had been brutalized or murdered, he wanted to spare Thea from that nightmare. "Wait out here," he said.

"No. You're the one who said none of us should be alone. Not even for a minute. We have to stick to that, Spence, or something terrible is going to happen."

She was right. "Stay behind me, then."

Spence pushed open the door. A sudden flash of light turned the glass walls opaque against the dark skies outside. Was it brighter in here? Had Rosemont set this scene for optimum effect? The branches of dead trees cast eerie shadows. The damp cold washed over them, reminding Spence of the hospital morgue. Heavy urns of brown leaves stood amid earthenware pots holding bare stems and countertops packed with lethal insecticides.

As Spence stepped onto the floor, he realized it was marble, rough-hewn and unpolished. He glimpsed color at the end of one aisle. Crimson. Spence went toward the only sign of life.

Dr. Mona Nance lay face-up on the marble floor, wearing her parka and colorful scarf. Her tiny fingers closed around a bouquet of dead roses.

"She can't be dead," Lawrence said.

"She's not," Spence said.

Mona's cheeks were scarlet, her eyes pinched shut in pain. Her teeth clenched. Her breathing was labored.

Spence knelt beside her. "Mona, it's going to be all right. We're going to take care of you."

As he removed the dead roses, her hands balled in tight fists. "Can you talk to me, Mona? Can you tell me where it hurts?"

Convulsively, she shook her head.

She was on the verge of seizure. Possibly a reaction to pain. But when Spence quickly examined her, he found no wounds. He assumed she'd been given a drug or a poison. That seemed to be Rosemont's preference.

Spence rose. "Let's get her out of the cold. We'll go back upstairs."

"I'll carry her," Lawrence volunteered. He bent down and slipped his arms beneath her shoulders and knees. "Do you know what's wrong with her, Spence? Do you have any idea?"

"None," Spence said grimly. And any diagnosis of poisons or drugs was impossible without lab analysis. He'd done a hell of a lot of work in emergency medicine, but he was terribly afraid he wasn't going to be able to prevent Rosemont taking this round.

He feared Mona Nance would die.

IN THE KITCHEN, accompanied by the reverend, Thea had warmed two large packages of cinnamon buns, while her eyes went again and again to the rack of hanging pots and pans. Dr. Mona's glockenspiel. She hurried up the servants' stairwell to the second-floor landing with two platters of buns, the reverend on her heels with the coffee-maker and a bag of ground coffee beans.

Joshua Handy rapped on the door to the nursery suite and Lawrence let them in. Handy set about making the coffee before Travis had a fit from caffeine deprivation.

Tucked into one of the nursery beds across from Jenny, Mona alternated between rest and seizure. She'd stopped breathing once, and Spence had had to perform CPR and mouth-to-mouth. She still hadn't regained consciousness.

Damn it, this wasn't fair! Rosemont had attacked the smallest and weakest. He shouldn't get away with this. Thea put the platters of warmed buns down on the coffee table in the sitting room. Travis descended on them and looked at her, ready to defend his boorish behavior, but she was struck for some reason with something Lawrence had said when they'd found Mona in the solarium. *She can't be dead.*

At the time, Thea had wondered at his phrasing. Did he mean "she can't be dead" as in a protest against the fates? Like "it can't still be snowing"? Or did he mean something else? It still seemed possible to her that Lawrence might be in league with Rosemont.

An untasted cinnamon bun in her fingers, she asked, "Why didn't Rosemont kill her?"

Both men turned toward her. They froze and gaped, slack-jawed.

The reverend spoke first, "Why would you expect murder?"

"Because Rosemont said repent or die," she snapped. How could these men be so incredibly obtuse? "Clearly, that implies murder. So, why didn't he kill Mona?"

"I won't guess," the reverend said. "How could I possibly comprehend the workings of such a sick, twisted mind?"

Lawrence sat spreading a napkin across his lap. He seemed to be avoiding eye contact with her.

Thea asked, "Do you have any ideas, Lawrence? Is there some reason you wouldn't expect Rosemont to kill anyone?"

"Not really." He glanced up and gave her a quick, uncomfortable smile.

"Well, when you first saw Mona, you said, 'She can't be dead.' What did you mean?"

"Perhaps you should eat your roll while it is still warm, Thea, and stop making mountains out of molehills."

"Of course," the reverend said, "they would have been

a good deal more palatable had you warmed them on a cookie sheet in the oven as I suggested.''

"Did you use the microwave?" Lawrence asked in disdain.

The reverend looked down his nose at her. "You're not much of a cook, are you, Thea?"

She couldn't believe they were jabbering about preferred methods for heating up breakfast. "We can't ignore what's happening," she said. "We can't just wait around passively waiting to see who Rosemont attacks next."

The reverend drew himself up tall. "I've put my fate in the hands of the Lord."

"What if the Lord wants you to take a more active role?"

"He will show me the way," Reverend Joshua assured her righteously. "In the meantime, I'll have my meager breakfast."

Faith could be a wonderful thing, but she was tired to death of the reverend wrapping himself in religion to avoid facing the truth. Or admitting the truth. No one had been more obviously distressed over Mona's guess that the person Rosemont was compelled to avenge had died. What was the Reverend Joshua Handy hiding?

She had to find out, but she had her suspicions of Lawrence's behavior too. Especially after his odd remark upon finding Mona. She looked at him. "You said you'd done some bodyguard work. Have you had any police training?"

"A bit."

"How would a cop analyze this situation?"

"I really couldn't say."

"Work with me," Thea said. "I'm trying to figure out what's going on. Why didn't Rosemont kill Mona?"

"He's not a fool," Lawrence said. "Some people would

say Rosemont is a genius. And a genius isn't going to prison for murder.''

Thea hadn't considered that twist, but in the next instant of reflection, she knew it had no merit or credence whatever. Rosemont would absolutely expect to get away without ever coming close to being caught—and it wouldn't matter how many dead bodies littered the castle. Did she have to repeat again Rosemont's message—repent or die? "What about his vengeance?"

"Perhaps he'll be satisfied by terrorizing each of you, watching you beg for mercy."

"Each of us? But not you."

"I'm not part of this. I keep telling you." His voice maintained a steady level, but when he finally looked directly at her, Thea saw tension in his gaze, bordering on anger. His frozen smile did nothing to dispel her impression. "Leave me out of your theories and discussions. I'm merely the butler."

Her aggravation at its keenest level, realizing that the conversation was pointless, Thea gave up and put her own roll down. The coffee was brewed, now, and Spence must need the infusion himself. She filled a mug for Spence and carried it into the adjoining nursery. He sat on the double bed beside Mona, holding her hand and watching her chest rise and fall with each ragged breath.

When Thea placed the mug on the bedside table and touched his shoulder, he flinched. "Sorry, I'm a little tense."

She glided her hand across his back and felt muscles bunched in hard knots. Lightly, she massaged between his shoulder blades. "How's Mona doing?"

"I wish I could tell you good news, but I don't know." He arched his back and exhaled a huge sigh. "Keep rubbing. It feels good."

"I brought you coffee. Black."

"Thanks."

He turned, accepting the coffee mug. His blue eyes were red-rimmed with exhaustion. Stubble covered his cheeks. The fine lines across his forehead and the corners of his lips carved deep in his chiseled face. No longer the handsome blond Adonis, Spence was ravaged by worry and fear for his patients.

Thea thought he looked magnificent. Her heart surged as she recognized the caring, dedicated man she'd once loved. Devoted to watching over Jenny and Mona, he embodied the finest attributes of a healer.

Spence lifted the coffee mug to his lips and took a gulp. "Caffeine. Good."

"Can I do anything to help?"

"Be a sounding board. I'm coming to a very weird conclusion, and I need somebody to tell me I'm not nuts."

He lifted the light sheet and turned Mona's forearm to show Thea a dark black and blue mark knotted at the vein. Harsh red streaks shot up to her armpit. Obviously, she'd been injected.

"Was she given a drug?" Thea asked.

"In a manner of speaking." He covered Mona again. "I've seen symptoms like this before. High fever, convulsions caused by a hemotoxic poison that works through the bloodstream, causing organs to shut down as if paralyzed. The victim generally dies of suffocation when the lungs stop working."

Thea's mouth felt suddenly dry. Had Rosemont killed Mona after all, only delayed the fatal moment? "You've seen this before?"

"Snake bite."

"Okay, Spence. That does sound a little nuts. Are you saying Rosemont *injected* a snake venom?"

"Yeah. That's what I'm saying. It could be a hundred different things. But here's the thing. The red streaks extending up into her armpit?"

"Yeah?"

"You sometimes see that when an IV infiltrates."

"What does that mean, infiltrates?"

"That the needle or catheter has worked its way out of the vein. I'm guessing Mona jerked when Rosemont started to inject her vein. He missed. He tried to induce a circulatory collapse, but the majority of the poison or venom or whatever the hell it is went out into her tissues instead."

Hope scuttled through her heart. "Is that good? I mean—?"

Spence nodded tiredly, but he couldn't conceal his own shred of optimism. "I think she has a chance anyway."

He stood, and they embraced, both too tired and fearful of the unexpected consequences to celebrate much more. Thea pulled back and cradled his grizzled cheek in her hand. He turned his face and kissed her palm. "You're a good doctor, Spence Cannon."

He shrugged. "It's not as if I've been able to pull off a brilliant save."

"Humble too?" She frowned fiercely. "All right. The jig's up. Who are you, mister, and what have you done with my boyfriend?"

"Boyfriend?" His gaze flew to hers. His Adam's apple bobbed, and he put his hand to his chest. "Be still, my heart."

"Not too still."

He kissed her, a brief but wet and ravenous kiss, then sank back onto the side of the bed where Mona rested, uneasy and fevered.

Thea buzzed around the room, tidying up Mona's

clothes, which lay where they'd been discarded after they'd stripped her down to her bra and panties. Thea folded Mona's turtleneck sweater and then began to fold the slacks, but a small wad in the pocket snagged her attention. As soon as she pulled it out, she recognized the paper on which Mona and Reverend Joshua had compiled their lists the night before.

Carefully, she read the reverend's spidery penmanship, then Mona's, searching for a name that might stand out. Not even one name was familiar. She sat cross-legged on the other double bed in the room and studied the list again. Nothing.

She folded the scrap and went to Spence, and again, she touched his shoulder. This time, he leaned back and nestled against her. Thea draped her arms loosely around his neck. The gesture felt completely natural. If anyone had told her yesterday that she'd be comfortable in Spence's company, she would've laughed out loud.

"You know, Thea, in all the times I've thought about getting back together with you, it was never like this."

"How was it?"

"I'd sweep you off your feet," he said. "All the romantic stuff. Great clothes. A nice dinner. Excellent wine. Maybe we'd go for one of those carriage rides."

"Exactly the wrong approach." Instead, he'd done exactly the right thing. He'd been himself. At this moment, she couldn't imagine a better man.

"I always felt bad while we were engaged. Not only did we never have enough time, but I didn't have enough money to treat you special." He gave a little chuckle. "Hell, I still don't have much. Private practice in Cascadia isn't the road to riches."

She leaned down and kissed the top of his head. "Do

you think money is important to me? I'm a schoolteacher, not a stockbroker.''

"I thought every woman was impressed by expensive things.''

"Not me," she said. She dug her thumb into the knots in his shoulders. "In my mind, there's nothing sexier than a man doing his job—whatever that job may be. And doing it well.''

"Work is sexy?''

"Very sexy," she said, more brave than she should be.

"Mmm.'' He melted into her hands, easing the tension in his shoulders. "Remind me to remind you what sexy is, when we get off this damned mountain.''

She showed him the list. "These are the names Mona and the reverend came up with last night.''

"There are less than fifteen names on either list.''

"Do you recognize any of them?''

He studied it for a moment and shook his head. "I don't know any of these people. Do you think either one of them left a few names out?''

"I think we can count on it," Thea said. "I don't know what to make of our Reverend Handy. Every time I turn around, I have the sense reinforced that he's got some dark secrets in his past.''

"Didn't he tell us that he'd come late to the ministry? Maybe he had a very compelling reason to turn to God. Maybe he was seeking forgiveness.''

"For committing a terrible wrong," Thea said.

But who had the reverend wronged?

Chapter Ten

"You should take a break," Thea said. "Eat something. Get some sleep."

Spence rose from Mona's bedside, stretched and yawned. "I'm not sleepy. Just tired. If I stretch out for a few minutes, I'll be fine."

"I've heard you say that before." She went to the other double bed in the room, pulled back the comforter and plumped the pillows. "When you were a resident, you were always getting called in for extra shifts. You never got enough sleep."

"Running on pure adrenaline."

"The workaholic's high. You're sleeping, mister."

He couldn't deny that he enjoyed the physical challenge, rising to the occasion, the sheer hormonal rush that came with pitting himself against death. "I always thought my brain was sharper at those times. That's how I feel now."

"Maybe that's how you feel." She came up in front of him, poked her fingertips against his chest and guided him backwards until his legs bumped against the bed and he sat. "But cowboy, you look like something that's been rode hard and put away wet."

"Sexy as all get-out, huh?"

"Oh, yeah." The looks zinging between them felt incendiary.

"Kind of an outdoorsy comment, coming from a city-slicker kinda gal."

"I used to ride all the time when I was growing up. I was good, too. Damned good."

He cleared his throat. "Nothing about that changed when you were all grown up, either."

She blushed wildly. "Stop." She snagged his mug from the bedside table and headed for the door. "I'm going to bring you a cinnamon roll and more coffee."

Spence slipped off his shoes and leaned back against the pillows, satisfied with himself for putting her so off-balance that she had to escape to bring him coffee when a minute before she'd been intent on his getting some shut-eye.

Though he'd thought their past relationship was good, he hadn't always been able to remember exactly why. He'd liked being with Thea. Who wouldn't? She was terrific—smart, quick and beautiful. But it seemed like they hardly knew each other. They'd both been busy with their careers and hadn't spent enough time finding out about each other. Except when they were together between the sheets. Oh yeah, those were hours well spent. And conversation hadn't been the first thing on their minds.

A slow warm glow spread through his body when he thought about making love to Thea again. There was nobody like her. Beneath her preppy, proper veneer beat the heart of a wild woman. She had been and still was a challenge. Would he find her as incredibly responsive, as demanding, in the best sense of the word, as he remembered?

Would their passion be different this time? He thought it already was different, deeper for what they'd been through together in the last day.

He wanted to make love to her. Wanted it like he hadn't wanted anything in a very long time. Over the years, he'd learned that patience was an art. He was willing to wait for the perfect moment.

Relaxing, his gaze floated around the nursery bedroom, resting lightly on the brightly colored accessories and the alphabet border around the ceiling. Aside from the field-hospital look of this room at present, and the chalkboard facade to the dumbwaiter that Travis had derailed and jammed shut, this room was an orderly one, without scuffs or crayon marks on the walls, no clutter on the floor, no sense that real children had ever lived here. Children?

That was a whole other issue. Spence wanted kids. Back when he and Thea were engaged, they'd talked about children. He liked the number four—two boys and two girls. But Thea had come from a big family and thought two were plenty. Maybe she'd changed her mind.

Thea returned, carrying two coffee mugs. With her was Lawrence who held a paper plate with cinnamon rolls. He glanced toward Mona. "Thea tells me our little Mona is improving."

"I hope so." Spence hitched up on one elbow and took a cinnamon roll. The scent had his stomach growling.

Lawrence set the plate on the bedside table and went to stand beside Mona's bed. His arms hung stiffly at his sides and his fingers twitched as if he'd like to touch Mona but didn't feel right about it while she lay unconscious. "I didn't believe he would do it. Try to kill one of you. I didn't believe Rosemont really had murder on his mind."

"Why not?"

"The threat alone seemed enough. If it's your repentance he wants, I would have thought—" He stuffed his hands back into his pockets. "Well. I obviously thought wrong."

"Do you think we're going to get out of here alive, Lawrence?" Spence lifted the coffee mug to his lips, wanting the caffeine even more than food. He held the so-called butler's gaze, waiting for him to flinch, to betray an untruth, but the man's facade showed perfect poise. Spence took a bite of the cinnamon roll which had probably been tastier before it grew cold.

"If we're very careful from now on. More careful than we have been." He gave a deferential nod. "I would, however, suggest that we pursue some sort of project during the day. The reverend and Travis are showing signs of serious cabin fever. Frankly, Mona was right about that. They might kill each other before Mr. Rosemont has a chance to wreak further revenge."

The last thing they needed was to start attacking each other. Spence needed to step up and provide a little leadership, to set forth some kinds of goals. "I'll be out in a minute."

When Lawrence left the room, Thea kicked off her shoes and stretched out on the bed beside him. In a quiet voice, she said, "You think he's hiding something."

"I do." Spence set the cinnamon roll aside. There ought to be some decent food in this castle.

"So many secrets," she said. "I guess we all have them."

"Not me. I'm an open book."

"But you must know something about Rosemont's mystery person. And so should I. Between us, we should be able to figure out the name." Turning on her side, she gazed at him. "Think about it. Five years ago."

He didn't want to go back there and pick through the ashes of their prior relationship. Not when they were doing so well in the present. "Personally, revisiting that time isn't very appealing."

Thea had already replayed her memories of the breakup a hundred times, but there was something she'd overlooked. Something important. She could feel the answer coming clearer. "What else was happening then? I was working with my project. Everybody got along okay. Maybe a couple of professional jealousies, but nothing serious."

"Not like Travis with his list of infamous demented competitors out to crack his kneecaps?"

"No way." She concentrated on the period in her life that had been so dominated by Spence. "I was trying to decide if I should fix up my apartment so you could move in with me. But I never really liked that place, and there wouldn't have been room for your piano. It was nowhere near as nice and roomy as that high-ceiling Victorian duplex I shared with Diane."

Fondly, she remembered the two-story, divided house near Cheesman Park. "Do you remember I pointed it out to you? It was a renovated mansion. Totally gorgeous, spacious with two bathrooms. I really loved the place, all the natural wood and antique fixtures."

"Did you tell me...? I don't remember if you did. Why'd you move?"

"Diane was driving me crazy. It seems cruel to say that, after her suicide, but—"

"Holy cripes, Thea. That's it!" he said. "That's got to be it. Rosemont's six degrees of separation."

He flipped to his side and faced her. She could see the excitement in his eyes. "Explain."

"I never told you this before... You were pretty torn up about your former roommate's death, and I didn't want to add to your stress."

"You could have fooled me," she said. "I seem to remember, after the funeral that you told me I should stop feeling bad about Diane and get over it. You said in your experience, you had to deal with life and death every day, and the sooner you put it behind you, the better it was."

He frowned. "I was a jerk."

"I never talked to you about Diane again."

"You were stubborn."

She nodded, accepting the fact that they were both at fault. "It's in the past. What were you saying about the six degrees of separation?"

"I was on duty in the ER when the ambulance brought her in. I was the one who worked on Diane. There was no way I could save her."

"Spence!" Thea sat up. "I can't believe you wouldn't tell me about that."

"I'm not proud of it, Thea, but it wasn't pretty and I didn't want to be the one giving you all the grisly details. I pronounced her DOA and signed her death certificate."

The significance of his words sank in. They were both intimately involved in Diane's death. On the night she killed herself with a gunshot to the head, Diane had tried several times to telephone Thea. She hadn't been home.

Thea had failed her as a friend. At the hospital, Spence was the doctor who couldn't revive her.

"Diane Moretson," Thea said. "Why didn't I think of her before? I felt so guilty when I heard about her death. I should have seen it coming when she broke up with her boyfriend. I should have been there for her. Damn it, Rosemont is right. I felt like I'd wronged her."

"Nobody's to blame," he said, warning her against self-recriminations. "Diane killed herself. Didn't she leave a note?"

Thea nodded. "She wrote that she didn't want to go on without her boyfriend. What was his name?"

"Not Travis or Joshua or Lawrence," he said.

"No. I would've remembered. It was John Hoffman, but there was another boyfriend before that. Diane was a spoiled princess who always ultimately decided that whoever was dating her wasn't good enough. She had lots of short-term intense relationships. One of them might have been Travis. Or the reverend, I suppose."

Spence pushed himself out of the bed. "Let me check Mona and Jenny again. Then we'll tell the others."

"Suppose Travis was a new boyfriend. Reverend Joshua could have been her minister—new at his job and not very good at it."

"But her name wasn't on his list," Spence said, checking Jenny's vital signs.

"Maybe it should have been." Thea wasn't about to let a little thing like facts withheld get in the way. "And Mona might have been Diane's psychotherapist. It's weird, isn't it? We didn't know each other, but we're all connected."

Spence checked Mona then, stroking fever-dampened hair off her brow with the back of his hand. "It makes you wonder who looked all this information up."

And what was Gregory Rosemont's connection? He cared so much about Diane that he'd arranged this complicated scheme of vengeance. He must have been obsessed with her. But how had Jenny's fiancé come to know Diane Moretson?

They'd have to find out. Thea was certain they were onto something. She almost ran into the sitting room when Spence indicated their patients were at least stable.

"I know we're supposed to stay cooped up in these quarters, but I wish to visit the chapel," the reverend announced as soon as he saw them. "I saw it yesterday when we were searching the middle of the castle. I'd like to spend a few moments there."

"Don't look at me. I'm not going with him," Travis warned. He sprawled across the sofa, sullen as a teenager in his baggy jeans. "Don't even ask me to do the buddy-system thing."

Thea ignored them both, anxious to test their theory. "We have a name. Spence and I remembered someone from our past who might be the person Rosemont is talking about. I feel bad about the way I treated her, and Spence signed her death certificate."

The three men stared at her. For once, they stopped whining and looked alert. "I hope you remember her," Thea said. "She committed suicide a little over five years ago. Her name was Diane Moretson."

"Suicide?" Reverend Joshua Handy shuddered from head to toe. "God rest her soul."

"Come on, Reverend. Think about it. You must have known her," Thea said, describing Diane to him—for them all. "I'll bet you were her minister."

Handy stared stonily at her. "You're mistaken."

She looked to Travis, who was shaking his head. "Sorry, dudette. The name's familiar, but I can't hook up."

"Of course, you'd recognize the name," Thea said. "The Moretson family owns a chain of sporting goods stores. As a professional skier, you must have run with some of the same crowd as Diane."

"Hey, I never knew the chick."

Frustrated, Thea turned to Lawrence. "What about you?"

"You're onto something." His expression was inscrutable. Was he nodding in agreement? "But I can't say that I knew Diane Moretson."

"I was so sure this was right."

Thea sank onto the sofa opposite Travis. She exhaled a

sigh as the air blew out of her sails. Another false trail? Or a path the three men were each, for their own reasons, determined to avoid?

She might have persisted, except that Spence took over. "Listen up. We've got a few things to figure out today."

"Yippy-skippy," Travis said. "Like what?"

"Last night, Rosemont came into this room, drugged you guys and grabbed Mona. He came in through the dumbwaiter, but he is moving around the castle without being seen, and he has to be holing up somewhere some of the time."

"Well, *duh*," Travis said. "He owns this joint. He's got the run of the place and he knows it better than anyone. He could elude us from now till doomsday."

"Which may come sooner than you'd like to contemplate," Lawrence snapped. Travis was wearing thin on them all.

Spence came to his point, which was at least in part to keep them all too occupied to fall into squabbles that would lead to more serious clashes. "I think we should search for secret passageways."

Frustration gnawed at her, but Thea's eyebrows raised. "I didn't think secret passageways existed outside horror movies."

"On the contrary," Lawrence said. "You are all familiar with the servants' staircase leading from the kitchen to the upper floors of the tower. The idea was that servants should not be seen. It's quite possible, in fact *likely,* that hidden corridors connect several other rooms."

"Sounds lame to me," Travis said, "but I'll give it a shot. What else?"

"While we're at it, since we know for certain that Rosemont is monitoring our conversations, we need to search for bugs and mini-cams." Spence bowed to Lawrence's superior knowledge of the castle, suggesting he take charge of their search.

"Very well," the butler said.

"Are you going to be watching over Jenny?" Travis demanded, "while we're out banging around?"

"Yes. I don't plan to leave the nursery bedroom," Spence said. "I'll keep a sharp eye on both Mona and Jenny." He got up and walked toward the bedroom. "Thea, would you step in here with me for a moment?"

She dragged herself off the sofa and shuffled into the nursery. Disappointment over her theory about Diane Moretson had colored her mood a dull gray. It seemed as if they were making absolutely no forward progress. Every step forward was followed by two paces back.

They had rescued Jenny, but Rosemont had got to her again in spite of them. They had barricaded the doors, but Mona had been snatched and nearly murdered. There was supposed to be some person, some nexus at which all their lives had intersected, but his or her identity eluded them.

Plus, Thea was tired. Having slept in her clothes, she felt grungy and wanted a nice, hot steamy shower.

Ironically, the only bright spot seemed to be her improved relationship with Spence. She joined him beside Jenny's hospital bed. "I don't want to look for secret passageways with the three stooges. Can't I stay here with you?"

"I'd like that," he said. "But one of us needs to keep an eye on those guys. We need to find out why they were lying."

"About Diane? Do you think they are?"

"Thea, I'm sure you got it right. Diane has to be the mystery person, and I think they're all lying about not knowing her."

"I don't get it. If we're right, and it is Diane, it's just

supremely stupid for them to refuse to admit it. Denying they even knew her is guaranteed to make Rosemont furious! Isn't it? Am I wrong?''

''No.'' A crease furrowed his brow. ''You're not wrong. Not unless we're both wildly off base.'' He moved toward the bed where Mona lay under a light blanket, breathing more regularly. ''If she were awake, I'll bet Mona would confirm.''

Possibly Mona knew more than anyone else. As Diane's therapist, she'd have heard an earful about Thea, the ungrateful roommate. Diane had been furious when Thea moved out, but no matter how much she loved the charming old Victorian, Thea really couldn't stand living amidst the clutter Diane generated. Thea had always done far more than her fair share of tidying up, and after a while, the trade-off no longer seemed worth it.

Diane had also enjoyed parading her exotic social life. If she and Rosemont had been lovers, Diane might well have mentioned him to her therapist.

Thea reached down and clasped Mona's hand. Her own heart was hammering in frustration. ''Spence, if you believe we're on the right track with Diane, I don't understand why you let them—'' she tilted her head in the direction of the sitting room ''—off the hook like that.''

''Like what?''

''You let the subject drop with Travis and the reverend and Lawrence…in fact, you changed the subject entirely. Spence, they need to get it, once and for all! Rosemont is going to pick them off one by one for being so arrogant and uncaring that they won't even admit having known Diane!''

Spence shrugged. ''Just a difference between us in styles, I guess.''

''What is that supposed to mean?'' She could see how

tired Spence was, and she knew he probably hadn't meant to be disparaging, but old echoes reverberated in her heart, and that was sure what it sounded like.

Spence blinked. "It's the difference, Thea, between getting in the face of the butler about carrying a concealed weapon and using a little finesse." The tone he took with her felt so patronizing she wouldn't use it on her middle-schoolers. "It's the difference between slamming the door on a man and—"

"Stop." A hot flush of anger spread upward from her neck to the roots of her hair. She held up a hand. "Don't even go there, Spence!" She looked at him and suddenly all she could see anymore was the same arrogant ass she *had* slammed the door on. Dismay ricocheted through her. Had she been a fool again, not only allowing an intimacy to crop up between them, but encouraging it?

She took a deep breath to steady her ragged emotions. "I'm confused," she began carefully, not wanting to fly off the handle for unintended offenses. "Last night you put the ball in my court. You said I was the emotional leader here, and that I should be the one trying to get their cooperation—"

"Thea." Spence touched a finger to her lips, then let his hand trail down so that his fingers molded gently to her neck. "I'm sorry. I was way out of line taking that tone with you—and dragging the past into this." She was defending her so-called style, but he ignored her words and instead, read the true source of her upset with an emotional precision that stunned her. "I'm tired, and I was stupid. Forgive me? Please?"

Her eyes glazed. Spence's face wavered before her. He *was* changed. He might still pop out with something arrogant and even mean, but he had never before seen the effect of it on her so clearly or so swiftly, or ever before taken responsibility and made amends on the spot.

She nodded. A lone tear spilled from her eye, and Spence moved in with his lips to brush it away, taking her into an embrace that thrilled her body and soothed her soul at once.

She backed away to grab a tissue and wipe her nose. She had her own amends to make. "I'm sorry too. I'm so frustrated that I want to scream." Spence nodded his agreement and she went on. "What did you have in mind by not getting in their faces about our mystery person being Diane? Do you have any idea why Travis and the reverend—or Lawrence, for that matter—wouldn't tell us the truth or own up to knowing Diane?"

"No. But it's obvious they're not going to cooperate under the conditions we've been operating in. To tell you the God's honest truth, Thea, I think we're at an impasse. And what I had in mind was this: maybe you'll have more luck with them one-on-one. But I'm having a lot of trouble convincing myself you should be alone with any of them at all."

She saw Spence's logic at once. "Rosemont only said we must each repent—not that we had to do it in full view of each other."

Spence nodded. "The thing is to arrive at the name of the person we're all supposed to have victimized, we have to cooperate, but—"

"Spence, that is absolutely inspired! One-on-one, each of them is far more likely to admit to knowing Diane, maybe even to admit that he failed her in some way." However, Spence's "but" hung in the air. "But what?" she asked.

"Nothing." He gritted his teeth a moment, and the muscles along his jaw tightened, then he cupped the nape of her neck and pulled her close, whispering so low even she could barely understand him. "I'm concerned now that Rosemont has no intention of letting any of us off this mountain alive, even if you get them to confess aloud."

Unease swelled within her like a slow-moving tide. She nodded her understanding and spoke as softly into his ear. "You're thinking if we search for secret passageways and Rosemont's surveillance, we can find him? Find a way to…take back control?"

Spence nodded. "The upside and the downside are exactly the same," he murmured. "We'll tick him off, maybe shove him into escalating or moving up his timetable. But that's the only way he's going to make a mistake we can exploit." He nuzzled her cheek with his grizzled one, and despite the seriousness of their circumstances, she felt a thrill of desire shoot through her. His hand trailed down her shoulder to her upper arm. His thumb strayed to the fullness of her breast and briefly, all too briefly, caressed her. His murmur took on a husky edge. "Whatever you do, Thea," he urged her, "don't be too brave."

She didn't feel heroic at all when she took her own ragged emotions back to the outer room and followed Lawrence's instructions to tap on walls and listen for hollow spots. After half an hour of pretending to be woodpeckers, they decided the room was, in fact, free from secret passageways.

"Now, we'll search for listening devices," Lawrence said.

"What do they look like?" Thea asked.

"Sound transmitters come in a variety of shapes and sizes," he said. "Most likely they won't be any larger than a dime."

"Dude," Travis said, "how do you know about this spy stuff?"

"Bodyguard work," he said, dismissive.

As Thea glanced around the room and its furnishings, she tried to narrow the scope of their search. "Am I right to assume you wouldn't put a transmitter near the floor because you'd hear too many footsteps?"

"Excellent thought," Lawrence said.

"Or stick them under a cushion because the sound might be muffled?" Lawrence agreed again, and directed them to think in terms of out-of-sight yet convenient locations.

She felt around the edges of picture frames and spent a lot of time at the windows, looking out at the relentless snow that masked the landscape behind a cold curtain of white. Was the rest of the mountain area held captive by this blizzard? The weekend forecasts in Denver had predicted nothing of this magnitude.

"I give up!" the reverend said, no more than forty minutes into their search. "I'm tired of this. I wish to go to the chapel."

"I'll go with him," Thea volunteered, aware of Spence's concern over her being alone with any of these men. But maybe if she was alone with Reverend Joshua, she might get him to open up.

"We'll all go downstairs," Lawrence said. "I think we should find something for lunch."

"Food's good," Travis said. "Gotta keep powered-up. Sleek. Gotta keep buff."

Gotta keep stupid? Thea could certainly believe he'd dated Diane. They were the same type of self-involved rich kids who expected the world to bend to their whim.

Though the temperature in the castle was regulated, she felt cold as she walked down the corridor beside the reverend. When Lawrence and Travis went left toward the kitchen, she and the reverend turned right. He stopped outside the second door down from the Grand Drawing Room. "I'd rather be alone with my Lord."

She resented his attitude that God was somehow his personal friend, but now wasn't the time for a theological discussion. "You won't even know I'm here. I'll be quiet as a mouse."

He drew himself up, emphasizing again his incredible height. "I'm afraid I must insist."

Thea only looked at him. He stepped inside the chapel and pushed the door, as silent on its hinges, closed behind him. Thea stood staring, trying to decide what to do when, as faithfully as the lights and gas fires sprang to life throughout the castle, the low comforting tones of recorded hymns on an organ began to play.

She made her decision in a split second and pulled open the door just far enough to slip through. She moved, wraith-like, through the narrow opening...and caught a break. The reverend, frustrated too long in his desire to visit the chapel, so intent on his conversation with God, sat in the front pew, his head already bowed, failing to notice that she had come in behind him.

The organ music played softly. Still as a statue, Thea let her gaze stray all around the chapel. At the far end, between Moorish arched windows, was a carved wooden pulpit and heavily draped altar. A driftwood cross hung on the white stucco wall. Four pews faced front. Small marble statues stood on pedestals in alcoves along the wall, but there was nothing ostentatious about the display. Unlike the rest of the castle, the chapel showed a modicum of restraint, a simple beauty, subdued as candlelight.

Though Thea had been consistently annoyed by his attitude, she didn't doubt the reverend's sincerity. In his simple black attire, he seemed entirely at home in the chapel.

She stood quietly beside one of two freestanding, high-backed chairs flanking the entrance, watching him, absorbing the peaceful atmosphere. She stole the moment, not to contemplate God or any sort of organized religion, only resting her brain, accepting the solace of this unexpected moment.

Subtly, the mood shifted. It felt somehow darker in the chapel, as if a cloud had moved in front of the sun. But there was no sunlight. Through the windows, she saw only the dull white of falling snow.

The reverend's shoulders began to quake, but she heard no sobs. He mumbled his prayers, but his voice was too muffled to pick out the words. Was he talking about Diane?

For a moment, Thea considered moving forward so she might hear him more clearly. She dismissed the idea. Eavesdropping on a man at prayer was despicable, and Reverend Joshua deserved his privacy.

From where she stood, she could pick out words here and there. Certain that the reverend could not even be aware that he was giving actual voice to his prayers, she concentrated hard on the splinters of sound. ''…poor sinner…thy will…never meant to…'' She thought she heard Diane's name once, but it might only have been *die*. But what else could that mean, given this place and these circumstances? Diane had died.

How good was Rosemont's surveillance? Would the transmitters he used pick up on the reverend's nearly silent prayers? It occurred to her that the chapel would be an excellent place for Rosemont to place a listening device. Where better to hear confessions? But where? Up front on the altar? She couldn't march up there and search while the reverend was praying. Where else? Not on the floor. Not attached to the bottom of a pew.

She glanced back toward the door. Lots of people hid keys on top of the door frame. Why not a bug?

She climbed gingerly up on the seat of one of the free-standing chairs and ran her fingers along the frame. And then, she found it. A small flat circular object. It was silver, thicker than a dime, but an electronic disk nonetheless.

Her heart hammered so she thought the reverend could not fail to hear it. Quickly, she replaced the disk and climbed down. If she removed the bug, Rosemont would know she'd found the hiding place. It was better to keep this knowledge to herself for now.

The reverend droned more loudly. "Forgive me," he said. "Oh, God, forgive me."

He'd spoken of forgiveness before, had said that only the Lord would judge him. What terrible deed had he committed?

Chapter Eleven

During the day, Thea had run the emotional gamut from terror to relief to elation to rage. By eight o'clock that evening, her predominant feeling was irritation. Despite her tireless pursuit of the truth, she still had no proof or idea why the three men would persist in lying about having known Diane.

Maybe they weren't lying. Maybe she and Spence were grasping at meaningless straws. But her irritation at her constant companions—Travis, Lawrence and the reverend—grew. Each man grated on her nerves in his own special way. Especially Travis. She had finally come to the conclusion that the unhappy familiarity he triggered in her must have to do with some facial expressions he shared with his sister Jenny. Expressions that rubbed Thea the wrong way, especially since Jenny had never acted like her prima donna of a brother.

Travis was with Thea in the kitchen now, supposedly helping to prepare a hot meal that could easily be transported to the nursery suite. She did all the work, though, while Travis offered pointless comments, punctuated by "dude" and weird little hops across the tile floor in what looked to her like a bizarre game of hopscotch.

"Travis," she snapped. "What are you doing?"

"Practicing my ski tricks. I can't do flips in here because I might bonk into something, so I'm visualizing the fly and the tuck. It's a Zen thing."

She tossed him a dishrag. "Zen the pots, dude."

"No prob." Hiking up his baggy jeans, he sauntered over to the stainless-steel sink and contemplated the greasy skillets and pans without actually touching them.

Turning away from him, she wiped down countertops. She wished Spence was here. Though nothing scary had happened with either Mona or Jenny, both of them, still unconscious, required Spence's continuing attention. The care involved in managing two semi-comatose patients was considerable, and Thea couldn't fault him for his diligence. But she needed to talk to him. Since before noon, when they'd figured out the Diane Moretson connection, they hadn't had a moment alone. There'd been no chance to tell him about finding the listening device in the chapel.

She hadn't told the others either. Finding the bug made her extra cautious. She monitored her every word, certain Rosemont was listening.

The door swung open, and Spence strolled into the kitchen. He'd cleaned up. He'd clearly taken the shortest break possible—his hair was still wet from the shower, but he'd shaved. When he smiled, the stunning blue from his eyes erased her gray mood and flushed her world with vivid color from the dazzling white of his turtleneck to the subtle greens and blues of his flannel shirt. Even his Levi's, snug across his muscular thighs, seemed richly hued.

In a blinding flash, Thea's simmering frustration was replaced by a new emotion: desire. She wanted to be with Spence, to talk to him, to hold him. She wanted to be with him in every sense of the word.

Though he greeted both of them, his gaze lingered on

her. "I figured I should take my turn with the chores," he said.

"About time, dude." Travis tossed him the dishrag and backed away from the sink. "It's all yours."

Without complaint, Spence rolled up his sleeves and started to work. "Good news," he said. "It looks like Jenny might come to by morning."

"Is she awake?" Thea asked.

"No. She's been to the bathroom three times now, but it's hardly more than sleepwalking. She doesn't respond to her name, just the biological imperative to void her bladder. She hasn't opened her eyes or said anything coherent. I hope, by morning, she'll be able to tell us something." Spence made quick work of the remaining dishes. "I set up a schedule for tonight, two at a time, to guard Mona and Jenny. I don't want Rosemont to get to them again."

"Cool," Travis said.

"Right now, it's your turn," Spence said. "You and Lawrence are on watch until midnight."

Travis started to make some smart remark, then must have thought better of it. He must have envisioned some fancy ski maneuver as he twisted his shoulders, executed a turn and leapt for the servants' stairwell.

Alone with her, Spence rolled his eyes and shook his head. "Maybe we'd best serve the gene pool if we let him ski down the mountain."

Thea laughed. God, but it felt good to laugh. She had never spent a longer stretch of stress-filled hours than this. But a laugh wasn't all she wanted. "I want to change clothes," she announced. "In my separate bedroom. Without a crowd of buddies."

"That can be arranged," Spence said.

"I need a shower. And some privacy." At the same

time, she wanted him to be with her. "Of course, I can't be totally alone. That would be dangerous. Maybe just you…"

He smiled. "I understand."

Did he? More importantly, did she? Had she really just invited Spence to join her in the shower?

After they'd checked that Travis had made it back to the nursery sickroom—and carried up more food for late-night munchies, Spence double-checked the schedule with them. He was worried about leaving his patients, and he took a few minutes to impress on the three men the importance of observing any changes at all in their conditions.

"Yeah, yeah, yeah," Travis interrupted Spence, making a gabbing motion with his thumb and fingers. "And just where are you gonna be, dude?"

Spence gave the jerk a level look. "With Thea. She's the only one who hasn't had time to herself. She's going to grab a shower in the other bedroom suite and—"

"In other words, you're gonna be screwing—"

Before he could get another word off, Spence planted the butt of his hand in the middle of Travis's chest and shoved. "Make my day, punk. One more word."

Travis drew an angry breath, but then took a clue and clamped his mouth shut. The other two men made themselves scarce, not wanting to make eye contact.

"We'll watch over Mona and Jenny," the reverend mumbled.

Spence turned on his heel and swept Thea down the second-floor hallway to the bedroom she'd intended to share with Mona.

Outside the door she looked solemnly at Spence. "Make my day?" she teased.

Spence scowled and pulled her into the room, and then

into a scorching kiss while he locked the door behind them. Finally, she was alone with him...except for the probable existence of Rosemont's listening devices. She didn't want to interrupt that kiss for anything, but she needed to tell him about the bug in the chapel. "Spence, there's something I have to say."

"Me, too." He took her hands and gazed directly into her eyes. "Thea, I'm sorry. Five years ago, I was a jackass. I didn't pay attention to how the way I acted was ruining what we had. You were right to break off our engagement."

His frank apology stunned her. When he squeezed her hands, a shiver chased up her arms.

He continued, "I never really took the time. I was caught up in my career...and my ego..."

She couldn't believe he was saying these things. It was as if he'd been possessed by an alternative spirit, that of a more sensitive man.

"...but I wasn't a complete idiot," he said. "From the first time I saw you, years ago, I knew you were the only woman for me. I knew someday we'd be together."

He lightly kissed her lips. The warmth of his nearness, his scent, his touch told her this was not a dream. Spence was here. He was real and solid. His words shimmered with the clarity of truth.

His voice was husky. "Someday is here, Thea."

She tore her hands from his grasp and flung her arms around his neck to give him a real kiss, deep and hard and passionate. Her back arched, pressing her torso against his chest, crushing her breasts. Her legs wrapped shamelessly around his thighs.

Their time apart vanished as her body instinctively re-membered how it was to love him with the frantic, earth-stopping passion she had never experienced before or since. Nothing else in her life came close.

His muscular arms supported her weight effortlessly, and she reveled in his masculine strength as he carried her to the bed. They fell together onto the mattress, still joined, with Spence on top.

He deepened their kiss. His tongue forced through her lips, through her teeth. His big hand cupped her breast. His thumb flicked the taut nipple, and a thousand trembles chased like static along her nerve endings. His arousal pressed against her.

Her hips ground against him. Thea was driven, desperate to make love.

And then she remembered the bug. Rosemont could be listening, eavesdropping on their perfect intimacy. She froze. Her passion went from white-hot to cold.

"Wait!" She pushed at his chest. "Spence, stop. You have to listen to me."

"No more talk," he growled. His hand pushed up her sweater.

She half-wanted him to persist beyond her plea to stop, but he read her urgent need to say something.

With a groan, he rolled away from her.

"This is important," she said. Her gaze flickered to the locked door. If she spoke, Rosemont would know everything. "How can I tell you this without words?"

He sucked in a breath and murmured, low, unconsciously aware of just what she needed to say. Aware that Rosemont heard everything. "If you don't want to make love, Thea, just say so."

"That's not it." She caressed his cheek, whispering. "Oh Spence, I want to—"

"What is it?"

She scrambled off the bed and went to the small writing

desk by the window. Rummaging through drawers, she found paper and pencil. Her hand was shaking so much that she could barely write the words: *Found a bug in the chapel.*

As he read, his eyes struggled to focus. Clearly, his attention was still distracted by his desire for her, another part of his body, somewhere south of his belt buckle. It thrilled her. He looked up and gestured, asking without words if she thought there might be a bug in this room.

She nodded.

He took the pencil and wrote: *Where did you find it?*

She wrote: *Door.*

His eyebrow lifted and he murmured aloud, "I don't understand."

It was easier to show him. She dragged the desk chair to the locked bedroom door and climbed upon it. Pointing, she reached up to the top edge of the door frame, in the exact center, where she'd found the chapel bug.

There was another! She held the silver disk between her thumb and index finger. Unbelievable! Was it possible that Rosemont had hidden all his listening devices in the same location in every room in the castle?

She marched to the adjoining bathroom, tossed the bug into the toilet and flushed. Then it occurred to her that there might be another in here. They should check every door frame.

Spence was way ahead of her. He searched above the closet doors and along the window frames. In the bathroom, he found another—centered precisely at the middle of the door frame.

He flushed it as well. "I think we're clear."

"How strange that he put them all in the same place."

"That's the compulsive behavior Mona described," Spence said, and Thea recalled the discussion in which

Mona had suggested that Rosemont was an obsessive personality. "I don't know much about the disorder, but if it's important for them to follow precisely the same pattern, again and again—like washing your hands three times, or counting a certain number of steps to get from one place to another—then this sure as hell fits the picture."

Thea was slightly familiar with obsessive-compulsive disorder. A couple of her students in the past few years had been on OCD meds. "So, Rosemont would need to hide all the bugs in the same location. Exactly in the center of the door frame in this case. There's probably some kind of twisted logic in that plan."

"Probably." Spence came toward her. His eyes shone with an unmistakably sexy glow. "At the moment, I don't give a damn about Rosemont. All that's important now is you."

She held him back. "I'm really filthy, you know."

"Don't care."

"I'd like to take a shower," she said, ducking behind the bathroom door.

"Why? You're just going to get all hot and sweaty."

"Showers are nice." Peeking coquettishly around the edge of the door, she teased, "And I need someone to scrub my back."

She eased the door closed, leaving it unlocked, and slipped out of her tired sweater and slacks while the water in the shower got steamy. The modern combination tub and glassed-in shower must have been a recent renovation to the castle. That and the pulsing showerhead.

She stepped behind the sliding-glass shower door. Dipping her head under the water, she shampooed and rinsed until her short chestnut hair was squeaky clean. The hot water pelted her shoulders and splashed between her breasts.

The bathroom door clicked open. Through the frosted glass of the shower, she saw him. As naked as she was.

He slid the shower door open and stood staring. His gaze caressed every inch of her body, lingering on her breasts, her belly and the triangle of dark black hair. Slowly, his mouth curved in an approving grin.

She returned his admiration, wantonly perusing the span of his shoulders, his chest, his flat stomach and his full, thick arousal. "Come on in," she said. "The water's fine."

"It's nice to look." He reached toward her, lightly tweaking her breast.

"Your fingers are cold," she said. "Get in here."

"Don't want to rush," he said.

"I want you now." She touched him where he could not possibly resist—or delay.

"Minx," he growled, but he stepped inside the shower and whisked it shut. Thick steam surrounded them with melting warmth. He pulled her close, joining their slick, wet bodies. He devoured her mouth with a deep, penetrating kiss.

She rubbed against him, excited by the rough texture of his chest hair. This wasn't the first time they'd made love in a shower, and her memories collided with present reality. She'd never dreamed this chance would come again.

He whispered, "Time for your scrubbing."

With lemon-scented soap, Spence rubbed his hands together, making a thick lather. "Hands up over your head."

Willingly, she obeyed, lacing her fingers behind her head. The hot shower sluiced down her back.

His hands skillfully massaged her shoulders and collarbones, then descended to her breasts. He laved her slowly, thoroughly. Shaping her waist, he trailed the fragrant lather down her body until he pressed at the juncture of her thighs.

Her eyelids drifted closed, and she gasped as the first shuddering wave crashed over her. She whimpered with pleasure, knowing the best was yet to come.

''Turn around,'' he ordered.

The shower water rippled down her swollen breasts, aided by tantalizing strokes from Spence. Then his attention turned to her backside, her shoulder blades, her hips. He squeezed her bottom, fitted her backside against his wet, hard body.

She turned again and draped her arms limply around his shoulders. Her gaze searched the rugged planes of his handsome face. She wanted to say something but was too overwhelmed by sensation to form coherent words. Softly, she moaned and purred.

And he turned her again. This time, she faced the wall of the shower away from the water. Spence tilted her forward, and she braced her arms against the tile wall as he grasped her hips and thrust hard into her waiting, yearning body.

A burst of exquisite pleasure took her breath away. But he wasn't done yet. He rocked against her, driving deep and hard in intense natural rhythm.

She climaxed again, more completely than ever before. And Spence held her, shuddering convulsively with his own fulfillment.

When he withdrew, she almost collapsed, limp and boneless and utterly satisfied. He held her gently in the swirling steam. His lips grazed her forehead.

He didn't speak. There was no need for words as he turned off the shower and guided her onto the soft rug on the tiled bathroom floor. With great care, he dried her from head to toe and wrapped her in a giant towel.

Still naked, he carried her into the bedroom and placed her on the bed where she curled into a cozy little ball of contentment. How on earth had she ever found the will or the courage to leave a man who could make love like that?

AS SOON AS Spence entered the nursery bedroom, he knew something was wrong. The atmosphere crackled like the aftermath of an explosion. Travis slouched cross-legged on the floor, not bothering to look up when Spence and Thea entered, while Lawrence paced back and forth, wearing a hole in the carpet.

"It's about time," Lawrence said coldly. "You were due on shift twenty minutes ago. That's too long."

Not long enough. Spence glanced down at Thea. She was dressed in black turtleneck and black velvet jeans, an outfit she said would be appropriate for a cat burglar. There was a certain feline resemblance with her big hazel eyes and sleek chestnut hair. He could've spent hours looking at her, admiring the sweet curves of her body. "Too long for what?"

"Dude," Travis taunted, "it isn't my fault the rev flipped out."

Spence only now noticed the absence of the Reverend Joshua. Alarmed, he turned to Lawrence. "What happened?"

"The reverend became suddenly agitated, mumbling to himself and fidgeting in a most awkward manner. Then he demanded to return to the chapel. I tried to dissuade him, reminding him of the danger inherent in being alone."

"There were three of us," Travis said, holding up three fingers. "Me and Butler Dude here had to stay here to watch over Jenny and Mona. We couldn't make a trip to the chapel, now could we?''

"But the reverend insisted," Lawrence said.

Spence groaned inwardly. His memory of the incredible sojourn in bed with Thea was fading fast as he focused on the immediate problem. Reverend Joshua, meandering around the castle by himself, was an easy target for Rosemont. "Let me check on Jenny and Mona, then I'll take care of the reverend. Wait for me in the sitting room."

"I wanna come with you," Travis said. "I need a little excitement. It's dead around here."

"Let's hope not," Spence said as he herded Travis and Lawrence out into the sitting room. "Thea, stay here."

She closed the door and sauntered toward him. A sultry smile curved her lips. Since they'd made love, she's hardly stopped grinning—a fact that pleased Spence. Though five years had elapsed, their passion was as fresh as tomorrow.

"I can't believe those guys," she said. "You can't leave them alone for five minutes without them getting into trouble."

"They made the right choice by staying here," Spence said. "Chasing after the reverend isn't as important as guarding Jenny and Mona."

Leaning over Jenny's hospital bed, he checked her pupils and vital signs. All were stable. "Are you awake?" Spence asked. "Jenny, can you hear me?"

She murmured, rolling her head from side to side on the pillow.

"Open your eyes, Jenny."

Lazily, her eyelids pried half-open.

Thea clasped her friend's hand, beaming delightedly. "Oh, Jenny! You're going to be okay."

She gave a feeble wave. Her lips parted. With great effort, she said one word. "Bathroom."

"You bet," Thea said, and put an arm beneath her best friend's shoulders, helping her to rise up.

"Let's try to keep her up a little longer," Spence said. "It will help to get her metabolism revving a little."

Spence disconnected the needle from Jenny's IV portal, and Thea helped her shuffle across the floor. One slow step after another. While they were in the bathroom, he quickly checked Mona's vitals as well. Her improvement was not going to be dramatic. She no longer seemed to be in pain, but her blood pressure remained elevated and her fever dangerously high by Spence's estimation. They needed to get her to a hospital as quickly as possible.

He waited for Thea and Jenny outside the bathroom and Thea talked to her, trying to encourage her to walk about a bit more. But Jenny's knees threatened to buckle and Spence caught her before she passed out again. He carried her to the gurney and reset the brakes on the small wheels when the cart moved a bit.

Her features slack again as she sank back toward unconsciousness, Jenny moaned. Spence hoped she was dreaming, as it sometimes indicated a lighter level of sedation. He wasn't looking forward to the moment when someone had to tell her that her beloved Gregory Rosemont was a psychotic who had used her to seek revenge.

"How's Mona?" Thea asked.

"Not out of the woods. She needs the kind of treatment she can only get in an ICU. All we can do is make her comfortable and hope."

Thea sent up a prayer for Mona. "Do you think we should tell Travis about Jenny?"

"No," Spence said. He didn't want Travis bouncing around like a demented puppy, pestering Jenny. Nor was Spence certain that any of the others—Travis, Lawrence or the reverend—could be trusted.

"What next?"

"I want you to stay with me." If anything happened to her, if anyone touched one beautiful hair on her head, Spence would be nearly as crazed as Rosemont.

She flashed a vixen's grin. "Are you protecting me?"

"Damn straight."

"That's so sweet." She went up on tiptoe to kiss his cheek. "But it's not necessary. Spence, I can take care of myself."

"Just in case," he said, reaching around to pat her perfect, round buttocks. "I've got your back."

In the sitting room, Spence issued decisive orders. "I want you guys—both of you—to stay close to Jenny and Mona."

Travis stepped away from the windows. "But I gotta get out and about. Let me go with you."

"Forget it, Travis. Look out for your sister. Thea and I will go find the reverend and bring him back here."

Spence commandeered Travis's handgun, under whining protest, so that he would have one and Thea could still have the one she'd been carrying that belonged to Lawrence. He tucked Travis's pea-shooter into the waist of his Levi's. "Pay attention to your sister and Mona."

He and Thea went out into the hallway, roaming again in the castle from hell. The lights splashed as soon as they stepped from the center staircase into the Grand Drawing Room.

"What's the deal with the reverend?" he asked. "You were in the chapel with him before."

"He's not my favorite person," Thea said. "His approach is a little too sanctimonious for my taste."

"Ditto." Spence thought Reverend Joshua was quick to call on God to excuse him from cooperation or from venturing into danger. In short, the reverend was a coward.

"From the very beginning, he's been scared. He was frantic to get out of here."

"Perhaps, a very sane attitude," Thea said dryly. "I think he's a truly religious man. The whole time he was in the chapel, he prayed, begging the Lord for forgiveness. He may have said Diane's name. I couldn't be sure."

They paused outside the closed door to the chapel. Spence drew the .22 and took off the safety. "Then you don't think the reverend is putting on an act, hiding behind his collar?"

She frowned at the closed door. Her voice lowered, "I don't, Spence. I think the Reverend Joshua is the real deal."

Spence placed his hand on the door handle and pushed the door wide open. Subdued lighting in the simple chapel tried to create an aura of peaceful contemplation, but Spence saw only shadows. As he eased around the rows of pews, he had a very strong sense of danger lurking nearby.

Behind the draped altar, Spence spied a boot, then the body of the reverend, lying face down in his black coat, his arms spread wide. Another victim.

Spence hurried toward him. "Reverend!"

With only a few feet to reach the prostrate body, Spence startled back when the Reverend Joshua moved. His long legs coiled beneath him, and he sprang backwards in a crouch with his elbows wide. His pale white hands dangled from his sleeves. "Keep away from me."

"It's okay," Spence assured him. "We're here to help you."

Joshua Handy's tongue flicked out to lick his lips. He had been lying there in some position of forgiveness-seeking, like nuns in old movies. His dark eyes burned like charred embers. He crept back, circling around the opposite side of the pews. "I was once a man like you, simple and in love, wanting nothing more than earthly pleasures."

Spence hid the gun behind his back. He held out his left hand toward the Reverend. "Come with me. We can talk about this."

"She lied to me," he cried hoarsely. "She had always loved another."

"Who?" Thea asked. "Who lied?"

"Diane." His lips curled hatefully about the name. "Diane Moretson." The same woman the good reverend had denied ever knowing.

Thea snapped her fingers. "J.H.—Joshua Handy. Your initials are the same as Diane's boyfriend, John Hoffman."

The reverend covered his ears. "John Hoffman died when I entered the seminary and started my life anew, answering the call of the Lord."

"Five years ago," Spence said.

So this was the deep dark secret in the reverend's past. He'd been in love with Diane Moretson, a woman who'd committed suicide and blamed her lover, John Hoffman. The guilt must have been more than he could stand.

Trying to appease his torment, Thea said, "Joshua, it wasn't really your fault."

"You don't understand." He began shaking his head. He looked nearly palsied. "The gun went off." He flattened against the wall, peering all around him. Haunted by the past, he looked as though he was being pursued by the hounds of Hell.

"You were with her," Thea said. Her voice was empathetic and kind. "That must have been terrible."

"God will forgive me. I pray and pray." He cried out, "Forgive me, Lord."

Spence eased closer. He might be able to tackle the guy.

Then what? He had to find a way to overcome him, to control him. He was within five feet when the reverend screamed. ''Murderer! I am a murderer. I killed her.''

He leapt through the open chapel door.

Chapter Twelve

As the reverend bolted through the chapel door on his long, spidery legs, Thea reacted without thinking. She went after him.

Since she was closest to the exit, she had a five-yard headstart on Spence. She raced along the corridor, passing closed doors on either side. The reverend outdistanced her with awkward loping strides he took as if he were jumping hurdles, but she managed to keep him in sight. It'd be impossible to lose him. Wherever he went, the lights flashed, pointing his route as clearly as a neon arrow.

"Reverend," she called to him. "Wait. We can help you."

Was he really a murderer? Had he really meant to say that he had killed Diane?

It wasn't until she reached the open doors to the ballroom that Thea put on the brakes. Spence was right behind her. His hand clamped a gentle restraint around her upper arm. "He's dangerous, Thea. Leave him."

"But you have a gun," she pointed out.

"I don't want you chasing after a man who just confessed to murder."

Gasping hard to catch her breath, she automatically asserted her independence. "I can take—"

"Yeah, I know. You can take care of yourself." His grip on her arm tightened, holding her back in case she decided to bolt. "But why? Why should we go after him?"

"The reverend just signed his death warrant. Rosemont was obsessed enough to put together this weekend of insane revenge because he thought we 'wronged' Diane. What's he going to do when he hears that the reverend killed her?"

"Because he didn't do it, Thea." Spence said. "Remember, I was the doctor who examined her body. Her wound was consistent with holding a gun to her head. She left a suicide note. The cops investigated *and*—"

"None of that rules out the reverend holding the gun to her head."

"—there was an autopsy. The forensic lab identified a powdery residue on her right hand from the weapon. She killed herself, Thea, and there's no way, with all of Rosemont's resources, that he doesn't know that."

"But why would the reverend, John Hoffman—whatever we call him, why would he confess to something he didn't do?"

"He felt guilty. Didn't Diane say something in her note about life not being worth living after her lover left her?"

"I think so."

"But the reverend just told us that while he loved her, she was in love with someone else. He had to have been traumatized by that discovery. If you want my take on it, Thea, he's spent these last few years convincing himself that there was no one else, and that Diane killed herself over him. He interpreted her accusation as evidence that he murdered her in spirit if not in fact," Spence said.

Thea shook her head in dismay. "Are you saying it was

easier for him to accept the blame for Diane's death than to admit the possibility of her having another lover?''

Spence shrugged. "I'm not saying it makes sense, Thea. Only that the theory fits the facts. He believes he killed her.''

Spence's reasoning made sense, but she couldn't abide her own next worry. "He might kill himself out of guilt if we don't find him, Spence. Or kill us all for our part in making the truth rise up in his face again. And all that is only if Rosemont doesn't kill the reverend first.''

As if on cue, ghostly piano music sounded from the ballroom, echoing eerily down the hallway, playing "Misty." Thea's muscles tensed as she remembered her helpless fear and anger when Rosemont had trapped her in the dark. He was taunting them, letting them know he was still very much in charge.

This was his castle, his territory. He controlled the lights, the temperature and the sound. Rosemont could do whatever he wanted.

Apparently fascinated, Spence entered the mirrored and marbled ballroom, pulling her along. The first time Thea'd seen this room, she'd thought it lovely and fanciful. Now, the chill from the French doors felt ominous. The crystal chandeliers seemed hung from a thread, ready to crash and shatter. This ballroom would never host beautiful women in long gowns and men in tuxedos. This was a place where demons would dance. She stared at the empty bench behind the Steinway as the music reached a crescendo.

"That's my music," Spence said. "A recording of me playing the piano."

"I told you."

He grinned. "I sound pretty damn good."

She stared at him, taken aback. "Have you lost your mind? We've just witnessed a man's psyche—if not his life—going down the drain! For God's sake, Spence, what is with you? Should we pursue your career as a piano man right this very second," she cried. "Let me call a talent agent. Oh, wait! No phone. No escape. We're trapped in a castle with a madman."

"Snap out of it, Thea." Spence gave her shoulder a serious shake. "I know you've just had a terrible shock, but it was a joke. A bad joke, maybe, but just a joke. And there's more than one psycho in this castle," he added when he had let her go.

"Meaning me?"

He grimaced. "Meaning Rosemont *and* Reverend Joshua Handy. I wouldn't say Travis has both oars in the water, either." He sauntered across the marble floor. "Let's go back upstairs. The best thing we can do is to keep a close watch over Mona and Jenny and stay safe until morning."

"Then what?"

"Then I'll think of something."

She fell into step behind him, feeling ridiculous for her outburst. She had overreacted. It seemed that whenever she was around Spence, her thoughts and emotions ran at a higher pitch. No one else could spark her anger so quickly. No other person could lead her to the pinnacle of arousal and bliss, either.

Living with him would be an emotional carnival ride. Round and round on a carousel, she'd see more vivid color, hear louder music. Was it what she wanted?

As they climbed the curving staircase to the second floor in the tower, Thea realized something was wrong. "There are no lights ahead of us."

"I guess the reverend didn't go this way."

"But it's not lighting up for us, either." The dark corridor gaped before them like a dragon's maw. Thea didn't have to guess at the presence of danger. She could smell it. Though she'd been anxious to find Reverend Joshua, she reversed her idea. "I don't like this. Let's backtrack."

"If the reverend got here first, he could have turned the lights off manually." Spence called out, "Reverend, you don't have to hide from us. We'll help you."

There was a whimper in the dark.

She and Spence were silhouetted against the light from the stairway. Windowless dark lay ahead of them. This was the perfect set-up for an ambush.

Spence took a step forward and called out, "Are you all right? Reverend, are you injured?"

Guttural, nearly feral sobs echoed in the corridor. When he spoke, the trained, sonorous tones of his preacher's voice made a terrifying contrast. "I've lost my soul."

"Spence, let's go," Thea urged. "He's dangerous."

"I can't leave him here if he's injured." Spence called out, "Reverend?"

"Stay back!"

Spence paused. He'd drawn the pistol and held it behind his back. "We want to help you."

"There is no help," the reverend said.

Thea stayed close behind Spence as he inched forward. Though she might be walking closer to danger, she didn't want to be left behind—alone and unguarded. Damn it, why weren't the lights coming on?

"It's dark here," Spence said in a calm voice. "Come over by the stairs where we can see you."

"I have no wish to be seen."

"Come on," Spence said. "You're going to be okay. I'm sure Diane would forgive you. Surely—"

"Not that witch!" the reverend moaned. Spence let him go on talking. "When I got to the house that night, Diane showed me the suicide note, but I didn't believe her until she held the gun to her head. Even then, I mocked her, called her a coward. Then she pulled the trigger. I killed her,'' he shrieked. One of the closed doors flung open. The reverend charged at them, arms flailing like a windmill.

Spence fired the pistol, obviously aiming high.

The reverend whirled. His black coat flared behind him as he raced down the hallway away from them.

This time, neither Spence nor Thea gave chase. Still holding the pistol, he wrapped his arm around her. "There's nothing we can do for him. Not when he's like this."

"Why didn't the lights come on?"

"He probably smashed out the fixtures," Spence said. "He wanted it dark."

"Do you believe his story?"

"It really doesn't matter, does it? Diane was set on suicide. He failed to stop her, but that's all."

"But is he sorry about that, or will Rosemont just find him the most culpable of us all?"

Spence didn't have a chance to consider before they heard a shout from far away. "Spence? Thea?"

"We're down here, Lawrence."

Spence held her close and guided her toward the lights at the end of the hall. He had the feeling that everything had spun out of control. At the same time, he figured Rosemont was getting exactly what he'd wanted. High tension. Nerves on edge. The reverend shattering under the pressure.

He heard Lawrence yell again. "Where?"

"Here."

Lawrence and Travis came running up the staircase from the drawing room. "Thank God, you're all right,"

Lawrence said. "We heard the gunshot, then it sounded like someone fell down the stairs."

"Did you see the reverend?"

"No."

Spence glanced down the hallway toward the sitting room. They had left the Jenny and Mona unguarded. There hadn't been time for Rosemont to slip inside, not with Spence and Thea coming directly down the hall. Still, he hurried.

The sitting room looked exactly the same. The door to the nursery was closed. Spence turned the handle. It was locked. "Lawrence, did you lock this door?"

"Not on purpose, certainly. I suppose the locking mechanism could have been pushed in when I pulled the door shut behind me."

"Have you got the key?" Spence demanded.

Lawrence holstered his gun and started digging through pockets. "I'm sure it's here somewhere."

Spence was beginning to have a bad feeling about this locked door. "Travis? Did you lock it?"

"No way, man."

Spence aimed the pistol at the door handle and fired once. Then he kicked. The door crashed open. Ice-cold air poured over him. The casement windows stood wide open. Blowing snow spilled over the sill and into the room.

"Close the windows," Spence ordered.

He went to Jenny first. A tiny drop of clear fluid glistened on the rubber port at her IV catheter, left there by a syringe used to inject Jenny yet again. Spence swore violently and checked her pupils and swore again. Jenny had been rendered comatose.

Rosemont had gotten to her again in the few seconds she'd been left alone.

Frustration bordering on rage churned in Spence's gut.

He'd given the idiots one simple task: Stay here and protect. And they'd stumbled out the door like a couple of nimrods.

He made the decision on the fly to pull the IV. If Rosemont got to her again it could be disastrous, the straw, so to speak, that broke the camel's back. Rosemont could still inject directly into a vein, but that took more time and skill, greater risk.

Jenny wouldn't get any more fluids, he explained to Thea, but at least the threat of continued quicky injections was put to rest. Spence stripped off the tape holding the tiny catheter in place, then pulled it out of the vein with practiced ease, and applied pressure until Thea could get a pressure bandage from the supplies into place.

He checked on Mona next. She seemed much the same. Resting comfortably. As he leaned down to take her pulse, her eyes opened a crack. "Get rid of them," she whispered.

"Gladly."

He turned on his heel. With both Travis and Lawrence struggling, they'd managed to close and latch the window.

"Dude," Travis said, "Rosemont must've flown in here like Dracula. I mean, it's still snowing and any normal human being would get blown off the window ledge."

"Out," Spence said quietly.

"Terribly sorry," Lawrence said. "When we heard the gunshot, it seemed prudent—"

"Get out!" Spence nodded to Thea. "You stay."

She glanced at the other two. "You'd better do what he says. Wait for us in the sitting room."

Shuffling their feet and muttering to each other, Travis and Lawrence exited. Thea closed the splintered door behind them.

Spence beckoned her over to the bed. "Mona's awake."

He knelt beside the bed and held Mona's tiny hand. "Welcome back. How're you feeling?"

"Been better," she said weakly.

"You need to rest," he instructed. "There's a hemotoxic poison working through your system. You're going to be okay."

"Diane Moretson," Mona croaked. The effort of speaking exhausted her. "Suicide. She's the one."

"We know," Thea said. "Spence and I figured it out. I was Diane's roommate. Spence was in the ER when the ambulance brought her in. He couldn't save her. And the reverend…"

"Her minister?" Mona asked.

"Afraid not." Thea shook her head. "The reverend didn't put Diane's name on the list of his parishioners because he never counseled her. Reverend Joshua Handy changed his name after Diane died. He transformed himself for the seminary from John Hoffman. He was Diane's boyfriend, and he found out she was cheating on him. It was probably losing her lover that made her want to die."

"Ah." Mona's eyelids closed. She nodded with a certain satisfaction from knowing the truth, but she was fading fast.

"Mona," Spence said, "can you tell us what happened when you were attacked? Do you remember anything?"

"Chloroform," she whispered.

"Did you see who did it?"

"No one," she said faintly. "No one came in. It was…one of us." She winced as she exhaled slowly. Her fingers went limp in Spence's hand.

He gave her tiny fingers a squeeze and stood. "She's asleep again."

"One of us," Thea repeated with a nervous glance at the door. "She doesn't know about the dumbwaiter." But a terrible presentiment formed in her mind. "What if Mona's right, Spence? What if one of them sneaked in here and opened the dumbwaiter to make us think whoever snatched Mona had come up on the dumbwaiter?"

Spence's hands fisted. "If it's true, then one of them *is* Rosemont."

One of them, he thought, angry that such a ruse hadn't even occurred to him, had then also slipped into the room just now, shoved open the window to create yet another distraction from the truth, and given Jenny another dose of sedation. But which one? Lawrence and Travis had run out the door when they heard the gunshot. Had one stayed behind? Or doubled back while the other was searching? Spence figured that each would defend his own actions, and neither could be trusted to tell the truth.

And the reverend was still at large. Was he Rosemont? Though it seemed unlikely that he was operating under a triple alias, if a double alias, then why not? Handy might well have convinced himself that everyone *else* around Diane had failed her long before he had. Wouldn't he then be well motivated to seek his revenge?

Which one? There wasn't going to be an easy answer to that question. The problem with having stuck together in their forays through the castle was that he and Thea couldn't possibly know which of these men had split off from the others in order to terrorize Thea in the ballroom and keep Jenny knocked out.

"Stay with Mona," he told Thea. He checked that she still had Lawrence's gun on her. "Don't be afraid to use it if anybody threatens you."

"What about you? Where are you going?"

"I'm calling an end to this game."

"How?"

"I'm going to admit that I've lost." In his work as an

emergency doc with SAR, Spence had never before given up. It was his job to treat the victims and make sure all of the SAR party returned safely to base. He didn't have the right to decide who deserved to be rescued, but this situation was different. "I can't protect everybody in this castle. So I'm making a choice. I'll stay here. In this room. With you, Jenny and Mona."

"What about the others?"

"They're on their own."

It pained him to cut his losses. Among the three men—Travis, Lawrence and the reverend—one was a dangerous psycho. The other two were innocent. Spence could only hope they'd be able to take care of themselves.

He entered the sitting room. Lawrence sat stiffly in the wingback chair. Travis sprawled on one of the sofas. When Spence stood in front of the fireplace, he completed the triangle. He looked from one to the other, seeking a clue. One of them was almost certainly Rosemont. Which one? Lawrence seemed clever enough to have staged this affair. But Travis had the ego to think he could get away with it. And the reverend had plenty of motive.

"Diane Moretson," he said, "is the person Rosemont believes we wronged. Thea knew her. I was the ER doctor who couldn't resuscitate. The reverend was a former boyfriend. Mona was her therapist."

"I thought so," Lawrence said.

"You *thought* so," Spence demanded, incredulous. "Are you now admitting that you did in fact know Diane?"

"No," he said. "I didn't. But as you might have noticed by my game playing, I am an aficionado of puzzles. After you and Thea came up with Diane's name, I wrote it out: *Moretson.* It didn't take long to recognize the obvious anagram."

"The what?" Travis asked.

"Anagram. *Moretson* can be rearranged to form another. The name is—"

"Rosemont," Spence supplied. A clue as big as Mount Sopris. And it had flown right over Spence's head. He studied Lawrence with new interest. Either the butler was a very clever puzzler or he was Rosemont himself, seeking to impress them with his game.

"What else have you figured out?" Spence asked.

"I must say that it makes perfect sense to me that only four of you had actual connections—through the six degrees of separation—with Diane Moretson. It was Thea who first recognized that there were only four daggers on the Rosemont coat of arms. A dagger for each of you."

Spence had forgotten about the coat of arms, but he was dealing with liars here. "Well, that's incisive thinking, Lawrence, except that there's another person connected with Diane. Rosemont himself."

"But he wouldn't paint himself as a dagger," Lawrence said. "He might be the blooming rose in the center of the coat of arms."

"Dude," Travis said, "maybe the rose is supposed to be that Diane chick."

Spence didn't want to travel too far down the path of symbolism. There were more important issues to discuss. "Mona woke up for a few seconds," he said. "She said no one entered the room to drug her. She was attacked by someone already in the sitting room."

"But there's that dumbwaiter—"

"And Rosemont could have easily opened it to lend the appearance that he hasn't been right here in this suite all along."

Outside the granite castle walls, the wind shrieked and the snow battered. In the firelit sitting room, there was uneasy silence as each man assessed the others, watching and wondering. One of them had staged this weekend. One of them was obsessed by vengeance.

"Not I," Lawrence said. "As I keep repeating. I am merely the hired help."

"Well, it's not me," Travis whined. "I just got sucked into this whole thing because my sister wanted her family here for the wedding—which is me since I'm all the family she's got left."

"I must also point out," Lawrence said, "that if—as you assume—Rosemont is not lurking elsewhere in the castle, unseen and unrecognized by us, he could also be you."

"Or the reverend," Travis said. "He seems pretty much whacked out."

Spence knew there was no definitive proof. No facts or logic could point conclusively to any one of them. At least, he thought ruefully, considering the dumbwaiter ploy, none that had occurred to him yet. It was still entirely possible that the dumbwaiter was not a ploy at all.

Spence drew a deep breath. "I'm telling you this as a warning," he said. "Protect yourselves. Tonight, I'll be locked in that room with Thea and the other women. If either of you comes through the door, I'll shoot first and ask questions later."

"Whoa, dude." Travis bounced to his feet. "How do we know you're not going to kill them all? *You* could be Rosemont."

"I must also object," Lawrence said. "You can't leave me out here alone."

"If you're not one of the four daggers," Spence said, "you should have nothing to fear."

Travis came at Spence. A spark of real emotion glittered in his usually laconic eyes. "Dude, I want my gun back."

"Not a chance," Spence said.

"You can't leave me out here with no weapon to defend myself. Man, that's not right."

Spence agreed with him, but he wanted at least two handguns to protect the women. Travis would have to fend for himself.

"I have a possible solution," Lawrence said. "There's a trophy room in the house. Locked in cases, there are several weapons."

Spence eyed the butler suspiciously. Hidden guns. Hidden secrets. Lawrence had buried a lot of vital information beneath his obsequious manner. "Why didn't you tell us before?"

"I truly didn't believe we're in mortal danger. He didn't kill Mona, either. Rosemont is merely toying with the four of you, playing on your guilt."

"In case you're wrong," Spence said with a nod to Travis, thinking of the possibility that the missing reverend was actually Rosemont—or even that Rosemont was still another man altogether, "we should be armed. Let's go."

Once again, they went through the Grand Drawing Room which seemed to be the center of the first-floor room. The trophy room was tucked away behind the library with the non-functioning computer screens, but it was a good-sized space, large enough for a regulation-sized pool table and a respectable display of taxidermy—heads and fish.

Spence made a beeline for the gun cabinet. Behind glass doors, there were eight rifles. Beside it, in a smaller case, were several handguns. "Open it, Lawrence."

"Unfortunately, I don't have the key."

"No prob," Travis said.

He grabbed a pool cue from the rack. His eyes lit with a maniacal glow as he approached the gun cabinet. He raised the cue, holding it in both hands like a baseball bat. For a moment, Spence thought Travis was preparing to attack them.

The glass on the case shattered with one blow, but Travis wasn't content with small destruction. He hammered again and again until all the glass had broken away from the frame.

"Cool," he said as he moved to the other case.

They found ammunition in the drawers at the bottom of the case and divided up the weapons. Armed like Rambo, the three men faced each other.

Spence felt the rush of adrenaline. If it was one of these men who wanted him dead, then he was powerfully armed.

Slow and steady, he walked to the door, not turning his back. Travis and Lawrence came after him, alternately watching each other. They eased through the library and into the Grand Drawing Room where Rosemont's threats had first been spoken.

Lights flashed from the hallway at the top of the stair. Was it the reverend? Spence needed to get back to Thea and the other women. But he couldn't take his eyes off these other two.

"A suggestion," Spence said. "I'll go up the stairs. Travis can take the first-floor hallway. Lawrence, you go toward the kitchen."

"If I turn my back," Travis said, "one of you guys could kill me."

"Don't be absurd," Lawrence said. "Any one of us could have killed the other right from the start. If one of us fires the first shot, the other two will kill him."

"On three," Spence said.

He counted fast and started backing up the stairs. The other men backed off in their own directions. Flashing lights signaled their movement in opposite directions.

At the top of the central staircase, Spence turned and ran toward the nursery suite. He charged through and entered the bedroom where Thea still sat on the bed, facing the door. She held the pistol in her hand, aimed squarely at his chest. "Where did you get all the rifles and—"

"Doesn't matter," he said. "Help me move stuff in front of the sitting-room door and the bathroom."

"What happened to Travis and Lawrence?"

"They're on their own."

He pulled the heavy elephant slide across the rug to barricade the doors. His only objective was to make it safely to morning.

In Cascadia at Spence's house, Emily and Jordan stomped through the front door, shaking off snow. Instead of the quiet weekend she'd anticipated, Emily had been called out twice. Once to help track down a couple of stranded hikers and this evening to perform emergency first aid on a little boy who needed eight stitches in his hand after a whittling accident.

She yanked off her cap. "Spence owes me. Big time."

"Me, too," Jordan said. "God, I hate snow."

"Don't worry. We'll be back to Florida before you know it. On the beach." Chagrined, she remembered how much she'd objected to the part-time move from her beloved Rocky Mountains. Now, she couldn't wait to get back to the lapping azure waves and palm trees. There was nothing as grand as springtime in the mountains, but she agreed with her new husband. A lot of the winter could easily be missed.

He was in the kitchen making coffee. "Turn the tube onto the late news. I want to see how the Avalanche did."

"Hockey," she muttered. Not her favorite sport. She'd

never understood the penalties. But the Denver-based team was one of the Colorado spectacles high on Jordan's list.

She flicked on the television set, then peeled off another layer of clothes and flung herself down on the sofa. The sportscaster came on with the top story. She called out the results to Jordan. "The Avs won. Nuggets lost."

The sportscaster moved on to a free-style ski competition in Utah. Snuggling deep into the sofa with a blanket one of the old ladies in Cascadia had crocheted for Spence, Emily nearly missed what suddenly jerked her upright. The winner of the Utah event was a local boy, Travis Trevain.

How could that be? She and Jordan had met Trevain at the gondola house. He was the bride's brother.

She stared at the screen, at footage of Trevain's winning run at Alta Vista. From a photo insert, she recognized the spikey white hair, but the face was different. If the guy in the castle wasn't Travis, who was he?

Chapter Thirteen

After a long night, sharing the watch with Spence three hours at a time, Thea stood at the nursery window looking at the most beautiful sunrise she'd ever seen.

Cloudless eastern skies of soft gentle pink arced above the distant peaks. Pristine snow drifted in mounds and weighed down the boughs of nearby conifers. As the sun rolled higher, the blanket of white glistened, sparkled, reflected. And the sky turned from lavender to pure blue. Hard to believe she was still wedging a gun into the waistband of her jeans.

Spence had told her about Lawrence's discovery of the anagram. The bit of information made it seem as if they were making progress when in fact, it contributed little to their understanding of Rosemont's quest for revenge. It was nothing but further proof of his penchant for games.

And Jenny had spent a restless, uneasy night, mewling sadly in her sleep. She'd been up once more during the night to use the bathroom. Thea had tried repeatedly in those few moments to get Jenny to describe her fiancé, but with no luck. Jenny could scarcely remember her own name. Thea's questions only confused and upset her.

Then there was the threat of the reverend. Where had

he spent the night? Was he prepared to pick them off the minute they emerged from the fortified nursery suite?

Thea wanted to wake Spence, to show him the promise of this brilliant new day, full of hope. She wanted to believe that today they would escape. She wanted desperately to indulge her desire for the beginning of a new life in which she and Spence would be together.

None of what she wanted seemed to have a snowball's chance in hell of coming true.

She tiptoed to the bed where he lay sleeping. In repose, he looked younger, more vulnerable. His sharply defined jawline relaxed. The lines around his eyes smoothed. At least he was here with her. She leaned down to lightly kiss his forehead.

"Five more minutes," he mumbled.

"It's stopped snowing."

"Okay." His eyelids remained closed. His nose wrinkled. "Ten more minutes."

She'd give him ten, maybe even fifteen. She wanted to give him a lifetime, to give him everything he'd ever wished for.

After a quick check on Mona and Jenny, who both seemed to be sleeping quietly, Thea nudged aside the heavy toy chest that blocked the door to the adjoining bathroom so that she could go in and splash some water on her face.

She could open the door just a crack. The pistol in the waistband of her jeans caught on the doorjamb, but she managed to slip through the opening.

Thea stared into the bathroom mirror. Her thick brown hair was messy. Every trace of makeup was gone. And yet, the face that reflected back at her looked better than on an average morning. Her eyes seemed brighter. Her mouth was relaxed.

Relaxed? How on earth could she be relaxed by a week-end at the castle from hell? Because she'd forgiven Spence and tossed aside the dark resentment she'd worn for five years? The effect was a flattering glow, despite the dire circumstances of their situation.

She turned on the faucets and tucked her hair behind her ears. The warm water refreshed her. She splashed again, then blindly groped for a hand towel.

A strong hand clamped around her wrist.

She felt the gun being removed from her jeans.

When she opened her eyes, there was another face in the mirror. Travis. His narrow cheeks were dingy with stubble. The bleached hair on his head formed a spiky nimbus. His eyes were red-rimmed and wild.

"Keep quiet," he whispered.

"It was you," she croaked. "You're Rosemont."

"Hell, no."

His face in the mirror distorted. His lower lip trembled as if he was about to break down in tears. Thea had seen that look before on her students when they'd done something wrong and were trying to pretend they didn't care about being caught. "How did you get in here?"

"I've been hiding behind the shower curtain all night," he said quietly. "I didn't know where else to go."

"How did you get inside the nursery?" she demanded. "We had the doors locked and blocked."

"I used the dumbwaiter," he admitted. "I wrecked it like I was supposed to, but then I fixed the mechanism."

Didn't he understand how a secret entry into the nursery endangered his sister? Disgusted, Thea snapped at him. "Let go of my wrist."

"Okay. Just don't scream."

"Give me my gun back."

"Sure. Whatever, dude."

He had stashed three other firearms she could see. He returned her pistol and backed away to sit on the closed toilet seat. His shoulders slumped, and he seemed to collapse into his baggy clothes. "I want to get out of here, Thea. I'm scared."

Though her instinct was to believe him, she kept her distance. "It's stopped snowing," she said.

"Okay." He looked up, suddenly energized. "I can ski out of here. I can make it."

The door burst open, and Spence crashed inside with a pistol in each hand.

"Don't shoot," she said. "It's only Travis."

He turned and glared at the young man cowering on the toilet seat. "What the hell are you doing here?"

Thea explained. "He spent last night in here, hiding behind the shower curtain."

Travis whined, "I didn't want to be all alone."

"Have you seen Lawrence or the reverend?" Spence demanded.

"No way. I tried to hide out in the video room last night, but I freaked myself out so I came up here."

Spence lowered one of his guns. "Why?"

"Because I figured if somebody came after me, I'd yell and you'd hear me. And you'd come and help me. You have to come, man. You're a doctor, and you took a hypocrite oath."

"Hippocratic oath," Thea corrected like the English teacher she was. "A hypocrite is a liar."

"Right," Travis said.

The sly twist of his mouth told her that he knew the difference, he was just being his smart-aleck self.

She addressed both of them. "Gentlemen, it's stopped snowing. We should pack up and figure a way out of here."

"I'm telling you I can ski down," Travis volunteered again.

"We'll check it out," Spence said. He pointed to the door. "Travis, go wait for me in the sitting room."

Grumbling, he shuffled out and slammed the door behind him.

Spence flicked the door locks on both doors—the one off the hallway and the bedroom. "How did he get in here?"

"The dumbwaiter."

Thea opened her arms to him for a morning embrace and gladly fitted her body to his. She clung tightly, greedy for time to rediscover their relationship. Time for the future.

She had to believe everything would turn out fine. They'd escape, start over. Fate wouldn't be so cruel as to offer these moments, so beautiful and true, and then snatch them away.

After a squeeze, Spence separated from her. He went to the faucet and began to wash up. "Here's the problem," he said. "It would be insane to let Travis ski down. We'd never know if he made it or not. We'll have to climb. That's a two-person job."

"Two-person." She daubed toothpaste on her brush. "You and Travis?"

"I don't trust that little weasel any farther than I can throw him, but I don't see another way."

She didn't like the idea of Spence making a difficult climb with a deceitful, possibly treacherous, companion. "I don't want you to get hurt."

"Neither do I."

Together, they brushed their teeth. Such a simple thing, but Thea's sense of intimacy with Spence felt remarkable.

"We can't wait," Spence went on after he'd finished.

"Mona seems to be improving, but I'm afraid of complications. She needs to be in the hospital. Today."

Thea nodded, agreeing with the need to end this ordeal as quickly as possible and fearing the danger that attended them.

She really didn't like the plan, but the only other option, to wait it out for another whole day and night, meant putting Mona at risk. And every moment they stayed, even though they had significant fire power, gave Rosemont the advantage. It was a chance Spence had to take.

"Thea, when we get away from here, I want to make up for five years apart. Come home with me to Cascadia."

"I can't just leave my job."

"Then I'll come to you. I'll stay in Denver." He took her shoulders and turned her toward him.

"Could you really leave Cascadia now?"

He frowned. "I don't want to be away from you. Not ever again."

She tilted back her head to accept his breathtaking kiss. Excitement shimmered across the surface of her skin and sank deeper, racing through her veins to her heart. She felt something stirring, something very much like love. His loyalty to the tiny mountain town had a little to do with it.

He gazed down into her eyes. "I'll be back as soon as I can. Don't let anybody into the room."

"I'll miss you."

"Be safe." He kissed her again, hard. Then, he exited into the sitting room to meet Travis.

Inadvertently, her hand raised. She wanted to call him back, to hold him and never let go. But they had to take this chance. They had to survive in order to have a future at all.

OUTSIDE AT LAST, Spence inhaled the fresh, crisp air. His lungs expanded, and his spirits rose. He slogged through the drifting snow that had buried the pathway in depths that varied from knee-deep to mid-thigh. It felt good to be out of the castle. Damn good. He stretched his arms wide to embrace the sunlight, the wind and the snow.

Travis smirked. "What are you doing, man?"

"Feeling free."

"We're still trapped," he said. "Until we get to the other side of the ravine and—"

"I know."

From here, Spence could see the onset of another problem. A thick bank of dark clouds was building in the north, but the storm was at least two hours away. They'd have enough time to make a descent and climb. In the equipment room, he'd found climbing gear: ropes, pitons, D-shaped carabinieres, even a harness and a couple of ice axes.

He was ready. The real problem was that Travis had insisted on dragging along boots, poles and a pair of skis which he planted in the snow at the edge of the trail.

Spence stopped beside Travis, not wanting to go first and offer his back as a target. No way would Spence trust him until they were climbing together, depending on each other for safety. If one of them fell, the other would follow.

"We'll make the descent from the area where the gondola fell," Spence said. He didn't like going down blind, but there wasn't much choice. "We can anchor onto the foundation of the gondola house."

"I'm telling you, dude. I can ski this."

"Don't be an ass," Spence said. "Some of these cliffs are straight vertical drops. Even if you could ski down, how would you get up the other side?"

"Scope it out." He pointed. "That side doesn't look half as steep."

Though it was hard to tell what lay under the mounds of snow, the opposite side of the chasm was marked by forest and rose at less severe angles. A strenuous hike, but nothing that required ropes and pitons.

"You'd need cross-country skis, not downhill," Spence said. He was thinking ahead. After he had the ropes in place for the descent, he could easily return to the castle. He could take Thea's car, make the emergency phone call and get back to her. "We'll do it my way."

"News flash." Travis stomped to a rock beside a tree. He sat and started changing from his regular boots into the ski boots. "I'm way sick of taking orders from you."

"What the hell are you doing?"

"I told you. I'm skiing down, man." He fastened the ski boots with practiced ease. "I don't need your permission."

"Come on, Travis. We don't have time for a hissy fit."

"It's your fault we got stuck here," Travis said. "If you weren't such a hack, you could have saved Diane Moretson." There was a hard edge to his voice. His eyes, behind red-tinted snow goggles, looked menacing.

"What do you know about Diane?" Spence asked. He slipped his hand into his parka pocket and closed his fingers around the handle of his pistol. "I thought you'd never heard of her."

"You couldn't handle the big-city emergency room. You had to slink off to the mountains where you could be a small-town pill pusher. You're a loser, Cannon. Diane Moretson died because you're incompetent. And if she hadn't died, we wouldn't be in this mess, now would we?"

Spence grimaced. "It was a miracle she survived the ambulance ride. She shot herself in the head."

"Yeah." Travis stood. "After lover boy, the late-blooming reverend, pushed her right over the edge."

Spence knew for damned certain he and Thea hadn't revealed what the reverend had told them. He took the gun from his pocket and removed the safety, prepared for the final showdown. "How do you know that, Travis?"

"I heard it." With a gloved hand, he tapped his ear.

The gesture reminded Spence of the earplugs Travis had been wearing all weekend long, a perfect device for keeping track of his bugs throughout the house while pretending to listen to music.

Travis clicked his ski boots into the bindings.

"You heard it," Spence said. "Where?"

Travis tilted his head skyward as if looking for the answer. "From Lawrence."

"I don't think so." Spence held the gun loosely. "I think you heard the reverend's confession through the bug you planted in the chapel. On the door frame. In the exact center."

Travis's mouth carved a hard smile. The loose-limbed immaturity vanished into the thin mountain air like a mirage in the desert. He tensed with a dangerous, wiry strength. "I don't know what you're talking about."

"Sure, you do. You like to have everything neat and precise. Especially your revenge."

"Blah, blah, blah. Nance's psychobabble makes me sick. She's some kind of diagnostician. Maybe a bigger quack than you. So long, sucker." Travis dug in the ski poles and slid down the slope beside the pathway.

Spence plowed through knee-deep snow, trying to catch him. What was he doing? If he was Rosemont, it made no sense for him to leave now. "Travis! No!"

"I'm out of here," he yelled.

At the brink of the precipice, he stopped. His skis kicked up a wake of white powder snow. He edged away from the gondola house, paused, then dug in his ski poles. For a moment, he soared. Then came the descent.

Staggering, Spence made it to the cliff. He peered down, barely able to see Travis skiing the moguls in expert style. He traversed the lip of a precipice. His downhill ski caught an edge. Off-balance, he slipped and fell.

Though Spence couldn't see what happened, he heard the outraged scream that echoed mightily up the canyon walls.

Fighting through drifts, Spence reached the gondola house. He crept along the side to the front and peered down. Far below, he saw the red parka, nearly buried in snow. Travis wasn't moving.

INSIDE THE CASTLE nursery, Thea heard a yell from outside. It was a human voice, distinct from any sound an animal might make. Spence! She ran to the casement window and peered frantically through the glass. Nothing! She could see nothing from here but snow and treetops and a sky that had already begun to thicken with haze.

Her heart beat in triple time. Her fingers clenched into fists, holding tight to her self-control. If anything had happened to Spence, she couldn't find the strength to go on.

"Thea," Mona said weakly. "What is it?"

Tearing herself away from the window, Thea returned to the bedside. There was no point in scaring Mona, but Thea couldn't keep the quaver from her voice. "Spence is out there with Travis. They're going to get help."

"You love him," Mona said.

"Yes." The answer slipped out before Thea had a chance to think about it. Her instincts had replied. She loved Spence. Just at the moment when she might lose him, might even lose her own life, she'd discovered love.

Mona whispered, "Then everything will be all right."

"That's a charming sentiment," Thea said, "but—"

Her eyes glazed and feverish, Mona cut Thea off with the weak gesture of her hand. "I wish to believe, just this once, in a happy ending."

Her eyelids closed, and Thea patted her shoulder. She wanted to believe it, too. She hoped at the end of this ordeal, she and Spence would walk off hand-in-hand into a Technicolor sunset. "Thank you, Mona. You should rest."

Mona began to squirm uneasily, trying to come more upright in the bed. "How long have I been out of it?"

Thea cast backwards in her memory to the moment when they'd found Mona in the solarium. It seemed like forever. "Two nights and a day. But you were awake for a couple of minutes yesterday. Don't you remember? You told us Diane Moretson was the one—" She broke off when what meager color Mona could still claim drained from her wizened face. "Mona? What is it?"

"Siblings." Mona's face crumpled, and she stroked her brow fiercely, squinting her eyes. "We were talking about your brother and—"

"But that was the night before," Thea said.

Mona clasped Thea's hands in her claw-like hands. "It only came to me in my dreams. The sibling issue. Diane had a brother. A half-brother. They had a very pathological relationship, Thea—" she broke off, torn by the need to betray Diane's confidences. "Oh, dear God. Don't you see? Diane could never break free of him. No one was ever good enough for his sister. She became promiscuous… Her last relationship—was it John Hoffman? Didn't you tell me…?"

Thea nodded. "Yes. After Diane died, he changed his name to Joshua Handy and entered a seminary."

Her fever still not dissipated, her eyes glazed, Mona shuddered. "It was the most dreadful mess, Thea. Undercurrents of true pathology. She had nothing left to do but to kill herself when her brother told her he would see John Hoffman dead before he allowed her to marry him."

Thea felt her heart constrict. How had she lived with Diane, and never understood what her roommate was going through? "I don't get it, Dr. Mona. How is it possible I never heard about her brother?"

Trembling uncontrollably, Mona clasped her head. "Ach, I should have known immediately Michael Moretson was behind this twisted revenge! This manipulation behind the scenes is exactly in accordance with his control over Diane's life. He lived abroad, in Gstaad, I believe. Yes, it was Switzerland. He was in and out of sanatoriums, drug rehabilitation, many times over, but he managed to call her every week."

"But why would she put up with him calling the shots in her life? Why—"

"You don't understand, Thea. It was not a matter of her brother calling the shots, but him holding sway over her very thoughts! He undermined her confidence in her own judgment about men time and again until she herself began to choose horribly inappropriate partners."

"Was John Hoffman so bad?" Thea asked. "How can he have been? He's a nutcase in my opinion, and a sanctimonious ass and a terrible coward, but—"

"You've answered your own question, Thea. Would you have wanted Diane to marry such a man?"

No. And the terrible irony was that Diane's brother, wanting in some twisted way to keep her to himself, had created a situation in which Diane had no way out but to kill herself.

But what was worse, Thea thought, in their current predicament, was that it didn't even matter. She and Spence had convinced themselves that Rosemont must be one of the men they'd arrived with, but she didn't know what to believe now. If Dr. Mona had it right, Rosemont's—or rather Michael Moretson's—obsessive-compulsive temperament would compel him to manipulate events from behind the scenes. And yet, they had found no trace of Moretson in the castle.

To have something constructive to do, Thea got a fresh cold washcloth for Mona to apply to her brow, and then checked on Jenny. She wished desperately that there were some way to get an answer from her friend, just a word that would reveal who her fiancé was. Jenny verged on waking, but close wasn't good enough.

"Thea, dear, is there any possibility of a bite to eat?" Mona asked.

"Yes, of course. Not a lot of selection," Thea apologized. "Bread. Peanut butter. Oranges."

"A bit of an orange, please."

Between peeling the orange and feeding sections to Mona, Thea returned to the window, looking out and worrying about Spence. Had he started the descent? Was he safe? *Please, let him be safe.*

At last she heard a noise from the outer room. Abandoning Mona, she stepped back. She drew the pistol from her jeans and held it in both hands, aiming at the door. "Who's out there?"

"It's me. Spence."

She flew to the splintered door and pushed aside the chest, diving into the sitting room, into Spence's arms. His wet, cold embrace encircled her. Holding him was like hugging a snowman, but she didn't care. He was here. He was safe.

He peeled off his parka and dropped it on the floor.

"What happened?" Thea asked. "I heard a yell—"

"Travis never intended to make the climb down. He took off skiing down the mountain. He fell."

She wanted to tell him what Mona had said, but she sensed there was something he hadn't revealed to her yet. "What else?"

"I'm not sure."

"Come on, Spence. I need to know."

"Before Travis took off skiing, he seemed different. Threatening. I had the feeling he was going to tell me he was Rosemont." Spence tapped his ear. "You know how Travis has been listening to music the whole time we've been here? I think his portable CD player was something else—a receiver to pick up conversations from the bugs."

Thea felt the blood drain from her face. "That makes sense," she said, "except that if Travis is Rosemont, why would he ski off down the mountain before he was finished with us up here?"

Grim-faced, Spence shook his head. "He wouldn't. Which means I probably should have gone after the jerkwad. Tried to rescue him."

"Could he have survived the fall? Will he survive in the cold, even if—"

"No." He gave her a look. "Not in these sub-zero temperatures. Hypothermia will kill inside of twenty minutes up here."

Thea trembled violently. "Spence, are you saying he's dead? That Travis is *dead?*"

"Yes."

Thea wrapped her arms around her middle, flatly unable to take in the fact of Travis's suicidal risk. She started to talk, just to keep herself focused, stopped, then started again in earnest. "Mona spilled her guts while you were gone." She took a deep breath and plunged ahead, filling him in about Diane's brother. She choked near the end, and tears began to glaze her eyes.

Spence sank onto the sofa, clutching his head, trying, Thea thought, just as she was, to wrap her mind around the scope of a disaster that had been in the making since Diane's childhood.

"What do we really know about each other, Spence?" She meant her question to be rhetorical, but it wasn't. Her throat thickened, and a terrible weight settled in her heart. "Jenny is going to be devastated and Diane killed herself. Love is a completely irrational emotion. It makes us believe in things that aren't there and never were! Why should I be exempt? How am I supposed to cling to some purely irrational hope that I'll get my Pollyanna happily-ever-after either?"

"Don't do that, Thea," Spence pleaded, his voice guttural with emotion. "Don't make this about us."

"How can I not, Spence? We can't believe anything we think we know! Any one of our stooges could *be* Moretson. What do we really know about any of them? Travis said he was Jenny's brother, but we don't *know*. What if he was really Diane's brother? I don't think Joshua Handy is a possibility. He's admitted his part in Jenny's death. But Lawrence sure could be Moretson.

"And then there's still the possibility," she went on, "that Moretson is none of the above. That he's the puppet-master behind the scenes."

Watching Spence watch her list the catalog of all possible deceptions, she felt clueless. Six degrees of separation was a joke. No one could ever be truly known by anyone else, and she didn't know where she was ever going to find the faith again to believe differently.

Spence got up and drew near her. She still stood with her back to the door, leaning against it for support. He braced his hands on her shoulders. "Let's just get through this nightmare and see where we are, okay? This is not the time to be swearing off each other." His troubled blue eyes searched hers. "Can you do that, Thea? Can you put all that aside and concentrate with me now on surviving?"

She brushed away her tears. "What can we do?"

"The only chance we stand is to make the climb down ourselves and head for help."

"Spence! How can we leave Mona and Jenny here alone and defenseless?"

"Hear me out," he urged. "We'll barricade them inside and leave Mona an arsenal, but I don't think we have to worry about them. When we make an escape attempt, we're going to force Moretson's hand. He'll have to come after us." He must have seen the fear rising up in her. "Thea, honey, we're sitting ducks in this place, and he is not going to leave us alive until help comes. If we make ourselves a moving target," he shrugged, clearly hating the idea himself, "at least we're moving. At least we have some chance."

Thea felt herself literally gulping. An escape attempt would be Mona and Jenny's only salvation too, if Spence was right. She plucked up her courage and nodded. "I'm with you."

THEY SCROUNGED through closets to come up with thermal underwear enough for each of them to survive their trek in the bitter cold, and donned it. They left Mona with enough firepower to protect herself against a virtual siege, with instructions to shoot first and ask questions later.

Mona swore she could do it, for Jenny's sake. It amazed Thea how quickly one could dispense with philosophical objections when precious lives were really on the line.

Before leaving the sitting room, she and Spence blocked the doors as best they could. Anybody coming in here would make a lot of noise, giving Mona and Jenny ample warning.

They went down the hall to Thea's bedroom where she grabbed her parka, hat and mittens. Rather than backtrack to the main staircase, they used the servants' stairs to the kitchen.

Spence went first. "Careful," he warned. "Remember, we don't know where the reverend is." But he came to a sudden stop at the landing before the kitchen. "Damn."

At the foot of the stair, Thea saw the reverend sprawled face-down. A butcher knife protruded from his back.

Chapter Fourteen

The rough brick walls in the servants' stairwell closed around her, dank and claustrophobic. Thea stood on the fourth step, looking down as Spence examined the body of Reverend Joshua Handy alias John Hoffman. His long legs pointed toward the door to the kitchen. His left arm bent backwards as if he had died trying to pull out the butcher knife stuck in the center of his back. She saw every detail, but her mind couldn't comprehend the reality of what lay before her. On some level, she was in shock, disconnected, and had been since Spence told her that short of a miracle, Travis was dead.

Her senses numbed. Her heart thudded, heavy as the aftershocks of an earthquake. Could she really be standing here, looking down at Joshua Handy's blood-soaked dead body?

Spence looked up at her. "There's nothing we can do for him." Dumbly, she nodded. He rose and held his hand toward her to help her down the last few stairs. "Be careful where you step. There's a lot of blood." She balked. He urged her gently down. When they were out of sight of the reverend's body, Spence wrapped his arms around her shoulders and held her.

She buried her face against his chest, squeezed her eyes

shut and tried to erase the horror of what she'd just seen. Later, there would be time for her brain to process what she'd witnessed. Later, she would weep. Right now, she had to pull herself together, to mute the scream that was building inside her lungs.

Spence hurried her along, and she soon found herself at the door to the coatroom, which in turn led outdoors. She was grateful not to have to think, only move according to instruction, but her mind wouldn't shut off, or forget the image of Handy's dead body. *Oh, God.* She didn't want to die. "I'm scared. Spence, I can't do this. I really can't do this."

His big hands stroked her shoulders. "I know you can manage, Thea. Because you're stubborn. You're too proud to let Rosemont win. You're the strongest woman I've ever known, and that's why I love you."

She wanted to do what he needed her to do. She jutted her chin high, hoping to summon her stubborn self. "Your timing stinks, Spence. We'll probably be dead within the hour."

He grinned. "That's the spirit. Now take out your gun before I open this door."

Immediately, the pistol was in her hand. Possibly, she gave the appearance of competence, but a million emotions swarmed around her head like a flock of buzzing bees. Horror at what she'd seen. Anger. Fear. A bit of joy that Spence loved her. Confusion. Right now she needed to concentrate on survival.

At the last minute, Spence grabbed up several pairs of silk glove liners and stuffed them into her pockets in case what she was wearing got wet, then snagged a compact bag of more survival gear. He took her hand, led the way outdoors and pointed out the pile of climbing apparatus he'd already collected for the descent with Travis. "That's where I'm headed. Follow along and try to cover our backs.''

She nodded. ''I'm ready.'' She'd never been more thankful for the hours she'd spent at the firing range.

Outside, the mists had descended, enveloping the Castle in the Clouds. The sting of cold on her cheeks felt good after the closed atmosphere inside the thick granite walls. In most places, the snow was past her knees. Even with Spence plowing a path toward the gondola house, it was slow going.

Though breathing hard from exertion, she held the pistol in both hands, frequently turning to protect their backside. Her gaze swept the castle tower, and she saw a light in the top floor bridal suite where this nightmare had begun with the discovery of the bloodstained wedding dress.

It occurred to her that if Rosemont was up in that tower with a rifle, he could easily pick them off. But that wasn't his game. Murder wasn't enough. He wanted them to suffer, to know the fear of approaching death.

''Are you okay?'' Spence called back to her.

''Fine.'' She caught her breath. Her gloved fingers tightened on the pistol in her hand—an automatic with a twelve-bullet clip. She remembered her self-defense lessons. Aim for the biggest target. Aim for the chest.

Determined to prevail, she searched the thick forest of evergreens for movement or signs of an attack. Halfway down the pathway, she noticed the parallel marks of Travis's skis in the snow. ''Spence, are there other tracks?''

''I can't tell. I churned up this area pretty bad when I was trying to stop Travis.''

''Where are we going?''

''Gondola house. That's the best descent.''

The words *gondola* and *descent* triggered a fresh concern as she remembered the wave of panic that had over-taken her as they ascended to the castle in the gondola car, swinging from a steel cable. Given her fear of heights, how was she going to climb down a sheer mountain cliff?

She brushed the thought aside. She wasn't frightened when she went skiing. The vertigo came when she was looking down from a tall building or from a suspension bridge or—as she'd discovered only a few days ago—from a ski gondola.

Near the gondola house, Spence stopped and peered over the edge. "I can still see Travis's red parka against the snow. It doesn't look like he's moved."

Thea came as close to the edge as she dared. Glancing down, a wave of dizziness swept over her, and she stepped back. Somehow, she had to do this. The trick was to keep from looking down. "Maybe this isn't the best time to tell you, but I've never done mountain climbing before."

"It's easy. I'll show you how."

She wanted to believe him. "You haven't forgotten, have you? I'm not real comfortable with heights."

"I'm good at this stuff. I won't let you get hurt." He smiled. "Do you trust me?"

"With all my heart."

The words left her lips and became a new reality. She trusted him. She was willing to place her life in his strong, capable hands.

From behind her, she heard a harsh command. "Drop the gun, Thea. And turn around slowly."

Dear God. She recognized the butler's voice. "Lawrence?"

"I said drop it!"

"Do it," Spence said.

Her fingers released. The pistol sank into the snow at her feet. Slowly, she turned toward the gondola house.

Lawrence stood in the doorway with an automatic pistol in each fist. "That's good, Thea. Now come toward me. I'm not going to hurt you. Move away from him."

She planted her feet. If now was the time for a final stand, she would face her fate bravely, side by side with the man she loved. "I won't leave Spence."

"For the love of God, Thea, I'm trying to help you." Lawrence stepped out of the doorway. "Don't you understand? He's Rosemont."

"What are you saying?"

"There's nobody else left. Travis was so desperate to escape that he crashed. The reverend is dead. There's only one man left standing." His eyes narrowed to slits. "Spence, you bastard! You promised me that nobody would get killed."

Uncomprehending, Thea questioned, "He promised you? What do you mean, Lawrence?"

"I'm a private investigator. He hired me to find one person who connected you, the reverend, Mona and Spence. I located Jenny Trevain. She and Spence were old friends. Mona was her shrink. She went to the reverend's church. She worked with you, Thea. I knew Rosemont intended to terrorize the lot of you, but he promised me no one would die."

The chill inside her went bone-deep. "Lawrence, Spence can't be Rosemont. He was one of the people you were supposed to find a connection for."

"That's what I thought." Lawrence came closer, taking a few cautious steps in the deep snow. When he spoke, his breath steamed in the cold air. "But last night, I searched every inch of this place again. There is no trace of another person. Not one single clue. No food scraps. No water glasses. Nothing. I had to conclude that we were the only ones in the castle. The wedding party and the bride.''

"Lawrence, I understand what you're saying, but you've come to the wrong conclusion. Spence—''

"I'm not wrong, Thea.'' His hands aimed with both guns. ''When I found the reverend's body, everything came clear to me. Rosemont had intended, from the start, to kill all of us. That's why he wanted me here. Because he couldn't leave me alive to tell any tales. He was always going to kill me, too.''

Spence must have made a wrong move behind her. Lawrence got off a shot that burned past her ear. The horrendous noise echoed and died. ''Move again, and you're history,'' Lawrence snarled at Spence. ''You see?'' he dared her.

"See what?'' she croaked, her dismay multiplying upon itself. ''Lawrence, *think!* Spence was with me every time Rosemont took some action—''

"Was he really? Where was he when you were terrorized in the ballroom? Think about it yourself, Thea. Travis was right. Who else knows his way around a hypodermic? And when the rescue party comes, Spence can produce an invitation to the wedding. He can swear that he knew nothing about the weekend, that he's been busy in Cascadia being a doctor. His lifestyle is his alibi. He's going to get away with murder.''

Her feet growing numb from the cold and lack of movement, her lungs burning, Thea tried to reason with him. ''What about Jenny? How could Spence convince her to stage a fake wedding?''

"He concocted some kind of story to make her happy, maybe said the whole weekend was a joke or a trick. Doesn't matter. He was planning to murder her. Thea, it's the only thing that makes sense. Spence Cannon is the last man left on the mountain. He's Rosemont.''

At the beginning of this weekend, Thea might have believed Spence was capable of such heinous duplicity. She might have believed Lawrence's rationale. But she'd rediscovered her heart. She trusted Spence implicitly, trusted him with her life. Defiantly, she turned on Lawrence. ''There's another explanation. There has to be. Spence is a healer, not a murderer.''

''Lawrence,'' Spence commanded with all the authority he could muster. ''Put down the guns. Let's concentrate on getting out of here. I can use your help in climbing down.''

Indecision flickered in Lawrence's eyes. ''I'm nobody's fool. Put your hands up over your head and walk over here. Don't make any sudden moves. I swear that I won't hesitate to shoot.''

Spence raised his hands. ''Come on, Thea. We'll do what he says.''

They were only a few feet from Lawrence when a gunshot shattered the cold mountain air again. Lawrence gasped in surprise. The guns fell from his hands as he clutched his chest and toppled face-first into the snow.

Before Thea could think of what should come next, Spence grabbed her and dragged her into the granite shelter of the gondola house. She sprawled backward on the flagstone floor, staring up at the giant cogs. The shot put an end to all speculation. No one was left to be shooting at them but the undetected Rosemont. ''Who is this guy?'' she cried.

''A lunatic,'' Spence ground out. He drew a pistol from the depths of his parka and flattened himself against the entryway. Without looking or aiming, he fired a shot.

''What are you doing?''

"Drawing fire to find out where he is."

She scrambled to her feet and stepped up behind Spence. Adrenaline pumped through her body, sharpening senses that only moments ago had been numbed. Through the doorway, she saw Lawrence. Splotches of crimson blood stained the snow around him, but his shoulders were moving. He was still alive. "Should we try to pull Lawrence in here?"

Spence leaned out and pulled back quickly. Another shot exploded. They were pinned down.

"Is that your only gun?" Thea asked.

"Within reach? Yeah."

"How many bullets?"

"Not enough," he said. "We're going to have to get down to the ledge below where he can't see to shoot us." But if he trapped them there, they would die of hypothermia in short order.

"Hey!" A shout came from outside. "You can't get away from me, dudes."

Her heart knocked to a stop. "Travis? How can that be?"

Spence swore. He'd been tricked by what he'd half-expected to see. "The bastard must've sent his red parka hurtling down the mountain wrapped around a rock or something."

Travis yelled again. "It's all over for you both. I suggest you make it easy on yourselves. Step out into the open."

His voice was different. He'd dropped the laconic drawl and every other semblance of a sane man. Thea knew there was no point in trying to reason with the man they'd known as Travis.

"What the hell else do you want, Travis?" Spence bellowed. "We all confessed—"

"Your so-called confessions," the voice hurled down

on them, ''were always going to be too little too late, doc. And the name's Moretson. My name is Michael Moretson,'' he screamed.

She shivered violently as the truth sank into her consciousness. She had been tricked by her own expectations as well. Every time Travis had triggered that vague uneasy sense of recognition in her, she'd chalked it up to a family likeness he shared with his sister. But his sister wasn't Jenny, as Thea had been primed by the very nature of the wedding event to believe, but her ill-fated roommate Diane.

The irony swamped her, and the diabolical symmetry that would appeal to the obsessive-compulsive Michael Moretson every bit as much as the name game. While pretending to be the bride's brother Travis, he was in reality Diane's brother.

Blindly, Spence fired off another shot. He grabbed Thea's hand and led her to the opening in the flagstone floor where the gondola had crashed through. ''I don't have the climbing ropes,'' he said. ''We'll have to make the descent free-style.''

She peered down, fighting a rush of vertigo. The foundation below the gondola house was constructed of heavy wooden beams, covered with blowing snow. Her vision blurred. ''I can't do it.''

''Think of it as a jungle gym,'' Spence lowered himself to the first beam. ''Let's go. There's no other way.''

She sent her mind off into oblivion and followed Spence's orders. Wrapped inside his arms, she descended one tortured step after another. Her legs and arms trembled with the effort of supporting her own weight. Somehow, they reached the relative safety of a ledge where the falling gondola car had gouged a deep space. A frozen drift of snow curled like a wave above them, shielding them from Michael Moretson's vengeance.

Shivering and afraid to glance down into the icy abyss, she clung to Spence. Her face was buried against his chest.

"Look at me, Thea."

Her gaze lifted to his face, and the love glowing from his blue eyes reassured her. Above them, the clouds parted and the winter sun reflected brilliantly on ice crystals.

"I've always loved you," he whispered.

"And I, you," she answered.

"Marry me," he said. "As soon as possible. I don't ever want to be apart from you again."

Strong emotion caught in her throat as she realized the irony of his wish. They might be killed at any moment. Then they would be together for a cold eternity.

Above them, Moretson had figured out where they were hiding. He hurled vile epithets and accusations. Frustrated, he began to slam the ice ax Spence had brought for their climb into the icy crest overhanging their precarious perch. If the slab broke away and fell, they would be buried beneath a ton of snow. Their only chance lay in keeping clear of the crushing fall.

Spence dragged her with him, deep into the gouge. Cradling her in his arms, he covered her face with soft kisses. "We'll get out of this. We're not going to die."

If only she could believe him. Bone-cold, Thea clung to him, crying and kissing him deeply.

"Wait!" He stiffened. "Do you hear that?"

She concentrated with all her heart. Above them, Moretson went silent, and Thea recognized a whirring sound. A rescue chopper?

"Emily and Jordan," Spence uttered.

How was that possible? Somehow, his friends, miraculously, had come to their rescue. "Please, God," Thea prayed, "let it be them."

Moretson roared in rage. They heard his footsteps on the flagstone floor as he charged to the opening of the gondola house. "Come on," he screamed. "Come and get me!"

Spence swore under his breath. "He's going to fire at the tail rotor!" He waved with both arms to get the pilot's attention, then motioned them away. "Turn back!"

Moretson blasted the air with several shots, yelling with insane fury.

Then, from above, Thea heard the mighty, desperate howl of another voice, Lawrence's, then a terrible *ooomph* as bodies collided. Moretson, his arms and legs flailing, hurtled past them in a deadly free fall into a yawning chasm of frozen death.

"Lawrence!" Spence called out. "Lawrence, are you all right?"

"Guess I was wrong about you, doc." He coughed weakly. "It was Travis. Rosemont was—"

"Hang on, Lawrence. The helicopter's coming."

Spence gathered her in his arms. "I told you we'd make it."

Tears of relief froze against her eyelids as she stared up at him. Her breath exhaled in a gasp, and she felt her lips curve in a smile. "Deep down, I knew I could trust you."

"Always. All I want, for the rest of our lives, is to prove myself worthy of your love."

Thea had no doubt of his worthiness.

After a last lingering kiss, Spence moved to the edge of their perch to direct the rescue operation. As always, he was taking charge, and she was content to sit back and quietly applaud the courage and endless competence of the man she loved with all her heart.

Epilogue

The tiny white clapboard church in Cascadia was about as far removed in opulence from the Castle in the Clouds as Thea Sarazin was from the woman who had sent her fiancé packing almost six years earlier.

Filled to overflowing with friends and all of Spence's patients, the little church teemed with anticipation. Spring had come early to the Rockies this year, and the Ladies' Crocheting Circle believed that must mean God was smiling on Spence and Thea. Colorful daffodils and butter-yellow tulips poked brilliantly through a dusting of fresh snow.

Dressed in a simple, elegant satin wedding gown with pearls bedecking her throat, Thea waited in the anteroom with her father, her maid of honor Jenny Trevain, and a gaggle of the most precious little girls, Spence's Brownie troop, with their gaily decorated baskets of rose petals at the ready.

She would carry her only extravagance down the aisle with her as she went to marry Spence, a bouquet of cat-tleya orchids. Her heart was filled to overflowing.

From above her, she heard the muted strains of the Cascadia String Quartet flow to an end, and then the organ music built to a crescendo of chords announcing "Here Comes the Bride."

She laughed till tears glazed her eyes as the little girls, Betsy, Callie, Allie, Margaret, Madeleine and Susie stepped solemnly into place and marched out into the church, every one of them unable to contain their peals of laughter at seeing their heartthrob Spence awaiting his bride.

This had to be the most unlikely wedding of all time. Not only had they conquered their stubborn pride and healed the wounds of a painful break-up, but Spence and Thea had to overcome a psychotic murderer and defeat his bizarre scheme for revenge.

As she stood at the back of the church, Thea spied Lawrence, the private eye, who had been able to summon a superhuman burst of unlikely strength to knock Michael Moretson off his feet, thereby stopping his assault on the rescue chopper. Beside him was little Mona who had made a full recovery.

Thea winked at Emily who had seen the real Travis Trevain on the nightly sports report while catching the Avalanche score for Jordan. That unlikely moment had been enough to convince Emily that a phony Travis Trevain at the castle spelled serious trouble.

As Jenny marched down the aisle, Thea realized that her friend's recovery was possibly the most unlikely event of all. Not only had Jenny suffered no long-term effects of the over-sedation, but she was even getting over her own broken dreams and even dating again. Spence had a friend who had a friend who owned the local snowmobile dealership, and he'd been courting Jenny's favor since they met. Nearly as handsome as Spence, best of all, he was almost as beloved in his sideline as coach of the local kiddie soccer teams.

But it was her luck in reuniting with Spence that took Thea's breath away. As she walked on her father's steady arm down the aisle strewn with yellow rose petals, she couldn't take her eyes off her husband-to-be. How did she manage to tame her own smile? What was she supposed to do about the tears that sprang loose again?

She'd thought she would never have the fortitude to believe in love again. In Spence's arms, she needed no fortitude, nor any faith. He was the man she had once fallen in love with. He was the man for her. They exchanged vows he had written for them.

There wasn't a dry eye in the house.

Creaking floorboards...
the whistling wind...an enigmatic man
and only the light of the moon....

*This February Harlequin Intrigue revises
the greatest romantic suspense tradition of all
in a new four-book series!*

Moriah's Landing
A Modern Gothic

Join your favorite authors as they recapture the
romance and rapture of the classic gothic fantasy in
modern-day stories set in the picturesque New England
town of Moriah's Landing, where evil looms but
love conquers the darkness.

#650 SECRET SANCTUARY by Amanda Stevens
February 2002

#654 HOWLING IN THE DARKNESS by B.J. Daniels
March 2002

#658 SCARLET VOWS by Dani Sinclair
April 2002

#662 BEHIND THE VEIL by Joanna Wayne
May 2002

from

HARLEQUIN®

INTRIGUE®

HARLEQUIN®
Makes any time special ®

*Available at your
favorite retail outlet.*

This Mother's Day Give Your Mom A Royal Treat

Win a fabulous one-week vacation in Puerto Rico for you and your mother at the luxurious Inter-Continental San Juan Resort & Casino. The prize includes round trip airfare for two, breakfast daily and a mother and daughter day of beauty at the beachfront hotel's spa.

INTER·CONTINENTAL
San Juan
RESORT & CASINO

Here's all you have to do:

Tell us in 100 words or less how your mother helped with the romance in your life. It may be a story about your engagement, wedding or those boyfriends when you were a teenager or any other romantic advice from your mother. The entry will be judged based on its originality, emotionally compelling nature and sincerity. See official rules on following page.

Send your entry to:
Mother's Day Contest

In Canada	**In U.S.A.**
P.O. Box 637	P.O. Box 9076
Fort Erie, Ontario	3010 Walden Ave.
L2A 5X3	Buffalo, NY
	14269-9076

Or enter online at www.eHarlequin.com

PRROY